*Playing for Love*

Also by Jilly Johnson

**DOUBLE EXPOSURE**

# Playing for Love

## Jilly Johnson

LONDON · SYDNEY · NEW YORK · TOKYO · SINGAPORE · TORONTO

First published in Great Britain by Simon & Schuster, 1997
This paperback edition first published by Pocket Books, 1998
An imprint of Simon & Schuster Ltd
A Viacom Company

Copyright © Jilly Johnson, 1997

This book is copyright under the Berne Convention
No reproduction without permission
All rights reserved

The right of Jilly Johnson to be identified as author of this work has
been asserted in accordance with sections 77 and 78 of the Copyright
Designs and Patents Act 1988

This book is copyright under the Berne Convention
No reproduction without permission
® and © 1997 Simon & Schuster Inc. All rights reserved.
Pocket Books & Design is a registered trademark of Simon & Schuster
Inc.

Simon & Schuster
West Garden Place
Kendal Street
London W2 2AQ

Simon & Schuster Australia
Sydney

A CIP catalogue record for this book is available
from the British Library.

0-671-85562-X

This book is a work of fiction. Names, characters, places
and incidents either are products of the author's imagination or are used
fictitiously. Any resemblance to actual people living or dead, events or
locales is entirely coincidental

Printed and bound in Great Britain by Caledonian International Book
Manufacturing, Glasgow

For Joyce & Dennis

*The world's greatest parents*

**Acknowledgments**

Lucy for always 'being there'

With heartfelt thanks to my fantastic team at Simon & Schuster, in particular Clare Ledingham and Jo Frank, who have been supportive friends as well as first class professionals.

To all at Marks Productions, especially Kay Silver and Mark Gregory for their patience, attention to detail and for generally looking after me.

To my manager and dearest friend, Linda Marks-Loftus – who makes all things possible!

# PART 1

# Chapter one

## London, 1996

'This is thy sheath; there rust, and let me die!' cried Grace dramatically, throwing back her head to reveal the silken ivory skin of her neck and heaving bosom and plunging the dagger deep into her broken heart. Gasping for breath she collapsed to her knees. Clutching at Friar Lawrence's robe, she slid to the floor of the Tomb of Capulets, the crimson blood spreading over her delicate cream chiffon-clad body. Life seemed to drain from her by the second, as her motionless body lay prostrate and still. The silence was deafening.

Grace continued to lie still, not allowing even so much as a muscle to move – professional to the very end, that was what she'd been taught to be. Friar Lawrence, distraught with grief, delivered his monologue to the audience. Although Grace knew everyone else's parts just as well as her own, she was suddenly unable to recognise the lines as her mind reeled, Friar Lawrence's voice appearing distorted to her. Her mind was doing somersaults.

Lying on the well-worn stage floor of London's National

Theatre barely allowing herself to breathe, her eyes closed in an agonised expression, she felt elated. She had excelled herself and she knew it – her performance had been flawless. It was almost impossible to lie so still when her body tremored with excitement, but knowing that not only the Producers and Director, but also the various critics and journalists were in the front rows, she contained herself and continued to play the part of the dead Juliet, lying next to her lover's, Romeo's tomb.

Struggling to stop her ribcage from moving, her heart from beating and her eyes and mouth from twitching, she reflected on how she had waited most of her life for this part, a classic such as Juliet. She knew she had at last 'arrived' and been accepted as a serious actress. Acting with the famous Royal Shakespeare Company at the acclaimed and highly prestigious National Theatre, spoke volumes in itself. The years of backbreaking touring and toiling up and down England's green and pleasant land with different productions and casts at last seemed worthwhile. On occasions in the past, Grace Madigan had screamed with frustration at the roles she'd had to accept in order to live and pay her rent. Those days were now over, she thought as the curtain came down and the roar of cheers and applause began.

Luc Fontaine, the devastatingly handsome actor cast as Romeo, leapt off the vault he'd been lying on. 'They loved it – you were absolutely wonderful darling! You had them eating out of your hand from the moment you made your entrance in Act One ...' he gushed.

'I could never have done it without your help, Luc. And you were incredible yourself ...' whispered Grace, as the cast scrambled around backstage preparing for the curtain call. The Assistant Stage Manager, Grant, rushed over to remove Juliet's dagger from her breast and help her to her feet.

'You were a knockout! Bloody brilliant, the pair of you,' he whispered excitedly.

'Listen to them, just listen to that!' said Luc grinning from ear to ear, nodding his head toward the auditorium where the curtain separated them from the enthusiastic audience. The props girl and stage hands were rushing around removing the tombs and Friar Lawrence's herb baskets to allow the rest of the cast on stage. The actors playing the Prince of Verona, Balthasar, Paris and the Montagues were fighting to get on the stage from the wings.

'Hurry up, hurry up, for Christ's sake!' whispered Grant frantically. 'All cast on stage. *Now.* We're going up in ten seconds. Positions please. OK. Enjoy.' He signalled for the curtain to rise and ducked backstage into the wings just in time.

At last Grace Madigan came face to face with her adoring audience, as they rose from their seats, cheering and saluting her and Luc. They took six curtain calls, but even so, just as the safety curtain was about to fall, the audience started up a chant, 'Grace ... Grace ... Grace.' For she had stolen their hearts and they wanted to show their appreciation. She looked questioningly at Grant in the wings, who nodded to her and signalled for the cast to disperse from the stage. Luc pursed his lips as he stood back in the darkness of the wings. Grant's gesture rose the curtain again and Grace stepped out into the spotlight, centre stage.

The audience stopped stamping their feet and roared their adoration to their shining new star. Grace had dared to prepare a speech should she be received so favourably, but suddenly she was choked up, unable to speak. To her horror, as she tried to submit the audience to her well-rehearsed words, the full impact of the emotion she'd been feeling hit her and tears began to cascade down her cheeks. The delighted journalists scribbled hastily in their notebooks as she brushed the tears away with the back of her hand, standing stock still in front of her audience, totally awed. At last, they ceased their cheering with impatient shushing. Quietly and humbly, she managed to stammer, 'Thank you ...' and with quivering lips and the tears threatening to begin again, she hurriedly left the stage.

'Jesus, talk about milking it for all it's worth! Anyone got a bucket?' asked Luc viciously, hissing through his teeth at some of the cast who were still loitering in the wings. 'That was pushing the boat out a bit far wasn't it old girl, turning on the water works like that?' he persisted, trying to hide his fury at being upstaged as he escorted Grace to her dressing room.

'That was for real, Luc, I couldn't help myself ... I don't know why ... Please, no criticism – it won't happen again,' she promised.

'I *do* hope so, Angel. I'm not talking just for myself, darling, but it upstages the whole cast,' he said superciliously, his hand on her dressing room door handle.

As Grace entered her dressing room, the heady scent of flowers almost intoxicated her. All day flowers had been arriving at the theatre from well-wishers and friends – but there had been nothing from her parents. Not a word from her family except for a ribboned wicker basket containing the most beautiful purple wild violets from her brother, James, with a miniature card reading 'Knock 'em dead, kid! From Little Bro.'

Poppy, her dresser, assistant and understudy, had arranged the bouquets beautifully, and there, almost engulfed by all the foliage and blooms, sat her beloved mentor, Sybil. Grace rushed across to the frail old lady of eighty-seven years, and threw her arms around her.

'Sybil, Oh Sybil, they loved me! Did you see how many curtain calls there were?' Grace sank to her knees and lay her head in Sybil's lap.

'I got out before all that pandemonium started,' said Sybil gruffly and unemotionally. 'And of course they loved you – don't sound so surprised, you silly goose,' she scalded affectionately.

'Well, I know that if you hadn't taken me under your wing and coached me I wouldn't be here today. I owe it all to you, Sybil ... everything,' she cried, tears beginning to well in her eyes once more.

'Stuff and nonsense. I simply recognised your raw and untapped talent when I saw you performing in a flea–pit of a theatre which might just as well have been in Outer Mongolia.' Grace smiled in spite of herself and sniffed, wiping the tears from her face with the back of her hand, smearing her make–up.

Their union had been formed when Sybil had announced herself to the stage door manager at a rather ramshackle, rundown theatre, asking to meet Miss Madigan. Sybil had been impressed by the young actress playing the lead in *Sampson and Delilah*, and immediately recognised a star in the making, in spite of the poor production. When she had introduced herself in the dressing room Grace shared with three other girls, Grace's mouth had fallen open. Of course everyone knew Sybil Grant, she was renowned on the British stage, and one of The Royal Shakespeare Company's principal stars. From that day on, Sybil had taken Grace under her wing, nurturing, coaching and developing her acting career. Their sessions were intense, with Grace often shedding tears, but slowly and surely, Grace Madigan had begun to make a name for herself.

With Sybil's expert guidance over the years, Grace was now in a position to be able to choose scripts, with directors and producers even allowing Grace's parts to be altered to the dynamic duo's liking, which was a very rare luxury within the theatrical world. It somehow made all the blood, sweat and tears of the years on tour seem worthwhile. Sybil had used her contacts and clout to full advantage. Many a time she would appear in the audience with agents, casting directors and producers from the RSC to assess Grace's performance. In 1995, Grace had signed an exclusive deal with Freddie Franks, one of London's most renowned and celebrated agents, and almost immediately landed the part of Juliet.

'Don't start dribbling all over my Jean Muir, girl! Now, we've got to work on a few notes ...' said Sybil authoritatively, waving her notebook and pencil.

'Please Sybil, not tonight. Tonight is *my* night and I've got to get ready for the reception,' pleaded Grace, as she reached for her Leichner cleansing cream.

'Oh, I see. A few curtain calls and suddenly you don't need notes. This, my girl is exactly the time you do need them. Your ego has been fed and your head's swollen. Now whilst you're entitled to that in small doses – God and I alone know how hard you've worked, one of the finest Juliet's I've ever encountered on the British stage – you must be a professional, constantly working to improve your craft. It's easy to slip into a false sense of security.' She softened the words with a warm smile. 'Arrange a time with Luc to go over a few sticky phrases in the balcony scene ...' she paused before continuing nostalgically, 'You know, Claude and I constantly strove to improve our performances by rehearsing relentlessly even after the opening of *The Taming of the Shrew*. And even though we had brilliant notices, we didn't allow ourselves ever to become complacent. Even when I played Ophelia opposite Ralph Richardson in *Hamlet*, we rehearsed constantly after our first night. An actress never rests; there's always room for improvement, as Dame Peggy Ashcroft says.'

Grace laughed and gave in, waiting for Sybil's next onslaught.

'Now, your first entrance in Act One, Scene One. I know you're only supposed to be fourteen, but don't look *too* wide-eyed and innocent, darling, you don't want to over act. I know there's not much dialogue for you there, but your stance and attitude looked like that of a six-year-old – remember Juliet is a *mature* fourteen.'

Sybil continued diligently going over more tedious notes, but Grace was too excited to absorb them. She stared back at her reflection in the mirror as she brushed out Juliet's ringlets. At twenty-eight, there was still not a blemish or line on her face, which was surprising considering all the battering, wear and tear and thick grease-paint make-up she'd had to endure over the years; she didn't look a day older than eighteen. With her luscious mahogany shoulder-length hair framing her heart-shaped face, it was easy to see why people hailed her as the next Vivien Leigh. Her milky skin lay taut over pronounced cheekbones; her arched ebony eyebrows gave her a questioning look and her emerald green eyes glinted and sparkled in the light. Naturally pink pert lips twitched animatedly as she spoke and her pointed chin completed the overall picture of fragile beauty. She suited her name – her long, slender neck balanced on tiny shoulders confirmed the fact that her frame was petite and elegant, with slight bones and the smallest of feet. Standing no more than five feet tall, she appeared almost fragile.

Sybil had resolutely fought to instil the grit, confidence and stance of a true performer into Grace, but like so many talented actors, Grace doubted her own ability and constantly talked down her unique gift. Somewhere within Grace was a born survivor – she'd had to be – she'd fought the good fight and come through with flying colours, albeit with a few emotional battle scars as well. Nobody knew of the anguish and agonies she'd suffered along the way. That beautiful, expressive face staring back at her in the mirror was now devoid of pain. Grace smiled wryly at her reflection – her public mask.

As Grace slapped on the cleansing cream, massaging well until the black eye make-up, lipstick and blusher congealed and curdled, Sybil's imperious instructions to Poppy as to where to hang Grace's final costume and rearrange the flowers, faded into the background. Grace always thought she resembled something from the Hammer House Of Horrors at this stage, and she eagerly wiped her face free of most of the gunge with tissues. Wriggling out of her tight, lycra, bandage-type bra – Douglas Crane, the Director, thought her a little over endowed for a fourteen-year-old – she slipped out of her briefs and stepped into the shower. As the water bounced off her onto the frosted glass door, Grace smiled to herself, listening to Sybil who was still trying to talk to her over the sound of the shower.

'Oh yes, darling ... another note ... in your suicide scene when you collapse clutching at Friar Lawrence's robe ... do remember to ...'

Grace interrupted bravely. 'No more tonight, Sybil. I stopped working when that curtain came down!' She awaited the predictable response.

'Huh! Your work has just begun, my girl. Do you know who's going to be at the reception? None other than those over-zealous Rottweilers commonly known as critics, not to mention all the journalists and photographers. So don't be getting too pleased with yourself, young lady. Hurry up out of that shower, now! I know you want to be a little late to make your "entrance", but it's considered arrogant to keep these blood-suckers waiting too long.'

A tremor of nervousness shook Grace at the thought of all the officials at the party, and the fact that she'd have to play the serene, confident actress, smiling graciously and accepting compliments whilst inwardly she squirmed with embarrassment.

She lathered off the rest of the Leichner cleanser and thought happily of seeing her brother, James, and friend, Lana. How she would have loved her parents to have been present tonight, to witness and toast her success and proudly acknowledge her as their own daughter. She reflected sadly on her estrangement from them for a moment or two and then pulled herself up short, refusing to allow melancholia to dampen her spirits.

As Grace emerged from the shower wrapped in a bathrobe and shower cap, Poppy was brushing the bottle green velvet Valentino evening gown in preparation for her. Never had Grace imagined she'd walk into such a famous showroom for her reception dress, but Sybil had absolutely insisted that her frock be none other than show stopping. As soon as Grace had seen it she knew it was made for her; it fitted like a glove, and only needed the hem taking up a little. It was the most expensive item of clothing she'd ever bought, but as Sybil had put it, it was an investment.

Sybil and Poppy continued to fuss, fiddle and lecture as Grace carefully applied her make-up, taking care not to overdo the foundation and blusher, but deciding to go overboard with a Paloma Picasso scarlet lipstick. Poppy tonged and styled her hair, sweeping it all over to one side so one half of her face was framed by her luxuriant locks and the other completely bare, showing her glowing skin and perfect features to best advantage.

'Stop fidgeting, girl, and let Poppy finish,' scolded Sybil gently. 'And stop biting your lip.'

Grace swallowed hard. Sybil had been right, her work had just begun. Although secure in the knowledge that her performance tonight had been breathtaking, the thought of being the life and soul of the party, rubbing shoulders with her critics, was unnerving. Maybe it's true what they say about actors and actresses: playing a part is so much easier than real life. Grace knew that to be true in her case – real life was far too painful.

She readjusted her hair to her liking, teasing the locks around her face and shoulders giving herself a softer and more natural look. Poppy finished lacquering her and stood back to observe the end result. As Grace reached for her delicate diamanté necklace with matching earrings, Sybil smacked the back of her hand and dismissed the jewellery as junk. 'Nothing but the best for my girl tonight,' she declared as she handed her a claret drawstring velvet bag. Grace gasped as she withdrew a double strand pearl necklace with matching pearl and diamond droplet earrings.

'Sybil, it's not ... I can't ... they mean so much to you ...' said Grace shakily.

'Exactly, my girl, that's why you're going to wear them,' retorted Sybil matter-of-factly. 'Dear, dearest Claude would have wanted you to wear them,' she continued.

'But they're yours! He meant them for you,' said Grace.

'Hells Bells, dear heart. Who wants to see an old baggage like me swathed in Jean Muir and fresh water pearls? It's your night, darling and you'll wear the bloody things if I have to strangle you with them first.'

Poppy stood back witnessing the scene with increasing awe.

'Sir Claude Clemments gave you these pearls? *The* Sir Claude Clemments ...?'

'Poppy, you're like a panting parrot. Yes, Claude did give me these on our first night in *As You Like It*.'

'Wow ...' said Poppy, suitably impressed, as she helped Grace with the diamond clasp of the necklace. Sybil looked away from the two sets of inquiring eyes, silent, as a vision of Claude in her dressing room after their first performance of *As You Like It* came to her. He had looked so suave, so debonair, the epitome of elegance as he had taken her in his arms and kissed her gently How she had loved him, this man whose generosity, artistically and materially, was legendary within the theatrical world. He had always been protective and adoring to his leading ladies, spoiling them with gifts and trinkets on first nights. She swallowed hard and blinked away the threatening tears.

This is not the time to get nostalgic or maudlin, she admonished herself. Claude would have hated it. Just enjoy your memories and keep a stiff upper lip, Sybil, old girl.

'Sybil ... Sybil. Grace is ready now,' said Poppy gently, patting her hand. 'We thought you'd dropped off there for a minute.'

Sybil pulled herself together quickly. 'About bloody time, my girl, now stand over there and let me look at you,' she demanded, gesticulating for Grace to stand across the room. Her eyes, not being what they used to, focused slowly on Grace. She took a breath, held it, and gripped her crocodile handbag so hard her knuckles went white as she sat mesmerised. It was as if she was seeing a reincarnation of a very young Vivien Leigh, but even more devastatingly beautiful.

She was captivated by Grace's pure creamy, porcelain skin, her high cheek bones... but most of all those eyes, those vixen green eyes. As Sybil slowly exhaled, her eyes inspected the glorious vision of her protégée, from her long slender neck showing off the pearl and diamond droplet earrings, to the double strand pearl necklace sitting tantalisingly on the swell of her full bosom. The dark green strapless velvet evening gown was full length and fitted like a sheath, showing off Grace's magnificent curves to the full. Although slender, she looked all woman, observed Sybil. In the six years she had coached, cajoled and trained Grace, she had never known her to restrict her passion for jam doughnuts or even consider doing a workout, which most women of Grace's age had been brainwashed into doing by the likes of Jane Fonda. Grace was simply a natural. In her tiny stockinged feet, weighing seven stones, a full thirty-four inch bust, twenty-one inch waist and hips a mere thirty-three inches, she was admired by almost every member of the cast, who christened her 'Pocket Rocket'.

Looking at Grace she was filled with an overwhelming sense of love and pride. 'Not bad, not bad at all, I suppose,' she said gruffly, looking nonchalantly at her watch. Grace and Poppy winked and exchanged grins. 'Just enough time for a stiff one, before facing this circus they call a reception.'

Poppy poured two double measures of Scottish malt and Sybil knocked hers back in one, dramatically slamming her glass on the dressing table. Graces's eyes watered as she tried to sip delicately at the burning amber liquid.

Sybil's arthritically gnarled hand groped for her beautifully carved walking stick with its antique silver embossed hilt and she made to rise from her chair. Poppy and Grace rustled to her aid.

'All right, all right, don't make such a bloody fuss!' she said belligerently. At eighty-seven, Sybil was riddled with arthritis, but never complained, only proclaiming her ailment a damned nuisance and inconvenience.

As Sybil fiddled with her black netting veil that had seen many a first night, she attempted to pull her time worn long black evening gloves over her distorted hands. Grace looked tenderly at the old lady who had nursed and guided her in her professional and private life. The love shone on her face as she fondly helped Sybil with her stole. The pity in her heart was intense as she thought of all the years her mentor had pined for, loved and mourned the loss of the only man in her life. For over thirty years Sybil had sat on the side lines watching Claude indulge himself in numerous affairs with his leading ladies. Her love for him never died, but a flame in her heart had been cruelly snuffed out when he'd died, aged eighty-two.

As Grace now prepared for the opening night party, she could still remember the overwhelming excitement she'd felt at the prospect of playing with the celebrated Royal Shakespeare Company. The only thing that continued to mar her happiness was the fact that her parents were not there to share in her glory. Was it merely pride that kept them away or had they really no feelings for her?

As Poppy and Sybil gathered their belongings and checked their appearances in the mirror one last time, Grace begged a few quiet moments to herself before she joined them. Suddenly rather emotional again, she needed time to pull herself together.

'All right, my girl. If you must,' agreed Sybil reluctantly, recognising that distant look she knew so well, but had never fully understood. 'But don't take too long.' And with that they left.

# Chapter Two

### Dorking, 1976

From as early as Grace could remember she'd always sought approval and craved affection from her father, George. A tyrant, who reigned over his family with a rod of iron, George left Grace feeling terrorised and repressed by his constant stream of verbal abuse and scathing attacks.

She was a pretty little girl, slight of bone with fine facial features and dark cascading hair. Her piercing green eyes were always animated and alert, defensively looking out for the unpredictable. Her vulnerability was often evident in the way she would wrap her arms around her hollow chest and speak in a rather strangled high pitched tone – and this annoyed George to distraction.

But his most violent crime of all towards his daughter was one of neglect – he rarely even seemed to acknowledge her existence. It was during these painful periods of rejection that Grace would find herself tiptoeing around the third-floor nursery, desperately trying to keep quiet to avoid drawing attention to herself. With the old rickety floorboards creaking at the slightest movement she restricted her activities to the attic where she and James had made 'camp'. Their hideout was known only to nanny Hannah, who regularly and precariously climbed the timber step ladder with cookies for her charges in her pinafore pockets. It was here that Grace would escape from the real world, acting out *The Wizard of Oz* with her brother James, dancing her way happily down the Yellow Brick road; here that she formed her happiest childhood memories. Many times she wished heartily that she could live in the attic for ever and not have to face the terrifying prospect of irritating her tempestuous father. Yet how she yearned affection and recognition from him – she even felt mildly envious of the regular horsewhipping that James endured, for almost anything would have seemed better than George's apparent indifference towards her.

Of course, when out in public George transformed himself into the traditional family man, proudly showing off his wife and family and putting on a united front. Grace lived for these occasions, when she could pretend they were 'normal', but in her heart she knew her family was different – seemingly unable to show affection or emotion in any way. Grace tried to look to her mother for comfort and support but Beatrice's insecurity, heavily disguised as passive indifference, just made her appear to be the proverbial doormat. Only much later on was Grace to learn that it was her mother's only form of defence – for she too suffered from her husband George's bullish, brutish ways.

On many occasions when Beatrice found Grace sobbing in her room she would push away her own pain and order her daughter to pull herself together. Elegant and refined as she was, she had been programmed by George to be second-in-command, and would stand quietly in his shadow, carrying out his wishes with an expressionless face. Only on rare occasions, and always in George's absence, would she ever laugh or play with her children and Grace couldn't help but think that she'd been deprived of what might otherwise have been a close and loving relationship with her mother because of her domineering father.

In her teens, when James was sent away to boarding school, Grace became more and more isolated. As a weekly boarder, she spent most of her weekends back at home in the attic or in Hannah's room, where she'd practise scenes from plays she'd been involved in at school. One particular rainy Saturday morning, when George had failed to return from London, Hannah and Beatrice sat in the formal sitting room of The Gables and watched Grace perform as Nancy, the female lead in *Oliver*. In a moment of rare luxury, Grace had basked in the glory of seeing her mother's habitually severe face break into a beaming smile when she'd finished, clapping wildly and calling out 'Encore!'. She'd wanted that moment to last for ever – that glorious sensation of feeling adored, treasured and important, and high on the adulation Grace had gone straight into another role, for whilst she had engaged her mother's attention she fully intended to keep it. But half way through her rendition their faces had frozen as they heard the sound of tyres crunching on the gravel drive, and they had silently rushed around putting the furniture back in position. Grace and Hannah headed straight for the nursery and Beatrice quietly went back to her study – the moment was lost.

To make matters worse, Grace also found herself the victim of bullying at school, for her tiny frame made it easier for her schoolmates to intimidate her. Towering over her, they antagonised her with cruel jibes about her flat chest and skinny legs. Pushing, poking and jeering at her, calling her 'Pygmy Seymour' they taunted her that if she didn't get good grades in her exams, she could always get a job in a circus as a midget or dwarf. Sports were an even worse nightmare for Grace, particularly lacrosse and hockey, where she regularly injured herself. Time after time she'd had 'collisions' with other larger girls or had her shins cracked with the back of a hockey stick.

Grace had tried her best not to let them get to her and would hide behind a good book, finding a safe haven in the library away from the overbearing co-pupils, with their Wonderbras and love-bites. But the hurt was always there – was she destined never to fit in?

Grace avoided boys at all costs, feeling awkward and out of her depth. To her they were aliens, altogether rather frightening creatures – James was the only boy she was comfortable with and she missed him dreadfully, but she preferred to stay away from home rather than return to the cold austere atmosphere of the family house. School holidays were always viewed with panic and trepidation and she had mostly managed to avoid going home by enlisting in some kind of extra-curriculum course. She wrote dutifully to her parents each week, informing them of all her successes and exam results, but her favourite letters were to Hannah, who by then had moved to London to work for a prominent aristocratic family, and James, who was boarding at Stowe. He would reply with badly written letters full of spelling mistakes telling her of his latest bouts of misbehaviour. If it hadn't been for James's prowess at sport his Housemaster would no doubt have recommended a transfer to a less academic school, but his excellence at rugby, swimming, basket-ball and in particular tennis, had won the school many a championship, resulting in an impressive display of trophies in the Great Hall. His colourful letters to Grace never failed to lift her spirits and make her laugh, and she drew great comfort from them.

James, too, avoided returning home to The Gables on holidays but when he did, it was always with his great pal, Lloyd Davies, a fellow boarder – and this only served to inhibit Grace further from spending more time with her brother.

At seventeen, after passing her three A Levels, Grace was sent to Le Vieux Chalet, a finishing school in Chateau d'Oex, Switzerland. She found it a lot more tolerable than her time at school, for there was an interesting mix of nationalities – her only complaint was that the girls were rather aloof and tended to form cliques, though this didn't worry Grace unduly, as she preferred to keep herself to herself anyway.

The advantages of Le Vieux Chalet were that she had far more freedom, and was at last treated as an adult, or 'young lady' as they put it. Also, geographically, it put many more miles between herself and her parents or, more particularly, her father, and this made her feel altogether much safer. They visited very rarely as her mother was terrified of flying, but this was a great relief rather than a sadness to Grace. Yes, life at Le Vieux Chalet suited her and she spent her time there fulfilled and happy.

An added bonus was that the dramatic society's facilities were second to none, and Grace eagerly took part in the musical extravaganzas they regularly put on. In fact it was during a lavish production of *A Midsummer Night's Dream,* when Grace was playing Titania, that she was hit like a thunderbolt with the realisation that she had been born to be an actress. Being on stage was no longer a hobby for her, it was a way of life – she lived and breathed for the moments when she was on the boards playing a character. It took away the pain of being Grace Seymour. She was good, and she knew it. Damned good!

She experienced an indescribable high standing at the footlights, filled with a euphoric feeling of power over an audience focused solely on her. She had a hypnotic effect on them and they ate out of her hand at every performance. She covered almost every inch of the stage and delivered her lines as if playing to each and every individual in her captive audience. They responded to her, passionately, and the more she felt their appreciation, the more of herself she gave.

It was obvious to all and sundry that here was a star in the making, so no one was in the least surprised when she announced at the careers meeting that she was planning to study thespian arts.

In between productions, when not rehearsing or helping build and paint sets, she would immerse herself in her other great love – books. Already acquainted with most of the children's classics, she ventured into the realms of adult reading, and it was thus that she came across D H Lawrence's, *Lady Chatterley's Lover.*

But this was one book Grace was not destined to enjoy – for on reaching a particularly explicit love scene, she flung the book face down on her bed, horrified, swallowing hard to rid her mouth of the sudden rush of watery saliva that was threatening to make her vomit. Her eyes burned, her stomach knotted up and her heart pounded alarmingly as her mind took her back to that horrendous scene she'd witnessed in the tack room at The Gables, so many years ago.

Grace had been eleven years old that summer's morning, when she'd wandered into the stable to visit the new foal. Her mother was busy with her seating plan for that evening's dinner party, James was playing tennis with his friend Lloyd and Hannah was tidying the nursery. Picking the straw from the mare's tail her attention was suddenly diverted by a strange, muffled noise from the tack room. She crossed the cobbled stable yard, stood on tiptoe to peer through the glass window, only to be confronted with a sight that would stay with her for the rest of her life: her father, his riding breeches around his muscular thighs, viciously lunging into the groom, Petra, who was bent over the table with her own jodhpurs peeled down to her knees.

Grace had frozen in her tracks, her eyes focusing on her fathers cruel sneering lips, the sweat dripping down his seemingly angry red face, and the bulging purple veins standing out on his temple. It was the aggressiveness with which he was thrusting and the indecipherable words he grunted through clenched teeth that frightened Grace – it was almost like an attack. And the fact that his riding gloves remained on whilst he wrenched at her long auburn plait, straining her neck with one hand, clawing at her buttocks with the other to steady himself. The onslaught of abuse became more intense, her father's voice rasping and increasing in volume. Sick to her stomach and unable to breath, Grace had run as far away from the tack room as she could on shaky legs, and buried her face in the neck of her beloved Labrador, desperate to find comfort. Swallowing away the bitter saliva and wiping her stinging eyes on the golden fur she had forced herself to think about the scene she had just witnessed. Was this how adults were supposed to make love? Was this an example of procreation? And what about her mother? Should she tell her? She shuddered, bewildered and shocked at the horrible scene of betrayal she'd witnessed.

Grace's heartbeat slowly regained its normal pace as she brought herself back to the present, her eye resting uncomfortably on that book again. Sighing, she determined not to dwell on the vision it had provoked and put it out of her mind. But try as she might, the unwelcome memory unleashed many more unpleasant thoughts and feelings.

For when, as a young teenager, Grace had begun to blossom, taking on the makings of a young woman, the physical change in her had only seemed to alienate her further from her father. For he was angered by his own reaction to her growing beauty, and from cruel indifference grew an even crueller obsession.

He did not know how to cope with his own feelings of sexual need, and to hide them he became even more verbally abusive towards Grace. Less and less able to handle the sexual tension he felt around her, he took to ridiculing her, sneering at the different hairstyles and new clothes she experimented with, stripping her of every last vestige of confidence she'd had.

On one occasion Grace suffered such utter humiliation during an Easter break from Le Vieux Chalet that she found herself desperate to return to the safety of her new environment, where she was slowly trying to rebuild her shattered self-esteem. She tried to take on a new persona – to be fun and frivolous like her counterparts – but felt repressed and somehow cut off from her own femininity.

With determination and practice she did eventually acquire the kind of captivating personality she needed in order to fit in, and her popularity increased ten-fold as she became part of the scene. However she still avoided close personal friendships, unwilling to trust anybody, and at parties always kept her eyes vaguely on the door, looking for her means of escape. On many occasions she'd heard her friends talk in breathless detail of their latest sexual adventures. She would turn away, not wanting to hear. Such things revolted – more than that – frightened her, and that hideous scene of her father in the tack room with his sweating sneering face, would repeatedly and painfully flash into her mind.

But there was a lurking curiosity somewhere within, and secretly she worried that there might be something wrong with her. She knew she was different from all the other girls, and battled with the thought that she was physically or mentally incomplete.

Most of the girls had regular lovers and were well past the

giggling stage, which made it even worse for Grace, as they spoke about sex as quite the normal, every day thing to do. When she did occasionally experience male contact, Grace would struggle against a growing sense of panic, but somehow force herself to show some kind of interest and even flirt if she was feeling particularly brave. On these occasions nobody would ever have guessed Grace's true feelings as she'd become quite accomplished at being the life and soul of the party; only those that knew her well might have guessed how nervous she was.

When it all got too much, Grace would climb into her ski-suit, grab her skis and go out onto the mountain as an alternative to the escape route she found with books. On one particular day she had rejected her ski-board – she didn't want to have to concentrate too hard today – and taken the lift to the highest point. At the top she ventured off-piste to the powder snow, her skis swishing crisply, slicing through the sparkling, white powder. Faster and faster she raced down the steep slope, twisting and turning through the forest of snow-laden, picturesque pine trees, icy particles splattering her frozen cheeks and stinging her eyes. Gaining speed and lowering her position she attacked the mogul field with a vengeance, her knees bent. She knew no fear out here, on the mountain. Only beauty, cleanliness, freshness and freedom.

Reaching the bottom she skilfully swung her parallel skis around, slicing and cutting through the snow as she came to an abrupt halt. She paused to catch her breath, removing her glove to brush the new fallen snow off her ebony eyelashes. Out here she was frightened of no one. On skis and on stage, she was master of her own destiny. It had been almost a year since she'd learned to ski and she was proud of the skills she'd acquired – she was certainly going to miss the refreshing and invigorating air of Switzerland when she returned to England. She tried not to think about going home, but the date was approaching fast ...

Determined not to let depressing thoughts ruin her afternoon, she headed for the nearest chair lift, knowing that it would deliver her on to one of Gstaad's most challenging slopes. On the long, cold journey upwards, she noticed her friend Leonora wrapped up in the arms of a ski instructor in the chair ahead. They were giggling and necking openly, the steam from their hot mouths rising into the atmosphere, their dangling skis entwining. Grace was acutely embarrassed – particularly when Leonora turned around in her seat to wave at her. The handsome ski instructor lit a cigarette and nonchalantly threw the empty Gauloise packet overboard, so that it buffeted in the wind before hitting the virgin snow below.

The temperature was rapidly dropping and snow was forming an icy crust. Grace's skis made that wonderfully exhilarating crunching sound as she ripped through the crusty snow. She decided to slalom, racing diagonally across the mountain before starting a death defying race, full pelt down the almost sheer drop. She exhausted herself going cross-country through a pine forest which was more like an obstacle course with its ditches, jumps and fallen tree trunks. Emerging from the dark forest covered from head to toe in snow, she prepared herself for the double black run downhill, which was for the true expert only. Putting on her goggles and zipping her suit up to her chin, she took off, the wind biting her face and her long hair flying wildly behind her.

She almost lost her balance when she caught sight out of the corner of her eye the bottom half of a fluorescent yellow ski suit and a tangle of skis, almost hidden by a boulder. Her first thought was to race to the bottom of the mountain to alert the rescue team, 'the blood wagon' as it's known. But deciding she ought first to see how bad the victim's injuries were, she tore through the snow chipping her skis on barely exposed rocks.

As she reached the boulder, the sight that greeted her eyes was not at all what she'd expected – in fact she was so taken aback, she fell backwards, her bottom landing on the back of her skis.

'Come to join us, pretty one?' laughed Jacques, the tanned, attractive instructor with the strong French accent. Grace, speechless took in the scene. Leonora, lying beneath Jacques, was naked from the waist down with her pretty Damart thermal vest pushed high above her ample breasts. She lay on her white ski suit and her bare legs, clad only in thick woollen socks, were wrapped around Claude's waist, her chestnut hair making a splash of colour in the snow. She turned to look at Grace, grinning.

'Look Jacques, a voyeur! I often wondered how you got your kicks, Grace,' laughed Leonora. Grace blushed furiously and tried to realign herself on her skis. Jacques made absolutely no effort to cover his bare buttocks, his yellow suit pulled down to his thighs.

'I guess this is what you English call a case of *coitus interruptus*,' laughed Jacques, as he reached for a crumpled new packet of Gauloise from his pocket.

'Do join us in a cigarette?' chuckled Leonora.

'Um ... no thank you ... sorry ... I didn't mean to ... sorry,' stammered Grace as she turned her skis south and headed swiftly down the mountain, tears of humiliation and embarrassment stinging her eyes.

Avoiding the jumps and slaloms, she sped, squatting down low in the racing position, poles tucked under her arms to get down to the bottom as fast as possible. Removing her skis, she trudged back to school in her heavy ski boots, passing through Gstaad village. Here she spotted several of her other school friends sipping coffee and eating pains au chocolate in the town's fashionable bistro. They all looked so happy, so confident, sitting behind the steamy windows, flirting and laughing with the international playboy set. What was wrong with her? Why was she so frightened? Why was it that sex or the very mention of it brought about a blind panic within her?

Back in the security of her room, after a steaming hot shower, she got out all the copies of *The Stage*. She read them from cover to cover, but was still unsure of how to go about starting her planned career: where to go, who to see. Now that she'd finally had the courage to admit to herself that her destiny lay with the theatre, nothing was going to stop her — she would find her way.

She knew it was something her parents would be wildly opposed to. She'd hinted at it once, on a weekend exeat, but they had laughed at her and dismissed the idea as ridiculous, insisting that she set her sights on getting a proper job. Well, she'd show them.

# Chapter Three

## The Gables, 1987

Grace stood in the middle of her old, childhood room, barely recognising it. Beatrice had had it completely re-decorated – gone were the pretty pink frills that adorned the windows and walls and in their place were sophisticated cream and coffee striped wallpaper and dramatic, sweeping, sumptuous cream silk curtains with huge coffee and gold coloured corded ropes for tie-backs. The cream carpets and Louis XIV dressing table edged with gold gilt gave the room an air of exquisite elegance.

She moved across to the window: nothing else had changed. The manicured gardens and grounds were the same as always. Her swing, hanging from the apple tree was still there, as was Hamish's, her deceased hamster's grave, complete with miniature headstone. She smiled and picked up her hairbrush. Distractedly brushing her hair she wandered to the closet, knowing her mother had been busily shopping for her newly 'finished' daughter's autumn wardrobe. There were the predictable Jaeger, Yves Saint Laurent and Acquascutum suits – her mother's taste and style entirely. Boring, stuffy and middle-aged, she thought to herself. But rifling through the rest of the hangers, she found to her delight a long black baggy Joseph cardigan with matching jodhpur pants; a casual cream loose weave trouser suit by Armani; and an ankle length tweed and corduroy skirt by Ralph Lauren with matching waistcoat, plus numerous polo and crew necked tops.

Wow! thought Grace. Her Mother really had gone to a lot of trouble and effort here and she was touched at the thought of Beatrice scouring the latest fashion magazines to acquaint herself with the current trends. There was a gentle tap on her door and her mother, classically elegant as always, walked in.

'Well?' she asked, smiling, her eyes sparkling. 'Do you approve?'

'Oh Mother.' said Grace crossing the room, hesitantly, to embrace her. Demonstrative or affectionate gestures were still not common-place within the Seymour family. 'The clothes are wonderful, just what I would I would have chosen, how did you ...?' Grace hugged her mother.

Beatrice smiled, somewhat embarrassed. 'I have to confess I cheated a little. I took a friend's daughter out on a shopping expedition to try and get a feel for what to buy you. I wasn't altogether sure of some of the items, but she assured me you'd love them. After all you're almost the same age.'

'She was right. Thank you so much, Mother.' They went happily through her new wardrobe together, and Grace was shocked when she realised that she was actually enjoying her mother's company. But then why shouldn't she? She'd always automatically judged Beatrice by the same harsh light with which she judged her father. How unfair she'd been.

Beatrice sat on Grace's bed as her daughter tried on each and every one of the new outfits, giving her mother an impromptu fashion show. They talked animatedly, rarely pausing for breath. Beatrice looked proudly at her daughter as she hung up her new clothes and acknowledged her new found confidence and happiness.

'Of course some of the garments will have to be taken up and in a bit, there wasn't a petite range, but that's the peril of being a tiny, size eight,' she said teasingly, herself only a size ten. 'You haven't tried on the Jaeger or Yves Saint Laurent yet ... you don't like them do you?'

'They're very nice, Mother ... but...'

'I know, I know,' Beatrice said with a smile. 'You consider them a little, how shall I put it, straight or prim?'

'Well ... a little...' confessed Grace hesitantly, anxious not to hurt her mother's feelings.

'Well, darling, I don't want to give too much away, but I can only assure you that you'll soon have good use for them, I promise you that.' She winked slyly. 'Come on downstairs, now, your father has an announcement to make.'

Mystified, Grace dressed whilst Beatrice chattered on. 'You must watch the video of James at Wimbledon. It was the thrill of his life to be ball boy ... Of course you know your Father and I are not at all happy with him, he's really become very irresponsible ... I don't know what's to become of him ... He'll soon be leaving school and ...'

'Beatrice? Grace? What are you two doing up there?' came her father's impatient cry from the bottom of the stairs. Grace slipped on her shoes and followed her still beaming mother downstairs.

The drawing room with its lavish furnishings was just how Grace remembered it. A chill swept through her when she made eye contact with her father. She averted her eyes as he approached to hand her a glass of champagne. Suddenly she was aware of a sea of faces all staring and smiling at her. James winked at her encouragingly, sensing her discomfort and his friend, Lloyd, nodded and smiled. The Williamsons were there with their soppy daughter Sarah, along with Reverend Thwaite and his perpetual, irritating smile, Craig Masters, one of the directors of Texoil, and two anonymous faces Grace recognised as her mother's associates from Sothebys. Bemused by the assembled group and wondering what the occasion was, she jumped when her father cleared his throat to address them all

'Ahem ... My good friends, as you can see, my one and only, much loved daughter has returned from her travels abroad and has arrived as one would say "finished".' He smiled at his own joke. 'This, my dear Grace, is an impromptu gathering to welcome you home, where you belong. There has been a long and deafening silence since you and James left to go away to school, and I'm looking forward to the chaos and mayhem one usually encounters when one's offspring return to the nest.' He paused. 'Your mother and I have thought long and hard about which profession you would now like to focus your attentions on and, knowing your love of books and the arts, we think we have come up with something that you'll be thrilled with.' He smiled delightedly. 'Over to you, Leighton, you do the honours,' he said, lifting his glass and nodding at Leighton Crown.

Grace felt the first stirring of alarm as Leighton stood forward clearing his throat. 'My dear Grace, I've watched you develop from a delightful little girl into a most intelligent and genteel young lady, and would be proud to have you on the staff of Sothebys. Your position would be as apprentice to Charles Collier, who is the most renowned restorer in the country of leather bound antique books. It is a highly accomplished skill, a position many would covet ... and your parents and I feel ...'

Grace's mouth fell open as the speech progressed. She was aware of everyone in the room celebrating and toasting her in her new found vocation, but all she could think was 'How could they do this to me? This is my life, to do with as I choose. How dare they take it upon themselves to arrange my career?' She fumed, reeling with shock and fury.

Her mother and Leighton approached her ready to plant congratulatory kisses on each cheek. But Grace stepped aside, holding her hand up.

'Mother, Mr Crown, I'm extremely flattered and honoured to be offered a job at Sothebys. But I don't feel ready to ... well, I feel I need time to sort myself out, to discuss with my parents the options *I've* outlined for myself. I'm not sure that I would be quite right for the job ...' There was a horrified silence. 'Thank you for thinking of me, but ... I really can't accept ...'

George yanked his daughter's arm roughly, pulling her to one side and hissed through clenched teeth, 'Have you *any* idea how sought after that particular position is? Stop being ridiculous. Leighton and Lawrence have driven down from London especially, as a favour to me and your mother ... you're sounding like an ungrateful, spoiled brat, Grace, and I won't have it. Now for God's sake pull yourself together and thank the people concerned.' Aware of the many pairs of eyes focused on them he straightened his tie and forcing a broad smile, said, 'Let's have no more nonsense. Your mother and I ... we've planned——'

Grace slammed her glass down on the grand piano thoroughly riled. 'Just what *have* you and Mother planned?' she demanded, raising her voice. She never knew where or how she found the courage to assert herself, always having been brought up to be subservient and respectful toward her elders, but her long pent up frustration was finally unleashed. 'How ... how *dare* you arrange my life for me with out any consultation. I'm nineteen years old! I do have opinions and ambitions of my own which you haven't taken into the least account!' She took a deep breath before the final hurdle. 'I'm not going to be manipulated any more – I'm going to be an actress ...' The room was silent. 'A great actress ...' she added.

George's face coloured in fury. He sucked in his breath through gritted teeth, gripped his glass and, trying to appear calm in front of the guests, forced a patronising smile. 'Let's not go through that again Pumpkin. You know how your mother and I feel about that. Be serious.'

'I *am* serious! Deadly serious!' Grace cried in frustration.

'Come along now Grace, we've all heard quite enough of your little outburst,' said Beatrice, embarrassed, as she tried to propel her daughter towards the door.

'I will not be sent to my room like a naughty child! I'll do what I want with my life, you can't stop me, none of you can!' And she stormed out of the room, leaving her guests shocked and silent.


'Wow!' exclaimed Lloyd later that night in James's room.'Your sister has got some balls ... *I* wouldn't like to challenge your old man when he's breathing fire.'

'She's got more bottle than most,' agreed James, 'but then she knows he's not going to get the horse whip out for her as he used to for me.'

'Did you see the way her eyes glinted and her face flushed when she told him she wasn't going to be sent to her room like a naughty child? That's one hell of a gutsy girl,' Lloyd continued in admiration.

'Oh yes! Got a bit of a crush, have you?' teased James as his friend coloured with embarrassment. The two laughed and continued to discuss the dramatic night until well into the small hours.

It was the dead of night when Grace crept stealthily down to the kitchen door and stepped over the snoring Labradors out into the garden. The rabbits cheekily darting in front of her up into the shadow of the cherry trees, and the magpies who'd all been her childhood friends tittered and squeaked as she trudged down the long, sweeping drive in her tracksuit, getting soaked by a sudden untimely downpour. She squelched on in her trainers, her sodden hair plastered to her head, until she reached Leith Hill where she knew she could get a bus to Dorking. From there, hopefully, a train would take her to London. She knew she had about eighty pounds cash and five hundred pounds in her building society – it was no fortune, but certainly enough to keep her going for a while. Her holdall contained her favourite clothes, old and new, jewellery she'd inherited from Grandmother Cooper-Smythe and a silver framed photograph of James.

Although there was a large element of drama and excitement about eloping into the night to seek her fame and fortune in London – it was good material for a novel or film, she mused – she also felt a measure of sadness about leaving.

Sitting, dripping on the train, she got out Hannah's most recent letter to check her address – for it was the only place she could think of to run to. Nervous, yet full of adrenalin, she contemplated her future, her new life. Hannah would help her, she always had in times of trouble.

'Today is the first day of the rest of my life,' she thought happily to herself. 'Everything is about to change and at last I'll be in control of my own destiny. I'll make a new life for myself in London and be able to follow my dreams.' Of course she would change her name, all great actresses did. She'd left Grace Seymour back in Dorking and she needed a new identity, a glamorous new name to go with her confident, ambitious new personality.

Lombard ... Grable ... Hepburn? No, she needed something unique and international, but not too clinchéd. Her mind enthusiastically selected and discarded names she plucked randomly from obscurity and she set about short listing potential stage names on the back cover of her address book.

'Madigan Avenue, Belgravia,' she called out to the driver of the black London Taxi cab when she reached Waterloo station. And then paused, excitement building. 'Madigan ... Madigan – that's it! Grace Madigan! That shall be my stage name, my new name. Seymour is no more – I am re-born, and the past is behind me!'

# Chapter Four

## London, 1987

Hannah wrapped her up in her ample arms at the entrance of her basement flat, the live-in accommodation supplied by the family she worked for as nanny to two little girls.

'Ma wee bairn! Let's be getting you out of those wet clothes before you catch your death. I'll explain to the Crawfords that you're my niece and that you've come to stay for a little while. They're a good lot, it shouldnae be a problem. But before we go any further I'm going to phone your parents – they'll be worried sick.'

George was clipped and curt with Hannah, intimating that unless his wayward, ungrateful daughter went home immediately and took up the very desirable vacancy at Sotheby's, he'd wash his hands of her for ever. Hannah was diplomatic, but made no promises and kept the conversation short. Then she and Grace sat up all night while Grace poured her heart out, revealing the whole painful truth to her dear old nanny.

Within the week Grace had accustomed herself to the sofa-bed and Hannah's micro-wave meals and was thoroughly enjoying herself in London. On Hannah's days and evenings off and when Grace wasn't busy desperately trying to get herself auditions, they would take themselves off to half-price matinées at the theatre, or to Covent Garden, Oxford Street or the Tower of London, though Grace found she was getting through her meagre savings at an alarming rate.

'So when am I going to see me darlin' girl, the great actress, Grace Madigan up there on that stage where she belongs?' asked Hannah one day, when they were leaving the Haymarket Theatre. 'When's she going to start going to some of those auditions advertised in *The Stage* and show them what it's all about?' To her horror, Grace burst into tears.

'Oh Hannah, I know I've got what it takes, but ... I didn't think it would be this difficult,' she cried.

'Stuff and nonsense, you're not going to be letting a little lack of confidence get in the way of your dreams. You've come this far, you'll not be turning your back on all that talent. Nanny Hannah will see to that,' she said, comfortingly.

'But it's not as easy as I thought, the whole city seems to want to get into "show business" and anyway I have to have an Equity card before I can do anything, and I can't do anything before I'm an Equity Member ... I can't even go to classes,' she wailed. 'And as far as getting an agent is concerned, I need to have experience before anyone will take me on. How can I get experience without an agent?' she finished, with a sob.

'Mmm, it's very much a case of the chicken and the egg, isn't it. I'll be having nae more of those tears my girl, dry your eyes. An Equity Member you shall become and an agent you shall have. Hannah's sure of that, Gracie love.'

The next day they scoured *The Stage* from cover to cover and made phone calls to theatrical agents, who all spoke in the same disinterested tone, giving the same rejection spiel. Eventually they came across an advert for Abe Cohen's agency on the back page, and he reluctantly agreed to see her.

He was a rotund, ruddy gentleman with a rather squalid office, but he was the only agent prepared to even consider taking her on his books without a show reel, biography or some professional experience, so she wasn't going to write him off. He grunted enthusiastically when he saw how striking her looks were and immediately set up a photo session for some black and white portraits.

Grace raided her building society account to pay for the two hundred blow ups with her name and the Abe Cohen logo printed on them, and for the first time since arriving in London thinking she might be in with a chance, excitedly set off on a round of 'go sees' and auditions.

At her first audition, Grace arrived at a run down basement in Greek Street armed with an A-Z, photographs and plenty of change for the tube fares. She was confronted by at least thirty other petite, dark haired actresses all going for the same Italian commercial for cheese. After waiting an hour she was called to sit on a chair, and say the product name in Italian whilst the cameraman zoomed in on her.

Within five minutes she was back on Greek Street, having had a polaroid taken and her details printed on a casting sheet. Disillusioned, she trudged to Abe Cohen's shabby office in Shaftesbury Avenue.

'You win some, you lose some. Don't expect too much too soon – you might have to do at least a couple of dozen auditions before you hit lucky. Now I've got a small supporting role here that's right up your street, it's a theatre tour of the northern provinces ... equity minimum, but good experience,' he thrust some type written copy into her hands. 'All the details are here for you, plus the lines for you to learn for tomorrow ... make sure you're not late.'

Hannah helped Grace learn the twelve lines of dialogue and the next day she treated herself to a taxi to the audition so that she could take her time getting herself into character as the painfully shy schoolgirl required by the script.

'Thank you Miss Madigan, we'll let you know.'

This was the phrase that Grace had become more than familiar with over the last few weeks and she seriously began to doubt her ability. But more seriously, she was going to have to do something soon about her dwindling finances. Panic and fear began to set in, as she wondered what on earth she could do to keep herself, though Hannah did her best to reassure her.

Abe Cohen continued to send her on auditions for small theatre company tours and Grace tried not to lose heart. Wearily letting herself into Hannah's tiny flat one afternoon, Grace picked up the message on the kitchen table informing her of an audition for coffee ice-cream. She looked at the time and, realising she had less than thirty minutes to get to the advertising agency in Tottenham Court Road, Grace flew straight back out of the door and threw herself into a taxi, arriving with just minutes to spare.

She was taken aback as she was shown into a waiting room full of beautiful, condescending creatures who looked her up and down disparagingly before continuing their conversations.

The blonde with endless legs, long hair, scarlet lips and black beret, was dramatically smoking a cigarette in a long black holder, and quipped, 'Well I'm well and truly pissed off with my agent. This, so I was told, was a commercial for a French yoghurt, so here I am done up like a French tart only to be told it's bloody Devonshire ice-cream.' She dragged on her lipstick caked cigarette holder and pouted as she exhaled the smoke.

'I know the feeling, honey,' sympathised a redhead in a minuscule leather mini skirt. 'My agent is definitely for the boot if I get sent on another bummer like this. I mean, really, it's as if we were a herd of cattle. I *never* go to castings, that's for bimbo model girls. Commercials can be pretty degrading for an actress, but if I've been specifically requested, that's a different matter,' she announced haughtily, applying another layer of lip gloss over heavily lined lips.

In the corner were two very striking females very obviously comparing each others portfolios. '... this was a still from a B movie I shot in LA. No big bucks involved but it looks good on the show reel ...'

An ultra thin girl, pacing around waiting to go in to audition drawing nervously on a cigarette, jumped like a startled rabbit when they called her name and grabbing her portfolio and handbag scuttled off to the video room.

'If you ask me, Charmaine's been going too heavy on the slimming pills, she's nothing but a bag of bones,' said the bottle blonde with the red pencilled lips.

'Mmm, well we could all do with a little help now and then,' piped up a pale brunette beanpole in the corner. Her eyes rested on Grace. 'I haven't seen you on the casting circuit before. You're new in London aren't you?' she asked, not unpleasantly.

'Yes,' Grace replied. 'I've only been here a couple of weeks,' she added confidently. Several pairs of eyes met and brows were raised, as the next girl was called.

The casting was relatively simple compared with the waiting room ordeal. The Director simply asked her to say, 'Mmm coffee cream,' and lick her lips. She was in there no longer than three minutes before the Director said, 'Very nice, dear, we'll be in touch ...'

To her amazement, Abe called that night and informed Grace that she'd got the job. She was ecstatic, and she and Hannah jumped for joy at the prospect of finally getting her Equity card. They celebrated long into the night, and Hannah even went so far as to enjoy a drink or two.

Four days later Grace found herself on a film set at Elstree Film Studios. The atmosphere was electric, and she was fascinated watching the set builders, lighting and sound engineers, make-up artists and hairdressers going about their duties. She took everything in eagerly, even the tea trolley with its huge urn and discarded plastic cups with their unappetising dregs of tea and floating cigarette butts.

When she went to wardrobe she was horrified to learn that she was to be dressed as a brown coffee bean with a huge cream polystyrene hat, supposedly fresh dairy cream. Grace was not impressed with her film debut, and felt quite absurd, but as Abe rightly said, it was a beginning.

On a giant sized turntable, she had to eat a spoonful of coffee ice-cream seductively and say 'Mmmmm coffee cream,' without getting any cream on her lips, so each spoonfull had to be carefully filled and arranged by the special effects man. By the end of the day, each new take became a nauseous nightmare, and eventually a crew member was placed beside her out of shot, so that she could spit the sickly sweet goo into a bucket before the make-up girl reapplied her lipstick. Glamorous this was not. But as it was termed a speaking part, Grace was granted her coveted Equity card and, with the money she'd earned, was able to enrol at The Actors' Centre for classes.

Here she met many exciting new characters; all the students seemed to be in a fashionable state of poverty in their threadbare Levis and oversized, well-worn sweaters, which when removed revealed more often than not a T-shirt that had seen better days. But they studied their art in the most intense manner, as if their lives depended on it, demanding extra time and coaching from the lecturers if they felt they needed it. The lecturers, it seemed, were nearly all famous directors or actors, whose time and patience for their dedicated students were limitless.

Grace had read on the notice board that some of the Vice Presidents of the Actors Centre were established names such as Dame Maggie Smith, Sheila Hancock, Michael Caine and Dame Judi Dench. She was impressed with her new surroundings, and to her great joy, she soon befriended Lana Logan, an extrovert from Ireland who would become the closest friend she'd ever had.

Lana was exuberant and exhaustingly funny – the class comedienne, always pulling stunts and making fun of herself. She was of medium height, with a stunning hour-glass figure which she did her best to expose by wearing micro-skirts with black T-shirts that were three sizes too small. These she mixed with fishnet tights and cumbersome black biker boots with metal clasps. Her hair was platinum blonde, and she'd attempted to grow dreadlocks: Cyndi Lauper was her fashion inspiration.

She was totally unlike the other students, who were all rather low-key and serious. At coffee time, she and Grace would sit together as Lana rolled up her cigarette. 'Us poor drama students can't afford to be buying regular ciggies, anyway it's rather uncool ...'

The two exchanged background stories over many a cappuccino. Lana revealed how she'd grown up in County Cork, where her strict Catholic upbringing had suppressed and restricted her to the point of suffocation.

Her mam and dad had never ventured out of their small village and were aghast when Lana, at eighteen, announced that she was leaving for the bright lights of London. All her life she'd dreamt of becoming a dancer and she had progressed as far as she could in her limited corner of Ireland. With money saved from a part-time job at the bakery, her baby-sitting services, and the small sum left to her by her Gran, she'd left Ireland with enough money for about three months rent.

Finding her flat in Battersea had not been too difficult – it was by no means The Ritz but Lana made the most of the small basement dwelling. Finding a job, however, proved to be almost impossible and the cost of living in London appalled her, what with the high tube and bus fares, the inflated prices for food and dance classes at Pineapple Studios.

So Lana took the only job she could find, filling a vacancy at The Gaslight, a topless club. She'd scoured the columns of 'Dancer Required' in *The Stage* and *Variety* and this was the best she was going to get, for now. So she brushed away any anxious thoughts at the prospect of dancing topless, and the even more horrifying prospect of her parents finding out.

The routine was hardly challenging choreographically – she found the hardest part of the act was rouging her nipples and having to embark on a full bikini wax, but with encouragement from the other dancers and a stiff gin and tonic, she attempted to deliver the goods on stage to the best of her ability. In fact, Lana began to surprise and excel herself, enjoying it to the full.

She strutted and thrust her way across the small stage, well aware of the effect she was having on the audience. She revelled in the adulation she received and consequently gave the 'punters' even more of what they desired. The audience, other dancers and the manager, Frank, were surprisingly friendly, and she found herself making lots of good friends.

She performed well in the chorus and soon became a soloist, with her own slot at the end of the evening. Lana met and drank with many important and affluent clients after her act, and they all told her that with her personality and looks, she would go far.

Like most people, Lana had the pre-conception that club members would be of the 'dirty raincoat' brigade, and was pleasantly surprised at the number of distinguished, high powered businessmen, politicians and aristocrats that were on the VIP guest list at The Gaslight.

A film director gave her a tiny part in a horror movie, and that was how she got her Equity card. She went on to play numerous extras in soap operas and had walk on parts in several BBC productions, plus a few roles with dialogue in a successful new detective series.

She enrolled at The Actors' Centre, loving the camaraderie and atmosphere she found there. When she tried to leave The Gaslight for greater things, the manager was so desperate to keep her he offered her the Saturday night top billing position for more money than she'd earned dancing all week, and he promised to let her choreograph her own 'Star Turn'. It was too good a deal to turn down.

So, Lana Logan became the resident Saturday Night Special Guest Star. Less committed to dancing now that she'd discovered her acting talent, she'd nevertheless grown fond of Frank and the other girls and found it hard to walk away. These people were supportive friends, who'd helped and advised her when she first came to London.

Grace couldn't get over the fact that Lana stripped – something she simply couldn't comprehend. But she couldn't help but admire her friend's resourcefulness and gumption, and her survival in the city tactics. How sheltered and confined her own life, not without its challenges, seemed in comparison. But she had left that behind her; she had only herself and her own resources to rely on now.

# Chapter Five

'May I join you lovely ladies?' requested a young man with a smooth, pleasant voice over Grace's shoulder, as she sat with Lana during one of their many coffee breaks. Before waiting for an answer the man placed himself confidently between them.

Grace guessed him to be about twenty-five, and he was certainly handsome facially, with a square jaw and a touch of dark stubble. Heavy hooded brown velvet eyes peered at her with blatant interest under black flirtatious lashes. She was unable to return his gaze for fear of blushing and averted her eyes to look instead at his body, observing long, denim-clad legs tapering down to tan cowboy boots. A baggy T-shirt didn't do anything to hide an olive skinned, muscular physique, and the man had dark, very attractive body hair on his arms and chest. Holding out his hand, he introduced himself.

'Hi. Hugo Finlay. Of course, I know Lana, but who's the newcomer?' he asked, smiling charmingly. 'I think I heard someone call you Grace in the sight reading class yesterday.'

'I *am* Grace, Grace Madigan,' she replied, as confidently as she could, holding out her hand. Their eyes made contact again as they shook hands and Grace felt her stomach lurch momentarily as they both acknowledged the chemistry of mutual attraction. A certain silence hung in the air and Lana raised her eyes to heaven as she chewed gum vigorously. Grace shifted uncomfortably in her chair.

'I am obviously interrupting a girly chat – my timing is appalling. Maybe you and I could get together for a coffee some other time, Grace?' He looked at her flirtatiously from under his beautiful black eyelashes. Grace felt the colour rising in her cheeks.

'Yes, some other time,' she agreed as nonchalantly as she could. Hugo took his leave.

'Don't take any notice of him – he thinks he's God's gift to women, and I do have to admit, he has the most biteable buttocks. But he seems to have targeted you as his next victim. Be warned.'

Grace looked alarmed.

'Don't worry,' laughed Lana, attempting to poke her tongue through the well chewed gum, 'I'm sure you can handle him.' And the incident was forgotten for the time being.


Over the next few weeks, Grace's confidence soared in leaps and bounds, as she lapped up everything she was taught and revelled in her new friendship with Lana. She even managed to overcome her inhibitions enough to perform a realistic kiss and embrace with a male student during a tender love scene. Her tutor had been extremely pleased with her, being accustomed to awkwardness in his new students.

And constantly in the background was Hugo Finlay, his eyes never leaving Grace. He seemed to scrutinise her performances with great personal interest, and though she did her best to ignore him and their mutual attraction, it was getting harder.

'He's closing in for the kill,' whispered Lana, one day in the green room, as he approached their table.

'Like a lamb to the slaughter,' Grace whispered back,

somewhat oddly feeling braver than she'd felt in her life.

'Three more cappuccinos here please,' he requested to Ted, the snack bar manager, who nodded in acknowledgment. 'So girls, you're looking very agreeable today, if I may say so. What's on your agenda?' he enquired affably.

Stuffing the rest of her carrot cake into her already packed mouth, Lana grabbed her bag and rose, managing to garble, 'My class is just about to start, so I'll have to leave you, Casanova, to utter your usual bullshit to Grace. Have fun.' She grinned amiably, and took off, her mouth covered in crumbs.

Grace and Hugo watched Lana disappear before Hugo turned back to look at her and spoke finally.

'So, Grace, tell me about yourself,' he said, lighting up one of his smelly French cigarettes and blowing the smoke into the air above her head.

'There's not much to tell, really. Anyway I'm really a rather private person ... are you always so nosy?' asked Grace, bravely turning the tables.

'I'm sorry. I didn't mean to be offensive,' he said visibly backing off. 'It's just that I find you so fascinating ... you're so talented.'

Grace smiled, acknowledging the compliment, and leant forward. 'Tell me about you, instead.'

Hugo needed no prompting. He reminded Grace of a modern day Clark Gable, except for his long dark curly hair. The way he spoke, his gestures and presence held Grace captive and she confessed to herself that he was indeed a charismatic man – maybe lacking in modesty, but then he was an actor after all.

Grace watched him talk about himself, which he obviously enjoyed doing, and deduced that he was a natural entertainer. Yes, indeed, Hugo Finlay had been first in the queue when they were handing out good looks and charisma. Grace listened attentively as Hugo continued his life story, unaware that across the room they were being observed by an amused Justin Clegg, a fellow student with whom Grace had struck up a friendship.

'Of course, I'm virtually potless, but I'm not about to start waiting tables or any other demoralising crap, because I know it's just around the corner – the big one. I've turned down several supporting roles, even though my agent says I should have done them, but I'm not about to scrawl and scratch about doing minor parts. I'm a leading man, not some "also ran",' Hugo paused for breath, flicking back the long dark lock of hair that had fallen over his eyes, and smiled.

'Gosh, your life story sounds like an Aaron Spelling production and you're certainly not short of ambition. I'm afraid my history isn't nearly so interesting,' she confessed. She condensed her life story into about five minutes, going into as little detail as possible.

He was impressed when he learned where she lived. 'Belgravia, eh?' he said and whistled. 'Most of the students here have rented rooms and live on baked beans, but you're different, what with your smart clothes and leather handbag ...' He examined her with his tantalising brown eyes.

Suddenly Grace felt self-conscious, she was the first to admit that she hardly looked the part of the penniless student. 'Well, Hugo for your information, I'm about as broke as you are. These clothes you see are about all I possess – in fact, in a few weeks I'm starting to work in the evening at the Texas Ranch. Lana works there too and managed to get me a job.'

'Oh, Grace, surely you don't need to do that? You're too classy to have to wait tables – you've got "star" written all over you. You shouldn't have to demoralise yourself with all that shit, you're far too good for it,' he said sincerely.

'Needs must, Hugo. I'm determined to pay my way.' Grace was beginning to find Hugo's interest in her a little too intrusive for her liking, but at the same time she felt she had in some way found a soul mate in him.

Over the next few weeks they spent more and more time together. They would talk for hours on end about their favourite playwrights, classic and contemporary, feeding off each other's passion for the theatre. Grace found herself looking forward to their daily debates and it became quite a regular thing for the handsome duo to be seen in intense conversation in the green room.

Eventually, the time came for Grace's initiation at the Texas

Ranch. Standing in front of the full length mirror in the dingy staff room she exclaimed, 'Oh my God, Lana, I can't wear this! You can see my knickers when I bend down. Look at me! Hannah would give birth if she could see me now – not to mention Hugo!'.

'Well, good job they're not here then. You should be grateful you get to keep your togs *on,* so stop whinging – we all have to wear the same thing and all the punters are interested in are the barbecued ribs and Mexican beers. Who the hell do you think wants to look at your knickers?' Lana laughed. 'Hey, did you know, we get paid extra if we get up on the bar and dance at the end of the evening?'

'Oh no, it gets worse,' Grace groaned, taking another furtive look at herself in the mirror. Her reflection showed her with her hair in plaits, a huge Stetson on her head, white drawstring blouse showing far too much cleavage for her liking, a red and white gingham bolero waistcoat, the tiniest A-line gingham skirt with matching knickers, bare legs and cowboy boots, complete with artificial spurs. 'Yeuch,' she shuddered.

Grace assisted Lana on her tables until she was accomplished enough to be allocated her own five tables. The atmosphere was that of a bar in the Wild West. Country and Western music blared above the noise of the rowdy customers; the wooden floor boards were covered in sawdust and the walls decorated in rifles, guns, 'Wanted, Dead or Alive' posters, saddles, bridle tack, bullock heads with horns and brass flickering lamps. The juke box never stopped playing the likes of Patsy Cline, Tammy Wynette, Johnny Cash and Willie Nelson.

Grace quickly learned how to serve food without bending over and showing her knickers or too much bosom. 'Don't be such a prude,' whispered Lana in passing, with a platter of ribs. 'The more you show, the bigger they tip. One thing's for sure Grace Madigan – I'd never get you on stage at The Gaslight!'

'Don't even think about it,' Grace whispered back, eyes wide at the very thought.

At the end of the evening after last orders, the dancing

started and the girls scrambled onto the bar to do their stuff, shrieking with laughter and throwing their Stetsons into the air. Before she knew it Lana had Grace up there with her, and much to her surprise she found she was laughing and genuinely enjoying herself, despite her shyness. To hell with her knickers!

Then, for a horrified moment, her eyes locked with Hannah's. What on earth was her old nanny doing here, tonight? Fearing she would strongly disapprove, Grace hesitated but found on a closer look that Hannah was laughing heartily and joining in the merriment. She smiled, relieved, and carried on enjoying herself.

After wiping down the tables, the girls got dressed into their own clothes. 'Hope you don't mind me inviting Hannah along,' explained Lana, as she zipped up her jeans. 'She was a bit anxious as to how and where you were going to work. I thought it a good idea for her to see for herself that this was a bona fide burger joint.'

'Of course I don't mind,' reassured Grace, as her friend ran into the kitchen to stuff the left over potato skins with soured cream and chives, into the bin. Grabbing her bags, she took off for her next appointment at The Gaslight.

On the bus home, Hannah was still singing along to the music the girls had been dancing to. 'I've not had so much fun since I don't know when ... eh, lass, there are times when I wish I was young again. What in God's name would your Mother be making of you tonight, I wonder? Still, it's all good clean fun, if you're asking me.' She chuckled away to herself all the way home.

Encouraged by how much she enjoyed the job, Grace enrolled in Lana's promotions agency for extra work and found herself in many more bizarre situations: hobbling around in clogs and Dutch national costume, handing out pieces of Gouda cheese at a food and wine fair; erecting and dismantling tents at a camping and leisure exhibition; covering her face and shoulders in Dead Sea Mud at a health and beauty show. But being a Marlborough Girl was the easiest: all she had to do was to mingle, handing out cigarettes to people. At the motor show she found herself draped across a Lamborghini wearing only a bikini. That hit the newspapers and Grace wondered what her parents would think. James wrote to her telling her he thought it was 'cool'.

It certainly was an eye-opener for Grace. Life was just full of surprises. She continued to study hard at The Actors' Centre and got more and more fond of her new friend, Justin. She found him kind, funny and a loyal friend, much to the annoyance of Hugo, who considered Grace his sole property. Grace often took Justin home to Hannah for supper – she felt comfortable with Justin as he was gay and made no secret of the fact.

Lana had taken up with a rather eccentric student, called Marcus, who was very in to the contemporary, off the wall fringe theatre productions. They engrossed themselves in such productions, working well together, and were both offered jobs at the Fringe in Edinburgh. Excitedly, they accepted the roles and took off, though Grace was devasted when Lana left.

But she recognised that she had to stand on her own two feet, and luckily she was more comfortable now with some of the other students, Hugo and Justin in particular. She was getting to know Hugo better and better and, to her surprise, even Hannah warmed to him when she stepped in as 'prompt' at their rehearsals in the tiny basement flat in Belgravia. He always arrived with shortcake or chocolates for Hannah and flowers for Grace, and more often than not brought a bottle of red wine. Hannah, for her part, would always make sure she had pasta, and the ingredients in her pantry for Hugo's favourite dish, *penne arriabiatta*.

One night, when Grace and Hugo quietly let themselves into the basement flat after a late night movie, anxious not to wake Hannah, they heard movement in her room and Grace peeped in to see her sitting on the side of her bed weeping silently.

Alarmed, she rushed straight in. 'Hannah, whatever is the matter, tell me?' demanded Grace, Hugo hot on her heels.

'All ma life I've been looking after wee bairns, now they tell me, at sixty, I'm too old. I'm as fit as a fiddle, I even gave 'em a blast of the Highland Fling to prove ma point, but they were having nothing of it. They said I shall have the best references, but they feel I should be retiring. *Me*, retire!' She sniffed. 'Ma whole life's been young 'uns, I'm happy here in ma work, those two wee darlings are ma pride and joy.' Hannah burst into floods of new tears.

'Oh Hannah, you're the best nanny in the whole wide world. I don't know how I'd ever have survived without you, and I'm sure there are many others who feel the same,' soothed Grace.

Hugo sat down on the bed and put his arm around Hannah. 'I wish I'd had a nanny just like you Hannah. I was sent off to boarding school straight after mother died. Don't you worry now, you'll be snapped up by another more deserving family just like that,' he snapped his fingers and held her closer to him.

'Apparently, it's not my ability, it's the fact I can't run about and get down on me hands and knees like I used to, due to the rheumatism, and 'cos I puff like an old billy goat. They've got a new Norland Nanny, a young lass, starting in three months. A new age Montessori type of thing.' Hannah's heart was broken. Her whole life had been devoted to looking after other people's children and now she had been rejected by the very people she'd worked so tirelessly for.

'Get some sleep now, Hannah, we'll sort this out tomorrow,' said Grace gently, leading her to bed, and staying with her until she closed her eyes at last.

The next day Grace telephoned all the nanny agencies in London, but they were all unanimous in their response, stating that they could not take on a sixty-year-old nanny, however highly qualified: the most they could offer was occasional babysitting. Grace's heart sank.

Defeated, she helped Hannah to start making plans to go back home to Scotland, where she'd be able to stay with her sister, Rose. They made a pact not to be miserable, to make the best of the three months they had left together, and Grace's worries over where she was going to live were relieved when Justin offered her the second bedroom in his flat. She could just afford the rent, what with the money she was earning at the Texas Ranch, promotional work and residuals from the coffee ice-cream commercial, and Hannah had fastidiously inspected the flat and given it her seal of approval. They all agreed it was the perfect solution.

As the date of Hannah's departure approached, Grace and Hugo decided to treat her to a performance at The Royal Court Theatre in Sloane Square, as they had some friends in the cast and their tickets were half price. On the way there, they were just passing down Cliveden Place in the taxi when Hannah tapped on the glass and asked the driver to drive slowly once around Eaton Square, where the Seymours had had their second home.

'Oh Hannah,' said Grace impatiently. 'That's all in the past, it doesn't mean anything to me.'

'To you, maybe m'lass, but I had many a happy time there. Of course, I preferred The Gables. But I have strong memories from here, too. Good memories ...' said Hannah sadly.

'Please Hannah, don't get maudlin.' Grace soothed, putting her arm around the old lady.

'You never told me you used to live in Eaton Square, Grace,' exclaimed Hugo, obviously impressed.

'Sometimes. But mostly my parents used to stay there during the week. My brother and I were based mostly in Dorking.'

'Oh Hugo, we had a grand time at The Gables we ...' started Hannah nostalgically, before noticing Grace's pained expression. She stopped abruptly leaving Hugo confused, though clearly impressed by the kind of background Grace seemed to come from. But he didn't pursue it further and the rest of the evening passed uneventfully.

Back at the Centre, Hugo and Grace started work on *Much Ado About Nothing*, concentrating hard on the relationship between Beatrice and Benedick. They worked day and night, Grace taking time off from the Texas Ranch to go over to Hugo's, where she often slept over on the futon. Although it was a bit of a journey to the Docklands, the warehouse he'd bought with an inheritance from his Aunt Tabitha was the perfect place for them to work: it was enormous, with natural brick and exposed beams and joists, huge potted palms and rugs on the polished floor boards. So full of character, so bohemian, so Hugo, somehow.

By now she was completely relaxed with Hugo, knowing he wasn't only interested in her in a physical sense. In fact, she even began to wonder if she was attractive to him in any way at all. Whilst they were putting every spare moment into the production, Grace learned to cope with Hugo's temperamental outbursts – he was so passionate about his craft, so ambitious – and would watch him fondly as he brushed back the lock of black hair from his eyes as he agonised over certain moves and lines.

Though he was impossibly arrogant and supercilious, she had grown extremely close to him, knowing that behind his façade he was just a lonely young man – his own worst enemy. When he stopped being an 'actor', they had many varied and interesting conversations, but whenever Hugo questioned her about her family, she would clam up.

'But I don't understand. Why don't you stay in Eaton Square, after all it's empty half the time ...'

'Hugo, I don't ever want contact with my parents – I need to be independent,' Grace insisted.

'OK, OK. I just thought it would be a lot more comfortable than sharing that pokey flat with Justin when you have to move out of Hannah's.'

'Oh Hugo, what am I going to do about Hannah, in a few weeks she'll be off,' wailed Grace, grateful to change the subject. 'Her heart's broken, she feels useless, on the scrapheap,' she continued.

At that moment the phone rang in Hugo's apartment, and uncannily it was Hannah, excitedly asking to speak to Grace.

'Gracie, love, It's a miracle to be sure. Rose's daughter-in-law, Edwina, has decided to go back to teacher training college. They've got three wee bairns aged six, eight and nine, all at school in Dundee, and they want me to go and be nanny. Isn't it wonderful?' she laughed happily. 'I'll have my own granny annex, and though the money's not grand or what I'm used to, I'll be part of the family. She's a grand lass is our

Edwina and her wee ones are dear little pets ...' Grace smiled to herself as Hannah rattled on and on. 'But, I'll not rest easy, Gracie until I see that you're settled in with Justin, you're still my responsibility, even through you're almost grown up.'

'Hannah, I'm nearly twenty, I can look after myself. Justin and I get on brilliantly and you know how nice the flat is. He even has two bathrooms, how's that for luxury?'

'As long as I know that you're fine. I'll expect a letter once a week and at least a couple of phone calls ...' fussed Hannah.

'Don't start, Nanny,' laughed Grace. 'I'll be home soon,' she added.

'Well, in that case I will be making you your favourite supper – macaroni cheese with grilled bacon on top, so I'll best be down the shops before they shut. Bye, Gracie love.'

Grace replaced the receiver, suddenly feeling lonely. What with Lana gone, and now Hannah, Grace felt she was going to be on her own once more.

Hugo sat down beside her on the enormous scatter cushions and whispered in her ear. 'You know, the obvious thing to do is for you to move in here with me. Lana and Hannah have been your life line, without them you'll be lost.'

'How did you know I was thinking of them?' she asked.

'I'm psychic, Grace ... I can read your thoughts,' he said knowingly. 'This place is so enormous, I get lost in here on my own. We could work together – we need each other. We're good together, Grace, we feed off each other's talent, and you'd have your own space.'

'But I've already arranged to move in with Justin, you know that,' replied Grace.

'You think you're better off going to share some flea-pit with a bloody poofter!' said Hugo standing up and pacing up and down, his cowboy boots scuffing the polished floorboards, hands in the back pockets of his jeans.

'Hugo, your reputation at the Centre goes before you – they all call you the resident Casanova. Apparently, your sheets are almost threadbare and always warm with your constant flow of female admirers. I don't want to cramp your style. You have an image to uphold ...' explained Grace as tactfully as possible.

'OK, sure, I was hardly a Trappist monk, but it was all a diversion until you came along. None of that interests me any more, I value your friendship more than anything else in the world.' He paused, and took hold of her hand. 'You're different Grace, you've got style, breeding and most of all, a blinding talent. We're on the same wave-length, we speak the same language, deliver a performance the way it should be delivered. You're comfortable with me now, I know you are. You used to be a nervous wreck in my company, so I respected that and never approached you amorously, though God knows I wanted to.'

Grace looked alarmed, but he continued, never moving his eyes away from hers. 'I've had to fight myself, and use all the self-restraint I could muster to keep my distance and my hands off you. I've sensed your nervousness and I've respected your need for space, but we're meant to be together, Grace. The sooner you realise that the better.'

# Chapter Six

All too soon the day came for Hannah to leave for Dundee. It was an emotional day for all concerned as Grace packed up her belongings, said her painful good-byes and headed for her new home at Justin's.

It was a lovely flat, larger and more luxurious than the basement she'd shared with Hannah, but she felt lost as she forlornly hung her clothes up in her new wardrobe. Justin, anxious for her to feel at home, cooked her supper and encouraged her to telephone Hannah and let her know she was happily settled in.

Most evenings Grace worked on the script of the Centre's new production, *A Streetcar Named Desire*, and Justin went to meet his friends from the Royal and National Ballets. Occasionally she would go over to Hugo's warehouse where they would rehearse and talk long into the night. They rarely mentioned Hugo's impassioned declarations and he never pushed her to accept his romantic advances. She looked forward to their evenings together.

Her brother, James, now in his final year at Stowe, made a

point of travelling regularly to London to see his sister, now that he enjoyed a little more freedom. They became closer than ever and revelled in their time together. Grace began to notice that James's most recent conquests were not just on the rugby pitch and tennis court, but increasingly of the female variety, and she found herself worrying about his dismissive, arrogant attitude toward women. Was he a product of his own father or merely a young stud out to prove his sexuality? Whatever it was, Grace convinced herself that he'd grow out of it and mature into a young gentleman like his friend Lloyd Davies.

James had made a special trip to The Actors' Centre to see Grace play opposite Hugo in *A Streetcar Named Desire*, and sat amongst the small audience enthralled. There were only makeshift costumes and sets, minimal props, and only an imaginary curtain, but as soon as this went up, Grace gave her all. In that performance she *was* Blanche du Bois, and the love scene was as passionate and fiery as could be. Hugo too, was captivating as Stanley, and together on that makeshift stage, they came alive, flushed with passion.

Grace had grown to look forward to these scenes with Hugo, as she knew from the script exactly what was going to happen and felt safe as his hands ran up and down her back and as he brought his lips down to meet hers. Each time, she felt an alarming churning in the pit of her stomach she couldn't explain, so to distract herself she'd concentrate on staring up into his nostrils, counting the hairs, whilst trying to keep her mind on her next cue.

They pulled it off brilliantly and their audience sat in mesmerised silence, utterly wrapped up in the moving scenes. So much so that, when the performance came to an end, they were so stunned by what they'd seen they were barely even able to clap, let alone provide the tumultuous applause the actors deserved. It took several agonising moments before they were able to show their true appreciation, and even James was subsequently quieter than usual, such was his awe at his sister's talent.

That night, euphoric and still on a high, Grace went with Hugo to his favourite bistro, having put James on his train.

They enjoyed a simple meal of French onion soup, garlic bread and a bottle of red wine, chatting incessantly about the evening, before heading back to Hugo's.

Grace stayed for hours, for she was far too hyped to be able to sleep, or to be alone. After they had talked animatedly for some time, she became aware that Hugo was looking at her solemnly.

'Why are you looking at me like that?' she asked, warily.

'I have a confession to make,' he sighed. 'All those rehearsals I insisted on calling for our love scene weren't strictly neccessary, I just needed an excuse to hold and kiss you again and it seemed the only way to get close to you ...' Sensing a more positive reaction from Grace than usual, he continued, watching her closely all the while. 'It fed my craving for a while, but now it's not enough. You were only kissing me because the script required it, but now I yearn to kiss you for real, without script, without direction, just us. I want to kiss *you*, Grace, not Blanche du Bois ... and more importantly, I want you to want to kiss me back.'

Grace was silent, mesmerised by the attraction she felt for this man with whom she'd shared such excitement. Further encouraged, Hugo leaned forward, gently took her face in his hands, and kissed her as he'd never kissed her on stage.

She felt the familiar lurch in her stomach, stronger than ever, and before she knew it, Grace was kissing Hugo back hungrily, wanting more and more of him. They lay back on the cushions, bodies and tongues entwined, exploring each other, and Grace found herself pulling Hugo's body closer to her. He sensed this and responded, all the time kissing her until she was totally intoxicated. Her face burned and her body prickled – so strong were the sensations that Grace felt slightly afraid. Don't be ridiculous, she told herself. You're twenty, you can handle this, Grace.

As if sensing her fear, Hugo broke away. 'Don't panic, Sweetheart, you're still in control,' he whispered. 'You call the shots.' And with that Grace pulled Hugo towards her again.

'Make love to me,' she whispered bravely, nibbling his ear.

'Are you sure, Grace? I know this is your first time.' He

looked concerned.

'How do you know? Is it that obvious?' He smiled kindly.

'Of course, you've had literally hundreds of girls, you know all about it. I expect you could rewrite and update The Kama Sutra,' she grinned, embarrassed.

Hugo, too, looked sheepish. 'Yes, you know I'm experienced, but none of that meant a thing to me. You are what I've been waiting for all my life, Grace. I've dreamt of this moment. I love you too much to want to risk blowing it by going too far.'

'You love me? You really love me?' Grace marvelled. And when he nodded seriously, she felt she would drown in the warmth that shone from his eyes. 'I want you to make love to me, show me what to do,' she begged.

'There's no manual or guide book, Grace,' he soothed. 'Just do as you feel.' She pulled Hugo's T-shirt over his head and buried her face in his burly chest, kissing his neck and shoulders, relishing the closeness of him, his scent, his taut body. Very slowly, he undid the buttons on her blouse, prepared for protestation, but none came. She eagerly helped him remove it.

Their kissing became more and more intense and Hugo gently removed her bra, tenderly stroking her breasts. Grace gasped, searching again for his lips, kissing him deeper, longer and even more passionately. How good their bodies felt together, naked. The sensation of her full breasts rubbing against his muscular chest was just indescribable, and they moved frantically, straining to be even closer together. Her body was burning with desire and her flushed face feverish with passion. Slowly, Hugo reached down to the belt buckle on his jeans, undoing his fly zip and lowering his jeans down.

But at this point Grace sat bolt upright as the ghastly image of her snarling father viciously plunging into the groom shot into her mind and broke the spell.

'I'm sorry Hugo, I didn't mean to ...' she whispered, appalled at herself.

'There's nothing to be sorry for, you just need time, that's all,' he smiled, knowing he mustn't show her his overwhelming frustration.

Grace heaved a huge sigh of relieve and looked back at the chocolate brown eyes staring at her. 'We really should be together, you know Grace,' he mused. 'I feel we are the next Elizabeth Taylor and Richard Burton, or Paul Newman and Joanne Woodward ... And imagine, it would read even more romantic in the biography to say that we met and married at drama school.'

Grace stopped in her tracks, her eyes wide. 'What did you say?' she whispered.

Sensing her panic, he lightened up. 'Arrogant I may be, but insensitive, I'm not. I know you have no real affection for me yet. But you will, I'm sure of it,' he said, confidently.

'Hugo, I do ... I have deep affection for you ... it's just that I'm ...' Grace floundered.

'You're the first girl I've met in a long time who has real talent, and I mean *real* talent. To me that's the biggest turn on there is. I also have a great deal of respect for the way you haven't tried to sleep your way through the city's casting directors, as most aspiring actresses do. You've got too much class for that – you're special, very special.' He gazed at her adoringly. 'Oh hell ... *would* you consider marrying me, Grace?'

Hugo's out-of-the-blue proposal stunned her, quite taking her breath away as she stared vacantly at him. True, she had become more and more comfortable in Hugo's company – he was the first male who didn't make her squirm and feel nervous. The first man who had recognised and respected the reasons for her anxieties.

'If there's anyone who understands you and has the patience to wait for your trust, it's me, Grace,' he continued gently. 'I'm willing to wait for as long as it takes. I desperately want to make love to you, the way a man should make love to a woman, with gentleness, kindness and tenderness. There's so much passion lying dormant within you, you just won't let it out. I'm your friend, colleague, critic, admirer, but I long to be your lover. I'll be here waiting for you when you're ready.' Hugo held her hands, kissing her fingers.

Still reeling, Grace remained speechless, unable to

assimilate Hugo's proposition.

'Look Grace, my clumsy proposal may seem sudden to you, but the truth of the matter is that I fell in love with you the first day I saw you at the Centre. I've waited all this time, biting my tongue every inch of the way. But there, now you know how I feel. I just hope I haven't jumped the gun and scared you off for good now.'

Grace's eyes filled with tears. Of course she was attracted physically to Hugo, what woman wouldn't be? But fear had held her back from admitting it fully, even to herself. But now it was different somehow; she trusted him, felt safe with him, protected. She had seen more than a little of Hugo's sensitivity and tenderness over the last few months, and knew that his often impossibly arrogant attitude was due solely to his professional creativity.

There was no denying the recent bond that had grown between them, nor the fact that her heart quickened every time she set eyes on him each day. They'd developed a closeness which Grace was comfortable with, and now she found herself boldly wanting more. 'I can't take all this in now. Let's discuss it later,' she whispered and with her heart pounding, she took his face in her hands and went to kiss him once more. He didn't move forward, he wanted her to make the move. She did, hesitantly at first, but finding it wasn't as terrifying as she thought, she began to move with more confidence. Only then did Hugo respond, kissing her back gently.

It was then that Grace realised just how well Hugo understood that it all had to be on her terms – the decision hers. This was enough to convince her that she, too, was in love with him, and she eagerly pressed her lips harder against his.

Hugo reluctantly broke away. 'I promised Hannah I'd take care of you, and I don't want you to do anything you're uncomfortable with. Say you'll marry me, Grace ... please say yes,' Hugo pleaded.

'But Hugo, I can't ... I'm not sure that ...' Grace started.

'The physical side of things will take care of itself in due course, I promise you. There's plenty of time for that, Grace – I told you, I can wait as long as it takes.' He smiled at her tenderly. 'The important thing to me is that you'll agree to become my wife.'

What a mature and understanding man Hugo had become ... but marriage, that was something else, something else indeed! 'I need time to think ...' Grace faltered.

'How long?' grinned Hugo looking at his watch.

'About two seconds!' she grinned back.

The ceremony was most unceremonious, the registry office dank and dingy, but Grace was unperturbed by her surroundings – the important thing was that she had with her the people she loved most in the world.

Hugo looked gorgeous in a dinner jacket, but wanting to add an element of the eccentric drama student, had substituted the normal shirt, tie and shoes for a white T-shirt and baseball boots. Hannah, having returned from Dundee for the wedding, wore her poppy outfit, that Grace could remember her having worn for garden parties and special occasions at The Gables. It was so Hannah; sunny, bright and full of cheer, and with the straw hat with its matching silk poppies jauntily bouncing on her head, she really looked the part.

Lana, who'd burst in and jumped all over the bride-to-be at six-thirty that morning, had caught the night sleeper from Edinburgh, and looked as only Lana could, in her own distinguished style. As bridesmaid, she'd decided on her 'Morticia' dress, which was full length, dark burgundy with long medieval sleeves. Grace had seen this dress on many occasions, but not alongside the vegetable rinsed claret coloured hair, with a scattering of woven turquoise beads plaited throughout!

Grace laughed at her best friend's latest look, and put her bizarre style down to too much Scottish spring water. She was as bubbly and dynamic as ever, and Grace realised sharply how much she'd missed her. So, selfishly, she was delighted to hear her friend had quit the Fringe, dumped Marcus and planned to come back to London.

Justin wore white Levis, with a ruffled, romantic looking shirt, his long blond hair swept back off his face. 'I'm happy for you Grace, and sorry to be losing a fab flat mate,' he said warmly. 'You're a very special person and Hugo's a very lucky man. Remember I'll always be here for you, should you ever need me.' Although Grace was touched by his sincere words, she was slightly annoyed by their pessimistic implication.

James, at eighteen, was already devilishly handsome. For someone so young he had a surprising number of laughter lines on his olive-skinned face, and crow's feet that fanned out into his dark hairline, showing that he liked to live life to the full. His mischievous hazel eyes – a mixture of Beatrice's green and George's brown – surveyed the scene. Although a little taken aback by Grace's unusual and eccentric friends, he made a big effort with everyone. He swept Hannah off her feet with an almighty bear hug when he saw her.

'Put me down this minute, Jamie my lad! You're not to big to be getting a clip around the ear from your old Nanny. Behave yourself, or else I'll be stinging your legs, you cheeky bairn,' laughed Hannah, tears in her eyes. 'You're naughtier than ever ...'

'You can say that again, Hannah,' laughed James, pushing a tall, stunning girl wearing a tight PVC cat suit forward. 'Clara will vouch for that,' he joked, pinching the blushing teenager's bottom. Looking suave and debonair in his tail-coat and silk cravat, he was proud to give his sister away.

Grace had dipped into her building society fund to buy her wedding dress, and after searching high and low she chose an antique twenties, cream lace calf length dress from Antiquarius. Hannah mumbled that it looked like it had seen better days, but knew better than to be critical. Grace was happy with it and that was all that mattered, she thought to herself. So with a simple crown of lily of the valley, and holding a single red rose with a ribbon that Hugo had given her, she married him.

Later on, when their guests were throwing themselves into the reception party with a vengeance, Grace and Hugo took a quiet moment together, their eyes locked in love and adoration for one other.

Never before in her life had she felt so happy and fulfilled, and Grace blinked back tears as she looked around at her new husband and all the people she cherished. She would remember this moment for ever.

# Chapter Seven

Grace and Hugo couldn't afford to go away on a honeymoon, but they didn't feel the need to, for they were happy re-arranging the huge converted warehouse, buying bits and bobs to turn it into a more marital home. They bought rugs, cushions, potted palms, huge wrought iron candle holders with large candles, a hammock which they attached to the original rough wooden joists, and aromatic incense sticks which filled the air with musky frankincense and myrrh.

Neither Grace nor Hugo had ever been so happy. But there was one enormous chink in the perfect shiney armour: technically Grace was still the proverbial virgin bride.

Although throughout their three month-long marriage they had been intimate and explored each other's bodies with relish, they had yet to consummate their union fully, and this had now become a major stumbling block. Grace tried hard to relax, but each time they reached the crucial moment she would feel every muscle in her body tense up and her mouth go dry.

'Man cannot live by bread alone, Grace,' said Hugo one

night, climbing frustratedly out of the enormous futon to pace the beautifully restored floorboards. Grace watched him nervously as he prowled up and down, lighting a cigarette, then running his hand through his thick wavy hair. His naked body was a work of art, thought Grace. She had never seen a man totally naked before, except in sculptures or paintings, but Hugo, she thought, was quite beautiful. She still didn't feel comfortable being totally naked herself, and at first Hugo had been touched by her shyness, re-arranging the sheets to cover her up a little. But now he was beginning to lose patience.

'I could understand it if you looked like an elephant, but the truth is Grace, you are quite exquisite – the daintiest and most feminine thing I've ever seen. Of course I don't mean for you to flaunt your body to all and sundry and do a "turn" like Lana, but just for your husband, once in a while, eh?' he smiled tenderly at her. 'Is that too much to ask?'

They had discussed the problem endlessly, but Grace could never bring herself to be entirely open with Hugo – or for that matter with herself – about the reasons for her sexual anxiety. As a form of defence, she threw herself even more vigorously into her acting classes, and began to avoid opportunities to address the problem with her husband.

Luckily fate intervened to give her a helping hand when Hugo's agent, Faith Goodman, saw Grace act and was immensely impressed with her, agreeing to represent her straight away. The best part was that Grace felt sure that having the same agent would give them more chance of actually working together.

Two days after taking her on, Faith called with an audition for a shampoo commercial for Grace. Hugo dismissed it as cheap, and tried to put her off, but Grace was determined to go ahead with it. Apart from anything else, they needed the money, for it was some time still until her trust would come through from her wealthy grandmother.

'Anyway, you've done advertisements and modelling – don't be so hypocritical,' Grace said crossly.

'That was before I knew my worth. You should know that you don't have to bother with things like that. Have you ever had legal advice about your grandmother's trust? I mean, they contest wills, maybe you could get the stash now, why wait until you're thirty?' enquired Hugo.

'Drop it!' was her only reply.

Grace went ahead with the commercial, shooting it the following week, and reaped the royalties. Although Hugo scoffed every time she appeared on television, he didn't turn his nose up at the frequent cheques from Faith.

Grace did two more commercials, one for an American sunglasses company who were captivated by her green eyes, and the other for a well-known liqueur. Once again, the royalty cheques flooded in and Grace was overwhelmed at how easy it all was. Like Hugo said, she knew she had more to offer, but at least it kept the wolf from the door.

As Faith had predicted, once she had become a recognised face on TV, Grace was approached for more and more bit parts and small roles. Together, Grace and Faith leafed through the potential scripts, choosing the most promising parts.

'I do wish that husband of yours would follow your example and be a little more open to these opportunities. He turns down every single part he's offered saying it's not right ... always insisting he wants to wait for the *big* one. I've tried to tell him it doesn't happen like that ...' Grace understood but there was little she could do to persuade her strong-willed husband.

In no time, it seemed Grace was rushing all over the country to different regional television stations, playing small parts in popular dramas. There weren't enough hours in the day, and instead of being supportive, Hugo became increasingly withdrawn, which made their lives together even more strained. So she was vastly relieved to hear an excited message from Faith on the answerphone one afternoon. 'This is the one, exactly what you've both been waiting for. *Macbeth*! Perfect for you both ... I can just see you in the starring roles. The audition's next week. Call me as soon as you get in so I can give you details. Bye Guys.'

Grace and Hugo rehearsed the allocated pages tirelessly for the audition, often working until the small hours, and Faith was impressed with their dedication. Consequently the audition went well and Grace spent five nerve-wracking days waiting for a decision, whilst Hugo was supremely confident. To Grace's alarm, he had begun to get more and more interested in mediums and clairvoyants, believing what they told him unquestioningly: in this case that that part of Macbeth would surely be his.

When Grace received a phone call from Faith, asking her to pop into the office to discuss which shot should be used for *Spotlight* magazine, she became alarmed. As far as she knew, this had already been arranged.

Her fears were confirmed when she went to see Faith who explained, 'Grace, this has nothing to do with *Spotlight*, I'm afraid. I got you here under false pretenses as I needed to talk to you on your own. I won't beat about the bush. The fact is, we've heard back from the Director, and though he definitely wants you for Lady Macbeth, they've offered the part of Macbeth himself to a slightly bigger name.' She paused, looking worried. 'How on earth are we going to break the news to Hugo?'

Grace didn't hesitate, stating flatly, 'As far as I'm concerned, neither of us got the job.'

Faith was horrified. 'Grace, are you crazy? You can't turn this down. As your agent, I'm telling you, it would be professional suicide.'

'And if Hugo knew the truth he'd be suicidal. Something else will turn up, I'm sure.'

'I'm not holding my breath,' warned Faith. Then she used her last card. 'You know that if the situation were reversed, Hugo would be there like a rat up a drainpipe.'

Grace studied her for a moment. 'I don't care. I just can't do it to him, he'd take it so badly,' she said sadly. 'I really am sorry.'

Lana was not at all sympathetic either, when Grace confided her decision, and wasted no time in telling her she was absolutely mad not to have accepted the part. But Grace had made up her mind and was convinced she'd made the right decision.

In spite of the minor setback, the next year was a very productive one for Grace, who'd gained quite a formidable reputation as a strong and professional actress among the casting agents. She was requested time and time again by production companies impressed with her performances, and Grace was away on location much of the time as a result – which was a great relief to her, as the tension between her and Hugo was becoming unbearable.

For his part, Hugo played two small cameo film roles for English Productions, but still wasn't happy, and was almost sacked for arguing with the Director. Faith grew more and more impatient with her impossible protégé, but continued to represent him as best she could.

Sexually, Hugo had now backed off from Grace; he was morose and moody, rarely attempting to show his affection and virtually never initiating intimacy for fear of being rebuffed. Grace tried her hardest to stimulate him in other ways, but he usually yawned and seemed indifferent. She cried private tears of grief, and considered counselling, but by the time it came to this sex had become a taboo subject.

Only once in their marriage had she been able to please him and that was when she'd allowed him to take photographs of her naked. She was quiet and subdued, but tried her best to look tantalising and erotic for his sake.

Uncomfortable thoughts began to creep into her insecure mind, and she worried terribly that Hugo might find sexual fulfilment elsewhere. She tried to quash the thought, as it was beginning to affect her professionally, but nevertheless determined to do something about it.

Finishing early one afternoon, Grace thought she'd surprise Hugo and go to meet him at The Actors' Centre. Entering the green room, she came to an abrupt halt as she saw her husband being rather familiar with an exotic, dark actress, whose appearance was not unlike her own. Grace watched him stroke her arm as they talked intimately over a cammomile tea. Those expressive, velvet brown eyes searched the girl's face just as they had done Grace's in the past, and she was shaken to the core.

Eventually Hugo spotted his wife, and he leapt up from his

chair as if he'd been scalded, crossing the room in his customary jeans and cowboy boots to greet her guiltily. In spite of herself, Grace didn't question him about the event, and he volunteered nothing. He had now become so jealous of Grace's success, and bitter about her rejection of him sexually, he didn't really care if he upset her, nor felt the need to try and redeem himself.

The realisation of this was what finally convinced Grace that, in order to salvage her relationship with Hugo, she was simply going to have to rid herself of her monstrous memories and consummate her marriage. The thought terrified her, but nevertheless she planned a seduction scene with great care, making sure she dressed and behaved in a way she knew would turn him on, and drinking almost a whole bottle of wine to help her relax.

Initially, she had great difficulty in arousing Hugo, reluctant because he thought, as usual, it would lead to yet another dead end, leaving him frustrated and angry. But she was determined to proceed with her mission – to rid herself of the past and move on. It was not a pleasurable experience and was somewhat painful, but she was sure it would get better with practise, and she did manage to grit her teeth through several further attempts.

Hugo was thrilled at first by his wife's change of heart and floated around on a cloud of happiness, but very soon reality kicked in. He was no fool, and soon worked out that his wife had manipulated these sexual encounters, pretending to enjoy them. Her theatricals in bed were unconvincing after the initial elation wore off, and his contempt at her deception enraged him. How dare she have the audacity to try and fool him? He was a skilled and thrilling lover and never in his experience had anyone had to 'pretend' with him.

'Save your performances for the paying public,' he spat at her, spitefully. And Grace had to face the miserable truth that her seductions had misfired badly and had only resulted in increasing the ever-widening gap between them.

The next six weeks were tortuous, the atmosphere strained, with Hugo taking to drink in a big way. But to Grace's great relief, Faith managed to come up trumps just at the best possible time, getting them both auditions for a new production of *Sampson and Delilah*. Grace was certain that this was her chance to put things right between them and aware that it might be her last.

Again, before he even auditioned Hugo was convinced that the part was his, having consulted his various clairvoyants. But to his disgust, though Grace did get the part of Delilah, Sampson went to another actor. This time, Faith, Lana and Justin absolutely insisted she accept the part. It was a six month tour with an impressive cast, an opportunity not to be missed and Grace accepted that it would indeed be sacrilege not to accept the part. The opportunity was just too good to pass up.

Hugo was gutted, and took to stumbling around the warehouse wallowing in his misery and fury with a bottle of Stolichnaya vodka. Fortunately for Grace, rehearsals started almost immediately so she was able to keep out of his way – and she found her co-star, Bradley James, a welcome distraction. He was a generous and talented actor and seemed to bring out the best in her professionally. More often than not she would stay after rehearsals for a drink with Bradley and Stewart, the Director, to delay her return home as long as possible. And when she did creep in the door Hugo would be lying around on the floor cushions playing his own show-reel on the video over and over, commenting on his performances, and swigging constantly on the Stolichnaya.

'So, how's our lovely Delilah, then?' he'd sneer, staggering towards her. 'Make the most of it, my sweet ... your success won't last. For I'm the star in this household, as you very well know.'

Grace found the situation trying, and did her best to console Hugo. But he became sexually aggressive, which frightened her, and when she'd reject his advances or try to calm him down, he'd head straight for the vodka again and lock himself up with the rather lewd photographs he'd taken of her.

He did make an effort on the opening night, at the Theatre Royal in Birmingham, where he appeared backstage, sober and holding a single red rose. He was even generous enough to proclaim her performance a 'knockout', but nevertheless had to criticise Bradley's portrayal of Sampson. He was at least civil to Grace's co-star, but to her utter humiliation, he insisted on giving Bradley notes on his performance.

James and Lloyd also made it to her first night, and Grace threw herself into her brother's arms at the stage door afterwards as they began to catch up on their respective news.

'Despite all that make-up, I can see that you're looking a bit peaky, Sis. Anything wrong?' asked James concerned.

'No no, just tiredness. Stewart is still calling rehearsals and changing the script before each performance, so you can imagine how stressful it is, remembering new lines and eliminating others ...' she trailed off, dismissively. 'But anyway, tell me, what's it like working for Texoil?' she asked, anxious to hear news of her family.

'You mean, what's it like working for the old man?' James grimaced as Grace nodded with a grin. 'Regimental would be the most polite description, but at least I get to stay in Eaton Square and enjoy what London has to offer. Lloyd is staying with me until he starts his new teaching post, so we've been having a right old time hitting the night spots, haven't we mate?' grinned James mischievously.

'Yes, but it's not much fun trying to get you up for work the next day,' said Lloyd dryly.

'The old man goes ballistic if I'm two minutes late,' groaned James. 'Which reminds me, we'd better make a run for that last train back to London.'

Grace's notices praised her as 'electrifying' and 'dynamic' and she was thrilled. But the travelling as she moved from city to city was getting to her and though she gradually got used to living out of a suitcase, she still felt exhausted and drained most of the time. So much so that she'd even requested a chair in the wings on a couple of occasions when she'd felt particularly faint and nauseous. What on earth was wrong with her?

One Saturday night after the curtain came down Grace decided to get away from it all and catch the last train to London. She planned to surprise Hugo and spend the Sunday with him before heading to the next venue in Peterborough on Monday morning.

She wearily let herself into the apartment, to be greeted by flickering candles and the arousing beat of Ravel's Bolero. The customary empty vodka bottle lay on the floorboards and the essence of frankincense and myrrh filled the air. Sensing something untoward, she made for the bedroom.

She stopped in her tracks, rooted to the spot as she took in Hugo's bare buttocks, lunging into a blonde student Grace had often seen at the Centre. She cried out faintly and Hugo stopped mid-thrust, turning to see his devastated wife. He scrambled off the bed, eyes wild, confused from the effects of the vodka and the overwhelming incense.

'Grace, er ... look, I can explain ...' he began. Grace swallowed hard, her mouth dry.

'There's no need. I'll just collect my things. Sorry to disturb you – pretend I'm not here, carry on ...' she said as coolly as she could, to hide the intense hurt and betrayal she felt. Grabbing a few clothes and possessions and stuffing them frantically into a holdall, she mechanically asked Hugo to send the rest of her things to Faith's office.

He was lost for words. She threw her keys onto the bed and silently staggered out of the flat with her bags, quietly closing the door behind her.

Only when the taxi delivered her to Lana's studio flat in Battersea did she finally allow herself to break down and cry as if her heart were breaking.

Lana was devastated to see her friend in such a state. 'I was going to tell you about Hugo playing away, but I wanted you to get settled in as Delilah on tour,' she explained, trying desperately to soothe Grace's hurt. 'I was going to come to Dundee next week and tell you everything, but ...' she stopped as Grace broke down again.

'Lana, you don't understand. It's even worse than you think,' she sobbed, almost making herself sick with grief. 'It's not just about Hugo cheating on me, though that's a shock in itself.' She paused, trying to control herself, breathing deeply and wiping the tears from her swollen eyes. 'You see ... Oh God, Lana, I've just found out that I am seven weeks pregnant,' she wailed.

'What?' whispered Lana, horrified.

Grace repeated her devastating news. 'What on earth am I to do?' she sobbed, burying her face on her friend's shoulder. Lana held her close, soothing her as best she could, whilst desperately trying to think what to do for the best.

'You deserve better than that snotty windbag,' she seethed. She had a good mind to go straight round to Hugo's now and put him in the picture – only she knew that a reconciliation with him was the last thing she wanted for Grace. No, she was going to have to think of some other way out of this mess.

Grace somehow managed to pull herself together enough to give one of the more brilliant performances of her life at Peterborough the next night. After all 'the show must go on' she told herself. No one in the cast knew of her secret misery and only Lana, who had come up with her, knew what this professional façade was costing her.

Her pregnancy had been a terrible shock to Grace, who'd never felt particularly maternal. She'd had mixed feelings about it since she had first realised it was happening, but had hoped that it might in some way help repair her troubled marriage.

So now her feelings were even more mixed. Could she cope with bringing up a baby on her own when her career was just taking off? Half of her wanted this foetus removed immediately – she felt sick and ill and wanted no further reminder of her ill-fated relationship with Hugo. But the other half already loved the tiny creature that was growing inside her – her own child.

She tossed and turned night after night, weighing up the various options and trying to work out what she'd feel for a baby born of such a disastrous union. Ultimately, after many a long talk with Lana, she came to the conclusion that in the circumstances a termination was really the only option for her. She agonised over the decision, mentally torturing herself, and struggling against the exhaustion that threatened to overwhelm her. For apart from anything else the tour schedule was tight and had another six weeks to run.

She decided in the end that she was going to have to

confide in Stewart, who was wonderfully sympathetic and diagnosed a 'mystery virus' the next week when they hit Dundee, allowing her some precious time off. 'Let's try and get you down to Leeds and see if we can get this sorted out,' he advised, kindly. 'I know a doctor there who may well be able to help.'

Lana arrived on the Monday morning at the clinic in Leeds and Stewart cancelled that night's performance so that he, too, could be with her. The two of them were a tower of strength to her, talking through all her worries and concerns and promising that no one would ever know about her operation.

Right up until the end Grace wavered as to what was the right thing to do. Her gut feeling told her she needed to do this for herself, and Lana and Stewart both pointed out that she had a brilliant future ahead of her, and that she'd be putting all that in jeopardy if she took time out now to have a child. This was what clinched it. How could she throw away all that she'd struggled so hard to achieve? However difficult a decision, and however much she knew it was going to haunt her for the rest of her life, Grace knew that this was something she just had to do.

Amazingly, Grace was back on stage just three days after her ordeal. This was where she belonged. Never again would a man jeopardise her career and self-confidence – she was a star in the making – all she needed was time to regain her strength. The rest of the tour was gruelling and her performances exhausting, but with the support of her many friends she was able, up to a point, to put Hugo behind her.

It was one day towards the end of the tour that a little old lady came backstage and changed the course of her life. Her name was Sybil Grant.

# Chapter Eight

## London, 1996

Grace stood at the top of the modern black open staircase at Blake's hotel with her agent, Freddie Franks on one side and Sybil on the other. The time had come to greet her guests at the first night party for *Romeo and Juliet*.

The hubbub of animated conversation rose to greet her, and she swallowed hard, checking her appearance one last time in the large mirror. Despite all her soul-searching the reflection looking back at her was that of a beautiful, successful woman with the world at her feet. Grace stood, wondering at the composed and confident image she put across. She could almost convince herself that this magnificent-looking female hadn't a care in the universe.

A flurry of unwelcome images raced through her mind: her father's furious face ... her mother's cool indifference ... herself as a lonely and frightened little girl tiptoeing around her bedroom ... James's yelping to the stroke of a horsewhip ... Hugo's deceit ... the hospital's glaring theatre lights ...

She closed her eyes and forced herself to blank these ugly images out of her mind. Now was not the time to go over old ground yet again, she told herself, fussing with her hair and pouting scarlet lips as she prepared to descend the staircase.

'Well get on with it, girl. What do you want? A bloody fanfare?' asked Sybil, poking her in the ribs with the hilt of her walking stick.

'No, it's just that ...'

'This is supposed to be Luc Fontaine's night too, remember. He'll get a terrible case of arse ache if you milk it any further,' Sybil said bluntly, though she knew exactly why her protegée was hesitating.

'And my good lady wife will most definitely get the arse ache with me if I'm not down those stairs in two minutes,' muttered Freddie. 'She still gets paranoid whenever your name's mentioned, my dear,' he whispered intimately in Sybil's ear.

Grace grinned to herself, remembering an old press cutting from the fifties she'd found in Sybil's box of memorabilia, which boasted the romance between Sybil and up-and-coming agent Freddie Franks.

Anxious not to trip, Grace lifted the skirt of her gorgeous green gown slightly and started her descent. As the guests caught sight of her, the animated laughter and chat faded into virtual silence, then in its place came roars of congratulations and appreciation.

The flash lights of the cameras dazzled her. She smiled, and slowly and exaggeratedly continued to make her way down the stylish black wrought iron staircase, giving the photographers plenty of different angles and expressions, knowing full well that these pictures would appear in the newspapers tomorrow along with the reviews.

Waiting for her at the bottom were Douglas Crane and Luc Fontaine, who threw their arms out dramatically and air-kissed her pretentiously.

The press closed in and Luc and Grace played to their captive audiences, inching their way around the room to talk to each and every one of their guests, stopping occasionally for photographs and answering probing questions about their professional partnership.

'So, Miss Madigan, how does it feel to be compared with

the late great Vivien Leigh?'

Having rehearsed answers to possible questions with Sybil, she replied, 'I'm extremely flattered by the comparison. Vivien Leigh was one of the most talented actresses of all time. I'm her greatest fan.'

Grace's eyes scanned the crowd in search of James. Her heart sank, for he was nowhere to be seen, but instead lighted on Hannah, who'd travelled all the way from Scotland, along with Lana. Grace hadn't expected to see either of them and threw her arms around them, touched that they had both gone to the trouble of being there for her big night.

Lana looked almost elegant and 'couture' in a simple, understated black evening dress, and her blonde hair fell naturally about her shoulders, devoid of dreadlocks, dye or beads. She'd matured recently, having outgrown her Cyndi Lauper phase, and now looked every inch the glamorous blonde, which meant she was getting many more varied roles.

Sybil shuffled toward her, winked and grinned slyly. 'Enjoy it while it lasts, my girl. One never knows what's around the corner in this business.'

'Thank you for those encouraging words, Sybil,' she laughed, happily.

'Who's the tall blonde almost wearing the black sequinned number?' enquired Sybil sarcastically.

Grace looked across the room to see Luc's girlfriend, champagne glass in hand, dramatically explaining something that was obviously vastly amusing to Mimi Franks, a celebrated casting director, and Freddie's daughter.

'Oh, that's Violet Valentine. Stunning, isn't she?' replied Grace, though she had no time for the woman.

'Bloody ludicrous name, if you asked me. Stunning, I agree, but I've been watching her work the room – she's doing one hell of a PR job on herself. Subtle, she is not. What does this Violet Valentine do?'

'Apparently she's a top international model – going to be on the cover of *Tatler* next month,' informed Grace. 'I'd kill for legs that long, she's almost six foot tall, you know.'

'I maintain it's quality not quantity, she's not to be trusted. She's been watching you, you know.'

Grace looked over at the blonde beauty, and agreed that she certainly was performing. She made an exciting picture in her backless halterneck dress, slashed to the waist and split to the thigh, and with her mane of artistically windswept hair cascading down her bare back. Her face was exquisitely beautiful, with pronounced cheek bones, heavily glossed full lips and enormous blue eyes, framed with expertly mascaraed eyelashes. Grace suddenly and for the first time that night felt a little frumpy, but quickly dismissed the thought, determined as she was not to be outshone on this of all nights.

Poppy sidled up to her, following Grace's gaze. 'Biliously beautiful isn't she, I loathe her,' she whispered, grinning.

Grace looked in amazement at Poppy, who could rarely see faults in anyone. They'd only known each other for a short time, in fact since they'd started rehearsals, but from the little she knew of Poppy, her instincts rightly told her that she was a loyal and loving person.

Standing no taller than Grace's five feet, and if anything of even slighter build, she looked rather like a shy schoolgirl. Her pale, pretty face with its smattering of freckles and its innocent amber eyes was framed by shoulder-length unruly golden hair. Poppy had just graduated from drama school and Douglas Crane had adored her when she'd auditioned for the part of Juliet. He hired her knowing that she'd had no professional experience on stage other than her training, to be understudy, personal assistant and girl friday to Grace.

Luckily the two women had hit it off instantly and Sybil took the younger girl under her wing too. Grace's hair accessories, make-up and costume changes were always laid out in preparation for the next scene. Poppy protected and guarded her, taking her phone calls and arranging her diary, and Grace had learned to depend on her.

As Grace laughed in disbelief at her friend's bitchy comment, Poppy went in search of the canapés and the press busied themselves in taking yet more photographs – this time of Freddie and Theo Palaris, an American film producer. White-coated waiters busied themselves refilling everyone's glasses and the atmosphere gradually became less frenetic and more relaxed.

Grace made sure she spoke to all the critics individually, being charming and articulate as was required. Sybil supervised silently from across the room, nodding approval as Freddie sidled up to her.

'Our girl did good, eh?' he grinned.

'Yes, Freddie, our girl did very well indeed,' Sybil replied, misty-eyed.

'See the fat guy over there with the cigar?' She nodded. 'Well he's the Producer from Universal who might be interested in Grace for the new Mike Russell film. Wouldn't that be something,' he beamed.

Sybil was momentarily rendered speechless. It was a notoriously difficult transition, theatre to film, but she had no doubts whatsoever that Grace would be more than capable of pulling it off. Well, well, well, she thought, mulling it over, though she wasn't going to show her excitement in front of Freddie.

Grace eventually returned to Sybil after working the room, for she'd noticed that the old woman's face was showing signs of fatigue. Aware of just how proud the old lady could be, Grace said, 'I simply must sit down, Sybil. My feet are killing me.'

'You kids have got no stamina,' she grunted. And Grace hid her smile as she arranged two chairs for them.

'Grace, dear, everyone here tonight loves you, quite rightly too. But tomorrow you will be public property and I will no longer be able to protect you ...' Grace looked puzzled. 'So it's important that we clear out any old skeletons that may be lurking in your cupboards.' She paused, searching the younger woman's face. 'By that I mean, get shot of any dead wood that may drag you down in the future. You see, today you're everyone's darling, but the bigger your name becomes the more the media will search for misdemeanours and unfavourable history to publicly shoot you down with. It's the unfortunate side of the business, but believe me I know what I'm talking about ...' she finished.

'But I haven't any ...' started Grace.

'I know Grace, you're a good girl. But there are a few loose ends you must tidy up – namely your divorce from Hugo.'

Grace flinched as she always did at the sound of his name.

'I know you tried to file for divorce nearly three years ago, when my solicitors couldn't track him down,' continued Sybil, 'but he must be out there somewhere, he can't have vanished off the face of the earth.'

'Oh Sybil, why can't we let sleeping dogs lie?' asked Grace, not wanting in the least to open up that painful old can of worms.

'Grace, you've been in denial, darling, all these years – and now it's time to close the book on that particular chapter. Really it is. You must put as much distance between you as possible.

'But I haven't set eyes on him since the day I walked out five years ago,' Grace persisted.

'Believe me, before you know it, he'll have sold some ghastly salacious story to some grotty little rag for a few quid, so officially terminating the marriage would make you much less vulnerable,' said Sybil, gently but firmly.

Grace looked at Sybil in anguish. The ache in her chest pained her. Was her dress too tight or was it the reminder of Hugo that was distressing her?

Reading her expression Sybil patted her hand affectionately. 'I'm sorry, darling. This isn't the time or place, I know. I just feel protective towards you.'

Grace sat up straight and concentrated on breathing through her abdomen, her professional smile perfectly in place. To her utmost relief, the painful spell was broken by the timely arrival of James, who was rushing down the stairs towards her. She excused herself from Sybil and ploughed through the crowd, hugging her brother closely to her.

'So sorry I'm late Sis, I had some business to attend to. Oh and by the way you weren't bad tonight,' he grinned and Grace playfully punched his arm.

They clearly adored each other and the few remaining photographers gathered around snapping and flashing at this unknown male who had his arms around the now famous Grace Madigan. Was this her lover? The whole room turned to watch with interest.

What a perfect end to a perfect evening, thought Grace happily, pushing all thoughts of Hugo and other 'dead wood' to the back of her mind.

# Chapter Nine

James Seymour lounged lazily on the floor of his parents' home in Eaton Square, swigging from a bottle of Becks beer. He didn't appear to notice that he was creasing the dinner jacket he wore in readiness for yet another evening out. If truth be known he was a little tired still from the previous evening's extravaganza with Grace, but he was sure a couple of drinks would soon sort him out.

'Get the door, Gordon. It'll be Amanda,' shouted James over his shoulder to the family's butler, glued as he was to the Grand Prix on the television.

'Wow, you look fabulous, babe. Sit down,' he said barely even looking at his latest girlfriend as she entered the room. 'Be with you in a tick. Eddie Irving has gone into the pits and Hill is about to overtake Schumacher ... this I can't miss.' His eyes didn't leave the set.

'Would you like a drink?' asked Gordon, politely.

'I'm sure she would, and so would I. Crack open a bottle of the champagne, would you?' said James nonchalantly.

'I don't think Mr Seymour would ...' started Gordon.

'Don't worry about it, Gordon. I'll square it with the old man,' James replied impatiently.

Throughout this exchange Amanda sat demurely in a black Lacroix strapless evening gown waiting for James to give her his attention. 'Yes!' yelled James. 'He's won, he's done it. Bloody good show,' he beamed, as he at last turned down the volume and focused on Amanda.

'Oh my God,' he said appreciatively as he ran his hands up her leg. 'Stockings! You know that drives me completely rabid, you evil woman.'

Amanda grinned knowingly. An evening with James Seymour was always sure to end in all kinds of wild sexual antics, and she was looking forward to it. He had something of a reputation as a ladies' man, but who was she to care? Although still young, he was well versed in the art of seduction, though it was rarely required, since most girls were virtually panting to get him in the sack before he even opened his mouth.

James looked down at Amanda's enticing cleavage, feeling a stirring in his loins as he pulled her to her feet and began to kiss her. He was just getting started, hoisting up her tulle gown to get a better feel of her stocking tops and suspenders, when the telephone rang.

'Bugger,' he thought angrily, as Gordon appeared at the door, discreetly averting his eyes from the sight before him as on many previous occasions.

'Seymour residence,' Gordon announced dryly into the mouthpiece. 'No, I'm afraid Mr James Seymour is ... indisposed at this present time, may I ask who's calling?' he asked professionally. 'That was Sophie Thurlston,' he announced sardonically, determined not to acknowledge Miss Amanda's display of stocking tops. His comment fell on deaf ears and he dismissed himself with dignity to return to the kitchen, shaking his head hopelessly.

Amanda's dress lay strewn across the floor, her hair dishevelled as James ravished her, thrusting for all he was worth. Her back was burning from the friction of the Persian carpet and James had accidentally bitten her lip, whilst trying to catch a glimpse of the football score chart on the mute television, but she couldn't have cared less. This man was insatiable!

When he was spent at last, he looked at his watch, yawning. 'We'd better get a move on old girl – crikey, you look a bit of a mess,' he muttered, eyes wide, before turning up the sound on the television. 'I wonder who won the rugger.'

Amanda pursed her lips in annoyance but said nothing, knowing that James hated confrontation of any sort and that if she were to become demanding in any way, he'd simply discard her for a more yielding playmate.

They tumbled out into Eaton Square to catch a cab, for they were meeting some of James's old school friends at Annabel's Night Club. Amanda had reapplied her make-up and adjusted her hair before they made their entrance, and she jealously eyed the other girls in the crowd who she suspected James had slept with in the past and tried not to let it bother her. Most of the men there had obviously come from privileged backgrounds and behaved like spoilt brats, all except for one: Lloyd Davies, who quietly laughed at his friends capers.

Lloyd had won a scholarship to Stowe on his tennis abilities, and although he enjoyed the company of his friends, he often felt uncomfortable with their very different upbringings. His mother had brought him up on her own, and the two had lived very frugally on a widow's pension.

James and Lloyd had made a formidable tennis doubles team at school, but Lloyd just had the edge on James and was already making a name for himself on the tennis circuit. Everybody, including Lloyd, knew that he was heading for the big time. Although James was envious of his best friend's success, he knew where his future would have to lie and couldn't afford to fall out with his parents, who would never have approved of a sports career.

James adored his sister and had maintained contact via phone calls and letters after she'd left home. But Grace's name was not to be mentioned within the family circle and James found it hard to accept that they could just cut his sister out of their lives because they objected so violently to her chosen career.

George despaired of his son, who'd flunked all his exams

out of sheer laziness and been threatened with expulsion because of his wild pranks and errant ways. Although Lloyd had always been his partner in crime, he was more sensible about pulling out of their escapades before they went too far.

So that was how James had ended up at Texoil, where he'd been told in no uncertain terms that he'd have to pull his weight and prove his worth for a year before joining the Board of Directors.

George had sent him off to his tailor in Saville Row who'd duly kitted him out for life in the city. He found it a little dreary apart from the secretaries and office girls that brightened his surroundings, and most lunchtimes he would play squash with a willing opponent from Texoil, before heading off to the winebar for a drink or two.

He'd had dalliances already with Sasha, who'd sway through the office in the shortest of mini skirts, finding any excuse to talk to the new office pin-up. James took to meeting her after his squash game, his hair still steaming from the showers. They'd share club sandwiches and a bottle of Chablis, sometimes two, and stagger back to work necking in the lift, much to the annoyance of the other members of staff.

Jennifer was another stunner, and even better, she was on a diet, so James didn't ever have to buy her lunch. She enjoyed working off calories by having a 'grub screw' in the ladies loo occasionally with him.

Then there was Louise, who he'd sometimes meet in the wine bar after work before they headed back to her flat in Fulham and fucked furiously until about seven o'clock, when he'd head home to get ready for yet another date.

Weekends were fun. Every Saturday morning he'd play tennis with Lloyd if he was in London, or go to the gym for a workout and steam bath, then have a long boozy lunch with old school friends or one of his gorgeous girlfriends and watch the sport on the television in the afternoon. In the evenings, James and his gang of friends nearly always ended up at Annabels or Tramp.

Sundays, James nearly always spent in the country, either at The Gables, where he could secretly scrounge a cheque off his mother, or sometimes playing rugger, polo or tennis at some function or other. James had endless invitations; he certainly was good entertainment value for any party host, and the more he drank the more amusing and witty he seemed to become.

Females flocked in droves around him and James Seymour took liberties with women that most men would have their faces slapped for. But somehow he was known as a lovable rogue. And to be fair, he didn't really mean any harm – he just enjoyed women. He never intended to cause pain or hurt but invariably did, in his attempts to live life to the full and experience as many girls as humanly possible.

The Monday morning after his weekend with Amanda, James had to be woken by Gordon as he'd overslept. He looked at his watch to see it was nearly ten o'clock and staggered out of bed with a horrendous hangover – it had been a particularly wild and wicked weekend and he was paying the price.

Later that day he was sitting at his desk, hardly able to focus on his notes for the afternoon's corporate entertainment schedule, when Sasha leant over him, brushing her full breasts against his arm.

'Lunch?' she whispered provocatively. 'You look hungry ...'

'I've got a squash match at twelve,' replied James, hoping, for once, to get out of it.

'You'll have a good appetite then,' she replied, leaving his desk with the required files. James grinned wickedly to himself, his penis straining against his pin-stripe trousers despite his exhaustion.

'Crikey', he thought, 'this place is positively wall-to-wall crumpet. Thank heavens for my reserve tank!' His grin widened.

James lost badly at squash, basically because he was exhausted from the weekend, and erotic images of Sasha, naked, kept flashing through his mind. Slamming down his racquet at the end he retired to the shower.

After two bottles of Chablis, Sasha and James headed back to the office as James had important clients to entertain that afternoon. His legs were extremely wobbly as he'd gone overboard considerably on his hair of the dog philosophy.

Sasha helped him negotiate the stairs to the impressive reception area of Texoil.

When the lift doors closed, Sasha made to run her fingers through his hair. James frowned, desperately trying to keep his mind on the very important presentation he was about to make to Texoil clients.

'This isn't like the super-stud I know, you're usually very frisky after lunch.' She nuzzled his ear lobe and slipped her hand inside his shirt. James felt that all too familiar stirring within his jockey shorts. The lift doors opened and they made their way down the corridor.

'Today's different, Sash. My old man will be there and ...' But before he could say more Sasha had pushed him into the photocopying room, slamming his back against shelves of Texoil headed stationery. Adeptly she unbuckled his belt and undid the old fashioned Saville Row fly buttons. James groaned in expectation – he could not argue with his massive erection, let alone the insatiable Sasha.

Pushing the unwelcome image of his father out of his mind, he mentally waved the white flag and allowed his over-active hormones to take over. Within minutes his trousers were around his ankles and Sasha was lying knickerless on top of the Xerox photocopier ... well, he had to do what a man had to do!

The longer and harder he thrust the more Sasha demanded. The photocopier was going berserk, the room was stiflingly hot, the green light flashing on and off beneath Sasha's body as the paper spewed out all around them. The sweat poured down James's face as the sexual gymnastics became more frantic. He hadn't anticipated such an athletically challenged session, he was still recovering from the previous evening's bedroom aerobics. 'Aghhh,' he howled, as someone barged into the tiny room knocking his hip hard.

The spell was broken. Suddenly the pair were aware of several sets of eyes gawping at them, as a large crowd gathered. Mustering up such dignity as they could, they adjusted their clothes and left the room, heading off in separate directions. The amused audience just stood with their mouths gaping.

James attempted to comb his hair with his fingers and tuck

his shirt in as he limped and staggered toward his desk. 'Christ,' he thought to himself. 'That was like doing ten rounds with Mike Tyson.'

Jennifer, from accounts approached him, her face a mask of fury. 'You're in deep shit, James,' she crowed. 'You'd better get your act together. Your Father's gunning for you ... you're supposed to be giving a presentation and overseeing that corporate event, *now,*' she whispered viciously.

'Oh my God,' he moaned, taking his notes as Jennifer pushed him in the right direction. As soon as he entered the room he tried to look officious, double-checking the catering, the seating arrangements, the PA system and rostrum. He weaved over to the microphone, before getting off the mini stage into the growing congregation.

'By jove, it's James, isn't it?' asked a faceless gentleman. James nodded stifling a belch. 'I say! Charles, this is George's son, James.' Charles held out his hand.

'Well well, the last time I saw you James, you were captaining the rugger team at Stowe. So how's it all going here at Texoil then?' James went to take his hand, but swayed and missed, bumping into some of the other guests, who backed away in disgust. He groped for his notes and turned around, managing to tread on someone's foot. He looked up to see that the foot belonged to his father.

'Just what the hell do you think you're playing at,' he whispered through clenched teeth. James reeled, swallowing hard, as he tried to keep his balance.

'This is your son, Mr Seymour?' asked an incredulous, white-robed gentleman.

'Er yes, Sheik Mohammed. This is James. James, meet Sheik Mohammed. One of our guests of honour.' George, hiding his fury for a second, managed an almost convincing smile.

James was about to greet him, but as he opened his mouth to speak he let out a loud belch. Sheik Mohammed looked him up and down with utter contempt and turned away disrespectfully. George grabbed James's arm and marched him to the corner of the room.

'How dare you embarrass me like this. Look at you. Your

shirt's torn and has lipstick all over it, you reek of booze, and your behaviour here is offensive. In case you hadn't noticed, I'm bloody furious.'

For some awful reason James saw the funny side to it all, the alcohol distorting his sense of values, and he grinned cheekily. 'C'mon Father, gimme a break. If a chap can't have a few at lunch time and get laid into the bargain, what is there in life? It's a lot more enjoyable than licking a lot of Arab arses,' he said, loudly.

George's eyebrows knitted together in fury. 'Get out. Now! Just get out!' He frog marched his son to the door and threw him out bodily.

The following day, when James had slept off his hangover, he went cockily into work, thinking vaguely that he ought to apologise to his father.

He had a good old chat with Bettina, his father's secretary, admiring the outline of her buttocks as she leant over the filing cabinet.

'I'm sure your father won't keep you much longer James. Can I get you another coffee?' James took in the mature but well preserved image in front of him.

'Mmm? Oh, no thank you, Bettina. So what sort of mood is the old man in today then?' he enquired.

'Oh, much the same as he has been over the last seventeen years ...' she smiled.

'Well I hope he's in better humour than yesterday,' James muttered to himself.

'You can send James in now, Bettina,' came the gruff voice of his father over the intercom. James winked at Bettina as he got up, making the older woman blush.

But the atmosphere of the room he walked into sobered him immediately. His father sat stoney-faced behind the huge antique desk. He motioned James to sit down as he began to speak in a barely controlled voice.

'You're a bloody disgrace, James! A damned liability. You've had more than enough warnings about your behaviour, but that appalling scene yesterday was inexcusable. I have an image to maintain here and you've been an increasing source of embarrassment to me and to the company from the minute you arrived. I simply cannot tolerate any more.' He paused.

'You've overstepped the mark just one too many times, my boy and you've left me no choice but to let you go, as I would any other member of my staff long ago.'

Until now James had been slumped in his chair barely managing to meet his father's eye. But at this he sat bolt upright, shocked to the core.

'Don't be hasty Father,' stammered James fighting to retain his composure. 'I think you're over reacting, let's have a drink and ...'

George looked at him contemptuously and continued as if James hadn't spoken. 'I want you out of Eaton Square by the end of the week. You've run the staff ragged and abused the privileges your mother and I have bestowed on you. You're to leave this building immediately and will receive one month's salary from Bettina on your way out. This, old chap, is where the gravy train stops.'

James was horrified. The whole fabric of his easy life was crumbling. In a last hopeless attempt he struggled to reason with his father. 'So that's it, is it Father? Just like that? You're giving me the old heave-ho for a couple of misdemeanours ... ?'

'*Misdemeanors*?' George was furious now. Had his son no concept of reality. 'I would have cut you off without a penny straight away, but I've reluctantly agreed with your mother to give you one last chance.' He paused. 'You can take up a position in the marketing division at Promosport, one of our subsidiary companies. If you prove you can manage a decent day's work you may live on the interest of your grandmother's trust, though as you know you won't benefit directly from it until you're thirty.' George sighed as he rubbed his stressed face with his hands. He looked old and defeated suddenly.

'So, here's the bottom line, James. Unless you're out of here, out of Eaton Square, and firmly ensconced at Promosport by next Monday, I will not sign the necessary documentation entitling you to receive the interest from the trust.'

At this, George turned dismissively in his large leather throne and pressed the intercom. 'Bring in Sheik Mohammed's file will you, Bettina?'

James sat motionless, his head reeling, but he refused to admit defeat so readily. 'So I'm really being shafted, Father, eh?' he asked, sourly.

Suddenly the full impact of his father's words hit him and he leapt up from his chair. 'Now I understand everything, you pompous old sod. You're control crazy and pissed with power. I totally understand why Grace did the moonlight flit and gave you the flick. You tried to control her too. The minute you knew she was serious about her stage career you got miffed because you'd lost control. It's the same with everyone – you have to be the Almighty and call the shots. Well, thank God Grace got out when she did! I only wish I had understood sooner, because from now on, as far as I'm concerned you no longer exist. Grace has invited me to live with her on many occasions, and now that I've been slung out of Eaton Square, I think I'll take her up on her kind offer.' James's eyes were cold as ice, his face filled with hatred.

'I don't want Grace's name mentioned in this office, do you understand?' bellowed George rising from his chair, all attempts at self-control abandoned. At that moment Bettina, from years of experience of George's wrath, knew it was time to make her entrance with the requested file.

James glared at George, turned on his heel and marched out of the office followed by Bettina, leaving his father standing with his head in his hands. Raking through his hair with one hand, George slowly unlocked the top drawer of the bureau and removed a dog-eared manilla file. Opening it, he leafed through wedges of typed surveillance information, press cuttings and photographs – all of his beloved daughter, the celebrated actress Grace Madigan.

Uncharacteristically, uncontrollably, tears ran furiously down his burning cheeks.

# Chapter Ten

James could barely believe his luck as he strolled through the high-tech offices of Promosport. The atmosphere couldn't be more different from that of the stuffy offices in the city that he'd become accustomed to. Informal dress meant he could wear slacks and a blazer or even jeans if he were not meeting a client. There was a sense of fun and banter amongst the young staff, and even better, the place was littered with babes, thought James. Living in Kensington with Grace was working out very well, too, and James saw this as the icing on the cake.

Promosport was an advertising, promotion and marketing company which used many famous sports personalities and athletes to endorse products such as training shoes, football boots, tennis racquets, swimwear and such like. James was responsible for all the corporate hospitality on and off site and had been put in charge of the Vitfizz account, a vitamin, energy, high protein drink whose direct competition was Lucozade. The job was tailor made for him; he had an unlimited expense account and was expected, largely, only to entertain the many clients who were sponsoring sports personalities and products.

Gregg Chappell, Marketing Director of Vitfizz, had found his advertising budget had soared since Pete Sampras and Stefan Edberg had been seen by millions drinking from the Vitfizz bottles during breaks at Wimbledon and the Australian Open and Gregg was looking to sign up more players to endorse his product.

Over just one boozy lunch James had managed to secure the appearance of the Vitfizz black and red logo on display around each tennis court at Wimbledon and on the back of the programmes. 'What a cinch,' thought James, thoroughly enjoying his new job.

Promosport, aware of their new wizz kid's success with Vitfizz, raised his salary and put him in charge of Pounce, a revolutionary new tennis shoe about to hit the market. Pounce's Marketing Director was looking for an up and coming tennis ace to sponsor their specialised footwear.

James organised a huge champagne reception for all the top seeded players, which turned out to be a riotous affair. As the party went on into the night James caught sight of Lloyd Davies, and pushing his way through the crowds in his usual tipsy way he slapped his friend on the back.

'Hello you old bastard, I've been looking for you. I haven't seen you in six weeks or more,' yelled James over the din of merriment.

'That's probably because you're so busy being Promosport's new golden boy. Everyone on the circuit is buzzing about the way you've revamped and upmarketed the Vitfizz image. Well done mate. Bloody good...' complimented Lloyd enthusiastically.

'Yeah, I'm pretty pleased with myself as well, and now Promosport have put me in charge of the Pounce account plus given me a substantial rise in salary,' said James grinning from ear to ear. 'Which is why I've been trying to speak to you for the last few days – every time I manage to track you down, some snotty tournament official tells me you're still on court. Didn't you get my messages?' asked James. Lloyd shook his head.

'Fraid not. I'm trying to stay as focused on my game as I can ... no distractions,' Lloyd said becoming serious.

'The word on the street – or should I say court – is that you are physically and mentally at your peak, and judging by all the results I've had faxed to me, I'd have to agree.' said James, pausing to smile at his friend. 'That's why I want to put you forward to Pounce to endorse their new tennis shoe.'

Lloyd was gobsmacked. 'But I've got no real track record yet, James. Surely I'm not a big enough name yet to endorse anything that big?'

'I know what you're saying, but all the big timers are too bloody expensive. The top ten seeds won't promote anything unless their fee's in telephone numbers,' he laughed. 'Let's see how you do next week and I'll approach the powers that be to see if they're interested.'

'That would be fantastic, James. I really appreciate it. By the way, how's that gorgeous sister of yours?' he asked slyly.

'Grace? Oh, she's doing incredibly well. Still playing in *Romeo and Juliet* at the National Theatre. I'm sharing a flat with her in fact,' said James proudly.

'I thought you were living in Eaton Square with the "olds"?'

'Yeah, well that's a long story ... I moved in with Grace nearly a month ago after a major falling out with the old man. He objected to my extra-curricular activities, so we parted company.' James grinned. 'Anyway, it's all worked out for the best. I'm really enjoying Promosport, and living with Grace is wonderful, well ... you of all people know how I adore my big sister ...' James tailed off and Lloyd, conscious he was no longer commanding his friend's attention, followed his gaze towards a gorgeous-looking Italian girl.

'That's what I call a serious skirt, look at the legs on that, Lloyd. Can you imagine her without her kit on? Ohhh yes, she is right up my boulevard, my old son.' Lloyd rolled his eyes. 'Duty calls ... international relations and all that,' James winked. 'I'll speak to you later.'

'You're incorrigible Seymour. All my energy these days is restricted to the tennis court,' laughed Lloyd as he watched his friend, glass in hand, wander across the floor in pursuit of the Italian player. 'Arrivederci, mate.'

\* \* \*

Grace wearily put the key into the lock of her beautiful new apartment near The Albert Hall only to be met, yet again, by a slovenly mess.

The obligatory champagne bottles and glasses stood empty amongst the strewn, abandoned rubble of stockings, high heeled shoes, underwear, trousers and loafers. She sighed as she brushed her hand through her hair. Did James really have to leave things quite as untidily as that? Twice before Grace had tried to talk to her wayward brother and asked him not to abuse her furniture and belongings – it just wasn't on to come home tired from the theatre only to have to tidy up after him.

Within a month of his moving in, she'd found a cigarette burn and a red wine stain on her new cream carpet, lipstick smeared across her cream couch, traces of red nail varnish on the cream phone and a couple of broken Lalique wine glasses.

He apologised profusely and swore he'd take more care, but the next time she came home with some friends from the cast to eat a late supper, they found James naked on the kitchen floor alongside yet another beautiful young woman. The Brazilian beauty was covered in Grace's natural live yoghurt while James fed her the strawberries she'd intended for pudding.

Fortunately the guests all found it hilariously funny and dined out on the story for months. But the amusement soon faded for Grace and harsh words were exchanged. James tried to make up for it by sending her a basket of purple wild violets, which he knew she adored. And sure enough she had forgiven him, for no one could ever stay mad with James for long – least of all Grace.

But this time he really had gone too far. Furiously, she systematically started clearing away the debris, piling the clothes, shoes and empty bottles into a black bin liner and dumping it outside James's bedroom door, where he was no doubt entertaining his current belle.

She went into the bathroom to run a bath, only to be faced with an even worse sight. For the top of her perfume bottle had been left off and the bottle knocked over, and her loose translucent face powder was all over the wash basin and tiled floor. She pursed her lips, turned on the spot and charged across the lounge intending to confront James, no longer caring that she might be interrupting something.

Just at that moment the telephone rang, distracting her from her mission. 'Hello,' she said hotly into the mouthpiece.

'We thought you'd be home about now,' came the familiar voice.

'Who's we?' asked Grace impatiently.

'Freddie? Remember me? And Sybil's here too.'

'Sorry Freddie, I'm rather preoccupied with wanting to give my brother a right hook. Why are you calling me this late? Everything's all right, isn't it ... is Sybil OK?' asked Grace with concern.

'Things couldn't be better. Sybil and I figured if we told you our news this afternoon, it would distract you from tonight's performance, which, by the way was brilliant as usual,' Freddie said mysteriously.

'What news?' asked Grace curiously.

'You know my contact from Universal Studios, the one I introduced you to at your party? Well, he's been showing great interest in you playing a supporting role in the new Mike Russell film, *Temptation*.' He paused, waiting for a reaction, but Grace was speechless. 'He's had your new photos and biog for some weeks now and last Friday he flew over with a colleague to catch you on stage. I didn't tell you as I didn't want to get you too excited.' He paused again, wanting maximum impact when he finally gave her the news. 'He phoned today from LA to confirm that they *do* want you to play the part of Sapphire. How about that?'

Grace slowly sat down, trying to digest what Freddie had said. Excitement was building in her stomach, but she was not prepared for this, not in the slightest. 'But Freddie, there's a whole different theory to working on film rather than stage. And isn't Sapphire a bit of a man eater, something of a nympho?' asked Grace in a daze, remembering the script she'd read.

'Yes to both questions, darling, but don't worry about a

thing – it's all taken care of. You'll be playing a red-blooded woman instead of a love struck fourteen-year-old. It couldn't be a better vehicle for showing off your versatility. Not many young actors get a break like this – the opportunity to play support to Mike Russell and Sally Field.' His response was met with silence again.

'Now Grace, all that's left to do is close the deal. Luckily you've only got nine more weeks of your contract with the National, so things are just coming up roses. Have a word with Sybil, she's breathing down my neck ...' Freddie laughed.

'Wait, Freddie ... I have to sleep on this. I'm not sure ...'

'Sleep on it! Oy vey, what's an agent to do? Are you kidding me or what? I've been sweating my guts out getting this part for you ...'

But Grace was having none of it. She didn't even want to talk to Sybil until she'd thought things through herself. Freddie was still mouthing off when she put the phone down.

Slowly trying to take in the news, she calmly went about bathing and preparing for bed as if in a trance. It was difficult to assimilate the pending new challenge. Hollywood ... Universal Pictures ... playing support to Mike Russell and Sally Field. She wanted to scream at the top of her voice with excitement but she was frozen by an overwhelming anxiety at the thought of playing to a camera rather than an audience. She'd never really thought about getting in to films, as theatre was her first love, but this was too good to miss. This was the beginning of a whole new chapter for Grace, and she fully intended to grasp the opportunity with both hands.

# Chapter Eleven

Hugo pulled the muffler tighter around his throat to keep out the damp and cold. The November dawn was just breaking over the Thames and the morning light revealed the damp rough brick of the railway arch.

All was still. The only sounds to be heard were the rumbling of the overhead trains, the constant coughing of his fellow dwellers and empty cider bottles and beer tins rattling along the cobble stones.

Hugo's chest was tight from the chronic bronchitis he now suffered from almost permanently, and he watched his breath vapourise into the atmosphere as he took stock of his life. Five years was a long time to have been living on the streets of London.

The cold and the hunger had bothered Hugo intensely at first, and were responsible for his deteriorating health. But these days he no longer even felt the cold, rarely acknowledged hunger and his appearance meant nothing to him. The alcohol in his system anaesthetised all sensations – he lived in a constant state of inebriation, senseless to the outside world.

He needed to drink to keep out the demons, the fury and indignation. Every so often in lucid moments the past would return to haunt him and he'd exorcise his anger by drowning his pain with liquor, which would lead him inevitably into oblivion. Last night those demons had returned with a vengeance, and this time even the special brew and cider he poured down him had failed to obliterate them.

His friend, Jock, had staggered into the dank shelter they shared along with others, with a bag of steaming chips wrapped in newspaper. He offered Hugo a share before sliding down the dripping arched wall to his assigned sleeping area: a sleeping bag on top of layers of newspapers which kept out some of the damp and cold and protected him a little from the hardness of the cobble stones. Within minutes Jock was unconscious, in an alcoholic stupor, his steaming chips spilling over on to the cobbles. Hugo stared vacantly at the newspaper, wondering if he should put his friend in a safer position, when his eyes focused on a photograph of Grace.

He started, and grabbed at the greasy paper, smoothing out the soggy report on Grace's forthcoming film, *Temptation*. He screwed up the paper in his fist, shaking with fury and outrage. He was beside himself, and desperate to vent his anger on someone or something, Hugo struggled to his feet howling like an animal.

Several voices from the gloom responded with slurred shouts of 'Shut up', but Hugo was out of control and in sheer frustration he lunged out and punched the brick wall with his left hand, crunching the bones and breaking the skin on his knuckles. He cried in pain and anguish and dropped to the ground, cradling his injured hand, the very hand that five years previously had damaged the face of a security man. America ... she was going to America.

If she thought she could just walk away from all the destruction and havoc she'd caused, she had another thing coming. For Hugo held Grace entirely responsible for his own decline, and he decided then that she would have to pay. He was convinced she had conspired to annihilate his career out of pure vengeance. Hell hath no fury, so they said. Well he'd show her, he'd show the bitch he was not to be trifled with. He'd destroy her just as she'd destroyed him.

Hugo winced as he clumsily reached across Jock to grope into the cavernous pocket of his vast overcoat and retrieve the almost full bottle of booze. He held it to his lips and finished it off without pausing for breath. Exhaling and belching loudly he wiped the excess moisture from his mouth with the back of his right hand and sank back into his unrolled sleeping bag to plan the demise of Grace Madigan.

He laughed maniacally, still clutching at the sodden newspaper and laid his head on the smelly canvas holdall that contained his few worldly possessions, angry tears streaking his dirty face. The searing pain from his left hand had transferred to his wrist, though very soon the booze would anaesthetise that pain too.


When Grace had upped and left him all those years ago, she'd failed to recognise that it was entirely her fault that he'd been unfaithful to her. Hugo had been temporarily thrown off balance by her desertion, but had been far too proud to try to win her back. Let her come to me. That's what he'd thought at the time. For they were destined by the stars to be together, of that he was more certain than ever.

With perfect timing, almost immediately after the break-up, Faith Goodman had got him an audition for a new production of *Othello*. He got the job and started rehearsals soon afterwards, revelling in the thought that as soon as Grace heard of his success she'd be back like a shot.

He'd studied the part of Othello many times before and knew it would be a piece of cake for him. He scorned the rest of the cast and resented the fact that he had to work with such inferior actors. He was dismissive of the Director, who he felt knew nothing of Othello, and Hugo tried to educate him on his character. Inevitably, sparks flew and Hugo was hauled up in front of the Producer and threatened with the sack if he didn't take direction. For the first time in his life, Hugo swallowed his pride, telling himself that they were all amateurs and that this was merely a stepping stone for him. He took to drinking heavily during rehearsals, convinced that this was the only way he could face working with such amateurs.

On opening night he calmed his nerves with double doses of Stolichnaya, knowing that his notices had to be nothing less than brilliant. Wherever Grace was, she'd hear of his victory and, realising her mistake would return to be his leading lady.

His entrance was, as always, breathtaking, but half way through the first act he stumbled uncharacteristically and fluffed his lines. In the interval he furiously polished off the rest of the vodka. Of course no one had noticed, he thought contemptuously. An uneducated, second rate audience wouldn't have detected his faux pas.

But halfway through the second act when Hugo was about to deliver his all important lines to the audience, he felt disorientated. The footlights appearing to fuse, he swayed and lost his balance, falling over. A titter swept through the auditorium as Hugo dragged himself to his feet. He was opening his mouth to deliver his speech when he dried, his vision blurring and his mind racing, searching and searching for the words which wouldn't come.

Hugo had never dried before in his life. It was as if he'd been struck dumb. The prompt whispered the crucial lines to Hugo but he stood motionless. Louder and louder came the prompts, but he made no acknowledgment, and the Stage Manager began frantically to search for the understudy, who typically was no-where to be seen. There was nothing for it – he was going to have to signal for the curtain to go down.

Seeing the green velvet partition come down brought Hugo to his senses and he turned to stare into the wings and lift his arms dramatically at the Stage Manager. Thinking Hugo had regained control, he cancelled the curtain, only to be faced with an even worse scenario.

Hugo took a large intake of breath and bellowed, 'Nobody brings the curtain down on me! *Nobody!* I am Hugo Finlay and I am a talented actor destined for greater things than this dump of a production. Just who the fuck do you think you are? And you,' he added, turning to the shocked audience. 'I'd get more out of playing to a bunch of corpses,' he shouted violently, spraying his saliva into the light. The curtain started to descend again.

Hugo's eyes blazed and his face distorted with fury as he faced the unfortunate stage manager, along with the rest of the cast who had gathered quietly behind him. 'Well, don't just sit there staring, you bastards. I'm too good for all of you ... just fuck off, the lot of you ...' he yelled.

Various people approached Hugo from the wings, attempting to whisk him away. But he turned violently on them. 'You're not fit to lick my boots. You're just robots ... you don't recognise my brilliance, my talent. Get off my stage,' he bellowed. 'I have to continue my performance.'

'Kill the lights,' ordered the Stage Manager. They were duly turned off and the stage was plunged into darkness. 'C'mon Hugo, let's go,' he cajoled, reaching out to him.

'Mr Finlay to you, you cock-sucking intefering bastard ...' At that moment the security men overpowered Hugo and they grappled to hold him down. Fists were flying and Hugo felt his knuckles crunch into someone's face as he heard an agonised howl.

It was an interminally long night that Hugo spent in the police cell and it did nothing to quash his feelings of fury at the world. Sitting on the coarse grey blanket, he heard a key turning in the lock and looked up, hopefully.

'Hugo Finlay, you've been bailed, you are free to go. Report to the Duty Officer for your belongings and your court date,' said the faceless uniformed official. He had been charged with assault after lashing out at one of the security guards.

Hugo smiled and stretched his hands behind his head.

'Don't you want to know who put up bail?' the officer enquired.

'It's irrelevant,' said Hugo arrogantly, getting to his feet. Hugo followed the officer up the stairs into the police station where he saw Faith waiting for him. He nodded at her and went to collect his belongings.

'Don't let me down Hugo.' said Faith quietly.

'I don't see what all the fuss is about, I simply defended myself against an over zealous security man,' replied Hugo nonchalantly.

'I can't say I blame him for pressing charges, Hugo. A broken jaw and shattered cheekbone means he won't be able to work for some time,' defended Faith.

Hugo shrugged his shoulders indifferently. Faith became annoyed. 'Apart from being pissed on stage last night, just exactly where are you going, Hugo? What is your direction in life?' she demanded.

'It's in the stars ... I know where I'm going. Everything has been taken care of,' replied Hugo superciliously.

'Stop all that ridiculous rubbish Hugo and listen to me. I may have bailed you out this time, but I'm also here to tell that you that ... it's me who's bailing out. I have to bail out of our professional relationship, Hugo. I simply cannot represent you any more. You're a brilliant actor, but you're too ... too troublesome, too arrogant, and I can't afford to have you in my stable any more,' explained Faith, sadly. Hugo only smiled whimsically, making Faith want to shake him.

'You don't seem to understand the severity of all this, Hugo. The Producers have fired you from the show, I can't continue to be your agent ... and because you're in such debt and refuse to deal with any of the correspondence, you're running very close to being declared bankrupt.'

'Don't worry Faith, it's not your problem. Everything's going to be just fine, believe me.' Hugo smiled and patted her hand. 'It's all part of life's rich and varied tapestry. There's a reason for everything, a reason which we may not appreciate or understand at the time, but fate is the key to our lives.'

Faith was rendered speechless as she watched him calmly leave the station and head off down Long Acre.

For the first two years of street life, Hugo had almost enjoyed the whole nomad existence. He'd met many varied and interesting characters and they all taught him a thing or two on survival techniques. They hung out together around Charing Cross, drinking heavily and exchanging stories of their past lives.

It was when Hugo was literally thrown out of the National

Theatre, trying to sneak in to see Grace in *Romeo and Juliet*, that his fury began to erupt. His life on the streets had begun to lose its lustre, his health was suffering and depression had set in. He began to question his future and wondered when his journey to success and fame would begin.

Jock and Giles were good mates and constantly shared their booze with him, and he promised he wouldn't forget them when his name was in lights. They agreed it was only a matter of time before his talent was recognised and that he'd be a household name. They drunkenly speculated for hours on their respective glittering futures.

But five years down the line nothing had materialised and reading in the papers that Grace was off to Hollywood to star in a film had completely unhinged him. The time had come to take matters into his own hands. He'd change his name and find a new agent – a new life!

# Chapter Twelve

'Ladies and Gentlemen, we have for you tonight our very own Star Turn: our Saturday night special guest. She's here with her brand new routine, and a style all of her own ... She's red hot ... Ladies and gentlemen ... I give you the one and only ... Lana Logan!'

Frank's introductions never failed to make Lana grin as the curtain went back. They'd become very close, she and Frank, and she'd come to look upon him as a father figure. He made sure the club retained its respectability, never allowing hookers to operate from his premises, and relied only on the heavy members fee and excessive drinks prices to fund the rent and licence. He stayed on the right side of the law - a family man with three children and one recent grandchild.

Lana stood dramatically, centre stage, giving Cyril time to pick up her dazzling red sequinned outfit with his ancient spotlight. He was getting slower and slower which frustrated Lana beyond belief, because if he didn't get a move on, she'd be behind beat with the music. However many times they rehearsed the quick moves, he could never seem to keep up with her.

But he was Frank's old school pal, and this time, luckily, he found her in time. Lana went straight into her routine with gusto, her firm dancer's physique looking magnificent in the red sequinned bikini, red satin stiletto shoes and matching red nails and lips. She was every man's fantasy.

'Simply The Best' had become her trade mark at The Gaslight and Lana danced a polished and stylish routine that she'd cleverly choreographed and rehearsed to perfection. She was on top form tonight, thought Frank as he watched his punters nodding in appreciation. Originally he'd not wanted a complicated routine, preferring the usual thrusting and grinding, but Lana had managed to twist his arm and to his surprise, the punters went wild for it. They couldn't get enough of Lana - she was the best crowd puller he'd ever had.

Her dancing was athletic and fast, and as she came to the end of her first number, sweat was trickling down her back. Luckily her next number, 'Private Dancer', was considerably slower and gave her time to get her breath back. She ended this with the splits and looking down at the audience she took in all the punters whistling, clapping and voicing their appreciation.

Lana was touched and smiled fondly at them. Frank stood to one side of the stage, grinning from ear to ear and shouting his applause, along with the customers.

She decided to do another number – the most erotic of her repertoire, and the audience sat in awe as Lana entertained them. Provocatively, she teasingly touched her own gorgeous, glistening body, then tantalisingly removed her bikini top and threw it at Frank. For it got to be expensive replacing all the scarlet tops she'd thrown to the clients, who were unwilling to return them.

Sitting alone at one of the small tables reserved for VIPs to the side of the stage, she noted a new disciple, his face expressionless in the shadows, his arms folded. The dark, handsome face looked familiar and his attitude intrigued her.

Frank was waiting backstage with a towel and dressing gown, and Lana dried herself down as she made her way back to her dressing room.

'Lana, love, you blew their minds,' called Frank, happily. 'We were packed to capacity tonight, so I think you deserve a bonus.' He took a roll of money from his pocket and stuffed it into her hand.

'Listen, love, the missus is laying on a big Sunday lunch tomorrow – all the kids will be there. Will you come and join us? After all, you're virtually family to us now,' he added warmly.

'Brilliant, Frank. I'd love to,' said Lana as she peeled off her G-string and removed the sequins from her nipples.

'Oh look, violets,' she exclaimed, remembering that they were Grace's favourite flowers. 'Where did these come from, Frank?'

'Could be the new punter who's panting to buy you a drink. He seems pretty kosher, not bad looking ...'

'Oh, not tonight, Frank. I was planning on hitting the sack early – it's past three in the morning,' she moaned, putting on her watch.

'Just a quick drink for ten minutes, Lana love. It's all good public relations for The Gaslight,' begged Frank. 'Do it for me?'

'Oh go on then. As long as it's only ten minutes,' replied Lana. It was difficult to refuse Frank.

'Good girl, I'll order a taxi for you. See you at the bar,' he said kissing her cheek and closing the door as he left.

When Lana was dressed she went back to the bar and sat down at the VIP table, sipping champagne with the 'new punter'.

It was to be the last time Lana Logan was ever seen alive.

It was a particularly grim and grisly scene that met the detectives and forensic experts at Lana's Battersea basement. It was obvious that she'd fought ferociously for her life, but she'd had no chance against the frenzied knife attack.

Justin Clegg had popped around to Lana's on Sunday morning to give her photocopies of a script they were to start rehearsals on, when he found her door open. He was confronted by the most horrific and gruesome sight he was ever to witness. Almost fainting at the sight of the mutilated body, he managed to garble a message to the emergency services using the blood stained telephone.

Justin sat with his head in his hands as the dispassionate professionals probed for clues. It was like a scene from a horror movie and Justin winced at the spattered walls and blood soaked carpets. The coffee table and chairs lay upturned, the curtains were torn from their rail and the glass in the framed photographs of Justin, Grace, Marcus and Lana's parents had been smashed to smithereens.

The pathologist timed her death at between three and five that morning. There was no evidence of rape, but her diary and gold watch could not be found, nor the rent money which Justin knew was usually kept in a jar on the mantelpiece.

Justin was grilled for hours by the detectives, and he told them as much as he knew. Could it have been someone she knew, they wanted to know. For they were convinced that the viciousness of the attack meant that it must have been carried out by someone with some kind of personal vendetta against her. Justin certainly couldn't think of anyone who would want to harm Lana, but he suggested they go and speak to Frank at The Gaslight.

Frank was absolutely devastated, and felt terrible for not making sure he had seen Lana into a taxi as he'd promised. He gave the police details on the man she'd been drinking with, but really couldn't tell whether he'd been known to her or not. For he'd had to cope with a disturbance at the other end of the bar when some of the customers had had a few too many.

Anyone who had had contact with Lana was thoroughly cross-examined by police and no stone was left unturned in their search to find her killer. If it wasn't someone she knew, it was very probably a psychopath on a sick mission to destroy women who sold sex, so they vigorously checked their computer files, cross-referencing for potential suspects.

After her parents in Ireland had been told the news, Lana's savage death was splashed over the front page of every newspaper with, of course, photographs of her in her dancing outfit. Because of her nudity she was described as a stripper, and in some tabloids, as a hooker, which was deeply distressing to all those close to her.

Lana's parents, justifiably, were particularly hurt by the salacious labels the press gave to their daughter. In their eyes, she was their little girl still, with a promising career as an actress ahead of her. All she had done is earn a bit of extra cash in the evenings to help finance her study. It was all so unfair.

Grace, as Lana's closest friend, was questioned at length by the two detectives. They shifted uncomfortably on her cream sofa as tears of grief poured down her face. Hardened as they were to what they saw regularly in their profession, this kind of pain and distress was something they could never become accustomed to.

'In your own time, Miss Madigan,' one of them said, softly. 'When you're ready, in your own words, could you tell us more about Lana? We have statements from Justin Clegg, the proprietor of The Gaslight and an ex boyfriend, Marcus. But we need the sort of information only a close girlfriend such as yourself would know.' Grace looked up, trying to calm her breathing and stem the flow of tears. 'For example, did she have any enemies? Was there a particular man in her life? Any clandestine or secretive liaisons?' Grace shook her head, still unable to speak.

'You see we haven't been able to find an address book or diary that could give us any clues, and we feel strongly that Lana might well have known her killer. She was last seen drinking with a man in The Gaslight, so obviously we'd like to question him, but we've no clues yet as to who he could be.'

Grace was baffled and could think of no one who'd want to harm, let alone murder, Lana but for her friend's sake she tried to be as helpful as she could.

The detectives quizzed Grace gently for nearly an hour before thanking her and taking their leave. Grace was distraught. She stood forlornly in her apartment, inconsolable and desolate, and even James was unable to comfort her. She needed to grieve, and she needed to grieve in her own time. Lana was the closest friend she'd ever had, and she didn't know how she was going to survive without her.

* * *

Grace took her final curtain call as Juliet the following Saturday night at The National. There was the customary party in the green room afterwards, which Grace only attended briefly, and only at Sybil's insistence.

Sybil and Freddie took her home afterwards, treating her with kid gloves, knowing how delicate she was feeling. James, for once, had made sure he stayed in and had even prepared a meal. He had abandoned all social engagements indefinitely in order to be there to support his big sister through her grief, and she appreciated it. He comforted and cosseted her and Grace leant heavily on her brother – the two became closer than ever.

'How can I leave for America now?' she'd wailed. 'How can I go when they still haven't found the bastard who killed Lana. How can I do anything without her?' But between them James, Sybil and Freddie had persuaded her that it was just what she needed, and that it was what Lana would have wanted for her. That finally persuaded her, along with the fact that Freddie managed to persuade Universal to fly Sybil and Poppy out to accompany her.

She had a week in which to put all her affairs in order and say goodbye to her friends before leaving for Los Angeles. The day before the flight, Sybil and Poppy sat on Grace's bed as she packed, offering advice on what to take.

'Isn't it brilliant that you're both coming with me? I honestly don't think I could make it without you,' she smiled.

'Well, how can you do without a coach and a personal assistant,' laughed Poppy, giving a wink. 'We're entirely indispensable.'

'Well all the same. I'm very grateful to you both for agreeing to come.'

'My pleasure,' said Poppy. 'I'd come even if I wasn't being paid – as would Sybil, as you very well know.' They smiled at Grace warmly.

'I wish I'd had time to go and see Hannah before I left, but what with Lana and everything ...' her voice trailed off.

'It's not as if it's for ever, Grace, just a few months,' soothed Sybil. 'There'll be time enough to see her when you're back.'

'I know. Oh God, I can't believe this is actually happening to me. I don't know whether I'm coming or going,' she muttered, gazing at the cases, trying to shrug off the pervasive sadness.

'Who wouldn't be excited at the opportunity to play support to Mike Russell and Sally Field?' exclaimed Poppy. 'It's a wonderful script, and the opportunity of a life time.'

'I know. I know all that, and I can't wait to get my teeth into it,' said Grace. 'Though I am a bit twitchy about the sex scenes,' she added nervously.

'Don't you worry about that now,' said Sybil. 'We'll be there, and anyway, Freddie has had a clause put in the contract insisting on a closed set for that scene. I made sure of that,' said Sybil officiously.

'What I wouldn't give for a scene in the sack with Mike Russell – now that's someone I could really get *my* teeth into,' joked Poppy, and they all laughed.

There was just one thing Sybil wanted to clear with Grace before they left for America, and she gestured for Poppy to leave them alone for a minute or two.

'Grace, love. I'm afraid my solicitor has had no luck whatsoever tracking down Hugo. I had hoped to get this matter finalised before we left for LA so all the loose ends could be tied up, but I'm afraid they've made absolutely no progress and are unable to issue the decree nisi until he's officially declared missing.' She paused, noting that Grace showed no reaction whatsoever. 'Faith apparently got rid of him over five years ago, when he was declared bankrupt, but that's the most up-to-date information we could get. My solicitor has even advertised in all the necessary newspapers and made numerous enquiries, but it seems he's vanished into thin air.'

Grace remained expressionless.

'I know you would rather forget all about the unfortunate episode, Grace, but I wanted you to know that I'd tried to find him.' She waited anxiously for a response. 'Well, I suppose it's more than likely that he's disappeared for good, so we can probably stop worrying.'

To Grace's immense relief, the front door slammed at that moment and James walked in. 'Stop worrying? What? About me?' he asked, grinning.

'We were just discussing the fact that Hugo can't be traced,' explained Sybil.

'Oh him,' said James indifferently. 'Least said the better, as far as I'm concerned,' he shrugged, looking carefully at his sister. 'Anyway, if he was going to cause any trouble he'd have done it by now,' he said firmly.

Sybil hoped that he was right, and put her worries to the back of her mind, as she watched Grace stare forlornly at the framed photo of Lana lying in her suitcase.

That night Grace went to bed surrounded by her packed suitcases. She tossed and turned, unable to sleep, her mind in turmoil. Hannah loomed largely in her thoughts and Grace worried that for some reason or other she might never see her again. She told herself that she was over anxious due all the recent upheaval: she could almost visualise the gruesome scene in Lana's basement flat. She tried to blot out all the unpleasant visions that invaded her mind but Lana's bloody end continued to haunt her.

Hugo appeared intermittently, too, his lock of black hair falling over one eye and his stance full of theatrical arrogance. Grace shivered under her duvet, as her father's face emerged. At this, she sat bolt upright in her bed, clammy and fearful. What about her mother, what about Beatrice? Surely she had the right to know that her only daughter was about to leave the country? It was possible of course that she'd already read it in the papers, or even that she wasn't interested, but Grace had the instinctive knowledge that Beatrice was not as cold and forboding as she appeared.

Feeling needy, Grace yearned for her mother's arms. She was surprised by her own feelings, but nevertheless her desire to see, or at least speak to her mother was overwhelming. As dawn broke, Grace decided to telephone her.

After a cup of tea and a few moments of pacing the floor of the lounge, she sat down on the settee and dialled the familiar telephone number. Holding her breath with anticipation, she clutched the telephone, listening to the ringing tone.

'Hello,' boomed the unmistakable sound of her father's voice. Even after almost ten years it made her freeze and she instantly lost her courage.

'Hello?' it came again, growing impatient at the silence.

Grace slammed the hand set back into its cradle, her heart beating wildly. Why had she thought her mother would want to hear from her? If she'd really loved her or was even the least bit interested she'd have made contact years ago. It was excruciatingly obvious she meant nothing to either of her parents. Grace bit her lip, refusing to allow the tears to fall from her welling eyes. She had never needed them before so why should she suddenly be seeking their love and support now?

Grace pulled herself up and stuck her chin out stubbornly. She'd show them something. If she hadn't achieved enough yet to gain their admiration, well she'd just have to make sure she became an even bigger star.

Grace efficiently finished her packing, and waited for the others to arrive to take her to the airport. These were the people that loved and cared for her, they were her real family. Other than them, her only love was acting, and that was what she intended to focus on from now on. To hell with her parents!

# PART TWO

# Chapter Thirteen

## Los Angeles, 1997

Grace strolled down Rodeo Drive drinking in the vitality and lust for life that Californians simply reek of. Every shop window enticed her from the sidewalk and she was indeed greatly drawn by what she saw.

Knowing full well that all Americans were brought up to say 'have a nice day' to all and sundry, this made no difference to the fact that she still felt heartened when she heard these cheerful, amiable words. She didn't really care if it was sincere or not, she was too busy enjoying herself in her new surroundings.

She swung her shopping bag and tossed her glossy, dark locks over her shoulders as she sauntered along, a skip in her step. Although tiny, Grace was slowly getting used to the fact that she turned heads and drew gasps, and she revelled in the admiring stares. Her light linen Armani suit clung to her tiny frame and the gentle breeze lifted her hair off her heart shaped face, exposing her creamy complexion in all its glory.

She had left 'Juliet' behind in London and here in Los Angeles she had become a sophisticated, elegant woman about to embark on a new and exciting career. She instructed her driver to take her back to the beautiful house in Coldwater Canyon that Universal had rented for her. Grace happily re-examined her purchases inside the cab. Sybil would be pleased with the new black evening gloves she'd bought her as her old ones were ancient and moth eaten. Grace knew that Claude had bought them for her over thirty years ago and she hoped the new ones would help act as a form of exorcism. For Poppy she'd bought a Gucci silk scarf, appropriately enough covered in wild poppies and forget-me-nots.

She had settled in very quickly, and become fond of Theo Palaris, an Alfred Hitchcock lookalike she found to be very accommodating and helpful. Likewise she had warmed to the Director, Kyle Zimmerman, who was flavour of the month after two box office hits in as many years. Grace found herself thinking back to the initial meeting with the two men when she'd voiced her concern about the seduction scene.

'Of course we understand your apprehension, Grace,' said Theo, puffing on an oversized Cuban cigar. 'Freddie has explained to me that you are a screen virgin, as it were, and we will take into consideration your reluctance to do full frontal nudity. It's not our intention to produce an "18" in any case, so I promise there won't be any unnecessary de-robing.'

'OK, but I'd still like a closed set. It is what Freddie stipulated in the contract,' she stated, categorically.

'I agree,' nodded Kyle. 'I don't want you to feel uncomfortable.' Grace smiled gratefully.

'I think we are going to be a pretty formidable team, guys,' added Theo. 'I know you haven't met Mike yet, but I know you're gonna love him, he's a real pro – always gets the best out of his leading ladies. Do you know how many actresses would give their left nipple to play a love scene with him? He sure has a way with the women ...' Theo stopped abruptly when he saw that Grace was not smiling. 'Hmm. Well ... let's have a toast to *Temptation*,' he said, clumsily changing the subject.

Grace felt her face stiffen, but rapidly regained her composure. She hadn't struggled this far, fought so hard and suffered such pain to be agonising over exposing a little flesh.

If Sharon Stone could open her legs for the world on screen, then she could seduce Taylor Redmond without batting an eye-lid. No, she could definitely handle it. She knew that *Temptation* was her passport to international fame, and recognised that she was just going to have to overcome her fears.

She had read the script over and over, getting to know the character she was to play as well as she might a close friend. Sapphire, a beautiful but psychopathic female obsessed by the occult, and a particular business tycoon. With witchcraft and voodoo she pursues Taylor Redmond (played by Mike Russell), who thinks Sapphire is nothing but another neurotic gold digger until he eventually falls victim to her spell when she seduces him. He is a family man, happily married to Elaine (Sally Field), but cannot control his lust for Sapphire. He becomes terrified of her and her powers and when he tries to escape her clutches, she destroys his business empire, murders his parents and attempts to mutilate him in an a desperate bid to own and possess him.

Sapphire could be bewitching and seemingly quite normal, but at the flick of a switch she'd become depraved and evil. No actress could ask for a better role to play, and Grace couldn't wait. She would *be* Sapphire, she decided.

'Minimise those gestures, Grace. Remember, the camera will be virtually up your nostril by this time. You are coaxing him, luring him ... just a twitch of the lips and lowering of the eyelids will be sufficient. You're not at The National now my girl – every little nuance will be picked up on the camera,' instructed Sybil as she read the script. 'Every tremor, every breath is very important here ... Do it again.' Grace delivered her lines to Poppy, who was standing in as Taylor, and attempted to keep her facial and bodily movements to a minimum.

'Yes, yes, better, much better. Go on ...'

Right on Poppy's cue, the telephone rang and she answered it, her face colouring when she realised who it was. 'It's for you, Grace. It's James,' she said coyly.

Grace's eyes met Sybil's. She too had noticed Poppy's strange attitude. She took the phone apprehensively, wondering if James had burned down her beautiful apartment or broken more of her glasses. She was pleasantly surprised to hear him sounding relatively coherent, telling her how much he missed her.

'What are you after, James?' she asked suspiciously.

He laughed heartily. 'Nothing at all, you baggage! I've simply called to wish my big sister good luck for tomorrow. Knock'em dead kid, I know you'll be just great,' enthused James.

'Thanks James, I need all the luck I can get,' replied Grace nervously.

'That's rubbish, Sis. You'll be breathtaking as always. By the way, I've got someone here who's foaming at the mouth to wish you good luck too.'

A deep voice came on the line. 'Hello Grace, how are you? It's Lloyd here.' He sounded almost nervous.

'Oh hello Lloyd, how nice to hear your voice,' said Grace warmly. She chatted to him pleasantly before putting the phone down to continue her coaching session.

The next morning a limousine collected Grace, Poppy and Sybil at five-thirty to take them to the studios for hair and make-up. Grace's stomach was churning horribly with nerves as she went over and over her lines in the car.

Kyle Zimmerman went out of his way to make her feel easy and indeed she felt comfortable in his company. After make-up Kyle brought Mike Russell to her dressing room, and to her pleasant surprise he was charming, unassuming and a total gentleman. 'So, Grace. I'm relying on you to tell me if there's anything you're not happy with – moves, delivery of lines et cetera, and I'll do the same. It's important we have a rapport and are able to voice our opinions,' he smiled. 'Kyle's a very cool director and is always open to options or suggestions – it's the only way to work. I'm a veteran within the movie world and I know this is your first picture, so if there's anything I can do to help, just say the word. See you on set in ten.' He squeezed her arm encouragingly and left the room closing the door behind him.

Sybil grunted. 'Forty years ago, he could have had his boots under my bed.' Grace grinned to herself, always amused at how direct the dignified old lady could be. 'I'm off to see how the lighting man is doing. Got to make sure you look your best, haven't I? And I'm not sure these foreigners know what they're doing.' Sybil rose from her chair and grabbed her walking stick.

Poppy and the woman from wardrobe fussed around Grace annoyingly while she withdrew into herself and prepared for the day. The scene they were shooting today was Sapphire making her entrance into Taylor Redmond's office as an interviewee for the position as his Personal Assistant. Sapphire could neither type nor take shorthand, but had bluffed her way through the preliminary interview.

There were many other scenes to be shot in Redmond's office so they were scheduled to be on that particular set for at least four days. Grace was itching to get on set to prove her worth.

She acted brilliantly, and was even more convincing on the second day. Taylor Redmond is convinced he's found himself a gem as Sapphire manages to convince him that she's indispensable. She schedules his days, vets his calls, collects his dry cleaning, arranges dinner parties and sends flowers to his wife, Elaine – through gritted teeth. Sapphire keeps her composure at all times, but slowly weaves her webb of subterfuge.

Grace *became* Sapphire, and she stunned Kyle, Theo and the crew as she acted out the perverse personality change. She was so brilliantly convincing that the crew were reduced to silence by the end of the day's shoot.

The only problem was that, unfortunately, Grace also took Sapphire back home with her. Wrapped up as she was in the character, she was unable to leave her behind at the end of each working day, and Poppy and Sybil had to tread on eggshells for weeks. It was extremely difficult to turn a deaf ear and blind eye to her stroppy and demanding behaviour, but as Sybil quoted 'One must suffer for one's art.'

Over the next few weeks and months, the pressure started to get to Grace, and she became utterly exhausted, but equally determined to carry on without a break. The rest of the cast and crew were getting pretty fed up with her, if truth be known, especially as Sybil was also becoming quite a nuisance, interfering and questioning all the time. Mike Russell and Sally Field were almost frozen out and *Temptation* was fast becoming *The Grace Madigan Show*.

Tension was building on the set and Grace's increasingly evil behaviour made it almost impossible for anyone to talk to her on a reasonable level. Everybody was stressed and overwrought and Theo Palaris started to become concerned about his production.

After one particularly gruelling day, the limousine dropped the three women back to their house in Coldwater Canyon at ten-fifteen, and Grace hit the bathroom with a vengeance soaking in the hot, steaming bubbles. She'd never felt so drained.

She scrubbed away at Sapphire's make-up, removing the thick pan-stick base, heavy black eyeliner and purple plum lipstick, luxuriating in the silken foam. Although suffering from immense fatigue, she felt elated.

She felt she'd found her true vocation with film work: everybody had crowded around her and Mike when Kyle called it a wrap today, congratulating her, kissing her and shaking her hand. Theo had opened bottles of champagne to celebrate reaching the half way mark, and toasted the professionalism of the cast. Technically, Sally was Mike's co-star; Grace, as supporting actress had second billing, which was the best Freddie could negotiate, as Grace was still unknown in the States. But as far as Grace was concerned, *she* was really the star of the show.

Grace was rudely awakened from her thoughts by Poppy's impatient tapping on the bathroom door. 'Will you be long Grace? I'm desperate for a bath before hitting the sack. I'm exhausted ...'

Grace raised one eye brow, Scarlett O'Hara style. 'Ten minutes, Poppy,' she replied irritably. Why on earth couldn't the studio have arranged for a house with three bathrooms? And more to the point, how the hell could Poppy be exhausted when all she'd had to do was stand around the set all day. *She* was the one who was exhausted.

She read through her lines with Sybil until midnight then set her alarm clock for five a.m. The telephone rang just as she was falling asleep, the familiar voice of Freddie Franks booming down the line.

'Grace, hope I didn't wake you but I've got great news. Remember the script, *Love All*, we read and liked? Well, Palaris and Universal have confirmed they definitely want you to play the lead. Isn't that brilliant?' he gushed. 'Universal have studied all the footage from the last six weeks and are convinced that you are perfect for the part of Paige Jordan. It's big bucks Grace ... I mean, *really* big bucks! I'm starting negotiations tomorrow.' He paused, giving her a chance to take it all in. 'It means that you won't be able to return to London, as you have to go straight into preparation as soon as you've finished *Temptation*. All I know at the moment is that the location is Florida. I'll let you have more details as and when I get them.'

Grace sat up in bed and grasped the telephone, hardly able to breathe. Well, that was proof if proof were needed, that she was no 'one hit wonder'. Incredibly, she was about to sign for her second picture even before finishing her first. And without an audition! Things were moving for Grace Madigan – she was about to be Hollywood's hottest property.

'Grace ... are you there?' enquired Freddie.

'I'm here, Fred,' said Grace, trying to slow her quickening pulse. 'Make sure you get me top billing when you negotiate the contract,' was all she said.

'Well, I'm pretty sure you'll be billed as co-star. I'm not sure you have enough track record with only one movie under your belt,' said Freddie cautiously. 'Remember, you're playing opposite some big household names.'

'That may be so Freddie, but I know my own worth and I also know the way the movie industry works here in LA,' retorted Grace.

'Come on, you've been in Los Angeles less than two months, Grace. As your agent the bigger your fee and the higher your billing the better it reflects on me. Trust me to do the best deal I can, will you? I've had a little more experience than you,' said Freddie tactfully.

At Theo's request, Grace met him the next day in his office after the shoot. Opening a bottle of his favourite champagne and lighting up a Cuban cigar, he said. 'Grace, what can I say? When I signed you, I knew you'd be awesome. But this ... well your performance, I gotta tell ya, is mind blowing. You're a shit-hot actress Grace, honey. A real pro.'

'Thank you Theo, I aim to please,' said Grace, calmly smiling through the cloud of cigar smoke.

'Apparently they're champing at the bit over in England too to get their hands on trailers and find out our release date,' Theo added excitedly. 'So you'll be numero uno back home, too. You should be feeling pretty proud of yourself.'

'I'm feeling quite happy, thank you,' she replied confidently.

'I know your agent has told you that the lead in *Love All* is yours, so I thought we ought to have a little celebration.' They chinked glasses and toasted their potential successes. 'I've decided you and Mike can have the next three days off for a little rest and recuperation. You're both looking shattered ...' started Theo.

'I don't need any days off Theo ...' interjected Grace.

'Actually, we've got to shoot another sequence and we've had a technical hitch, so while I panic about going over budget, I want you guys to chill out and rejuvenate.' He paused, looking slightly uncomfortable. 'I'd ... er, I'd like to take this opportunity to mention a coupla things that are not too cool and I'd like you to think about it over the next few days before you come back to shoot the sex scene.' Theo put his cigar to rest in the ashtray and placed his glass on the desk before lowering his portly frame next to her on the leather couch.

'I know you're in character most of the time, honey, and don't think me critical, but your behaviour and treatment of the crew ain't too hot. We're a team ya know, a little respect goes a long way with those guys.' Grace looked at Theo as if he were mad.

'You want me to kiss arse to lighting technicians and sound engineers?' she said, aghast.

'Take it easy, Hon, it's just a suggestion. It makes for a happier environment on and around the set if you could just be little civil to the crew. We're all working together ya know. They feed off you and need communication to know your needs, they only wanna help. Look at Mike, he's always got time to shoot the breeze with the tea boy, it certainly don't hurt none to be a little friendly,' tried Theo tactfully.

'What the hell are you trying to say?' seethed Grace, rising to her feet. 'How dare you criticise me. Nobody could play Sapphire as well as me. Nobody.'

'Well, all I can say, hon, is always be good on the way up, 'cos you never know who you'll meet on the way down. This is your big break – don't blow it. I've seen many actors get too big time too quick and start throwing their weight around.' He paused summoning up the courage to raise the other issue.

'Whilst we're clearing the air, I'm sorry to have to tell ya that Sybil Grant's studio pass has been cancelled. I'm afraid she's driving everyone up the wall. I know she means well, but she's a feisty old broad with an attitude an' it don't go down well here. No siree,' said Theo, shaking his head.

'Is that it? Or do you have any more complaints?' demanded Grace, coldly. She paced the room, tears of fury smarting her eyes. 'I'm a professional actress, not a public relations officer. Maybe we should discuss this further before I sign the contracts for *Love All*. I'm not sure you appreciate ...'

'I understand an actor's needs, Grace, and I'm sure you'll have calmed down and relaxed before the next picture. You're the new kid on the block ... now don't go getting your British arse all uptight, Gracie. C'mon here and sit down,' he patted the space beside him.

Grace, suddenly forlorn and exhausted, returned to the leather couch and let Theo affectionately put his arm around her shoulders. 'Now don't go taking this personal,' he said, brushing her hair off her face. 'Go take the next few days to unwind. Take a work out, catch up on some sleep, get ya face done ... or get laid ...'

Grace turned to look at him in horror. 'Thanks for the

advice, but I certainly don't need to get laid at a time like this,' she fumed.

'Maybe that's what you think. I've reason to believe otherwise; I don't think I've ever seen a broad that needs fucking as badly as you do.' Theo ran his hand up Grace's thigh and attempted to nuzzle her neck. In an instant Grace swung her arm around and slapped Theo's clammy face hard.

'Shiiit!' cried Theo, nursing his face. 'For a little critter you sure are ...'

'Don't fuck with me Theo Palaris, OK? Just don't fuck with me!' Grace spat.

'Sorry, Honey. I just thought you might need a little coaching or practical experience for your next scene.' He tried to make a joke of it.

'Fuck the next scene. Fuck *Love All* and fuck you, Palaris.'

And with that she strode to the door, slamming it after her. Her heart pounding nauseatingly, she made her way to her dressing room.

Theo smiled wryly to himself. 'Oh well, it was worth a try. Ya win some – ya lose some.'

The studios were virtually empty except for a few set builders. Running in the near darkness with tears still pricking her eyes, Grace ran to her dressing room. Struggling to unlock the door, she almost tripped over an envelope addressed to herself as she let herself in. Grace slung it on her dressing table while she gathered her things to go home.

She was overwrought, anxious and desperately tired; the shooting schedule had left her completely drained, and she knew she was going to have to take stock of things over the next few days. For although she was striding forth in her career in leaps and bounds, there was something missing in her life. Why did she suddenly feel so desperately lonely?

She sighed and opened the curious hand delivered envelope she'd found, her name scrawled in colourful crayon. Inside was a single piece of A4 note paper covered with the same scrawl in multi coloured crayons. In bold irregular print it read.

## GEORGIE PORGIE PUDDING AND PIE
## KISSED HIS GIRL AND MADE HER CRY
## WHEN HIS BABY RAN AWAY
## HE VOWED ONE DAY TO MAKE HER PAY

Grace froze, clutching at the piece of paper. Who would send her this? And why? She felt the hairs stand up on her arms. Who disliked her enough to want to threaten her?

Her first suspicion was Hugo, but then she dismissed that thought as he hadn't been seen for so long. Sybil had warned her that he'd 'rear his ugly head' at the most inopportune moment, but why write a silly note? Why not simply present himself? Or could it be her father? Again, she dismissed the notion. She hadn't seen him for over ten years.

A chill ran up her spine making her shiver and she anxiously pulled her coat around her. She couldn't deny that she was extremely frightened, feeling exposed and vulnerable. She jumped nervously as the driver appeared at the door and she stuffed the puzzling note into her handbag, deciding to try and forget about it.

# Chapter Fourteen

Grace slept almost solidly for two days and awoke feeling as if she'd been in a coma. Sybil and Poppy were relieved to find her in slightly better humour and were happy to hear she'd accepted an invitation to go out to dinner with Kyle and Mike that evening to discuss the next shoot sequence. As she waited for them, she flipped through the script, her stomach churning uncomfortably as she came across the sex scene. She'd read it many times before, but somehow now that it was only twenty-four hours away, it seemed an even more terrifying prospect. If only Lana were here to advise her on how to handle it.

She slammed the script shut, determined not to let it bother her. No. She could handle it. It would be a closed set after all, and she was a woman of the world ...

The limousine drew up outside Ma Maison and a crowd waiting on the sidewalk surged toward the car, calling out Grace's name. She looked at Kyle in bewilderment. 'Wow the movie's not even completed yet – imagine what it will be like once it's released,' said Kyle. The couple pushed their way through the throng of fans and paparazzi.

'Hey Grace, what's it like working with Mike Russell?'
'What do you think of Hollywood'
'Grace ... Grace ...'

Once inside they were shown to their table and sipped at vodka martinis while they waited for Mike and his wife. Somewhat against her better judgement, Grace decided to tell Kyle about the episode with Theo in the production room. He had become a good friend and she felt she could trust him.

'That turkey is *so* uncool. What an idiot! Please don't let it get to you, Grace. I'll make sure you're not left alone with him at all from now on,' he assured.

'Thanks Kyle, but I've a feeling Theo won't be bothering me again,' Grace replied assertively. 'Um, I did also want to talk to you about this sex scene before Mike gets here,' she added, looking up at him nervously.

'I know, I know, babe. I can sense you're uptight about that scene, but you gotta just trust in my judgement. I won't let you do anything tacky, just let me guide you through it. Look, if it helps I can give you something to help you be a little more er relaxed ... creative ... After all Sapphire is supposed to be the horniest woman on the planet,' he grinned, though his words only made Grace feel even more alarmed.

The Russells arrived and Grace found herself relaxing and even enjoying the evening, which was a major achievement, the way she was feeling. At the end of the evening Grace let herself into the house and went straight to bed, determined to get a good night's sleep before her big day tomorrow.


'Rolling ... and ACTION!' said Kyle, signalling Grace's cue.

She glided across the sumptuous set lit by huge freestanding candles, and decorated in rich, russet colours. The warm glow from the candles shone through her translucent tangerine voile, the fine mesh resting on her full inviting breasts and clinging to her thighs as she lay down on the bed, fingering her crystal beads.

Her eyes gazed sensually through the burning incense to focus on the door, where she knew Taylor Redmond was about to appear. Grace lay back, her mahogany hair spread out over the black satin sheets, and she licked her lips in anticipation. Slowly, sensuously, she touched her breasts, cupping them in her hands and rubbing at her nipples, letting out a gentle moan. Her heavy eyelids closed as she waited for Taylor to enter the room.

'Cut.' Kyle's voice brought Grace back to reality. 'Take ten, everybody,' he barked, crossing the set and pulling Grace up into a sitting position. 'Fan-fucking-tastic! You've been holding out on me Grace – what a horn-pot you are,' said Kyle, giving her a hug.

Grace laughed, happily. How ridiculous she'd been to have worried about this scene. 'To tell you the truth, Kyle, I felt a bit ridiculous lying there touching myself,' she confessed.

'You were absolutely mind blowing. I just need to do one more take for technical reasons and then we're on to the next.'

Taylor Redmond pushed open the door, not knowing how or why he was there. All he knew was, he had somehow found himself in the apartment of this exotic, exquisite creature. Entranced, he dropped the papers he was carrying to the floor and made his way towards the bed. Grace reached out, pulling Redmond by his tie and opened her mouth ready to devour him. Ripping open his shirt, she buried her head into his chest, and then slowly began to remove her tangerine robe, running her hands over his muscular body.

Redmond took her in his arms and kissed her, his hands exploring her breasts, her buttocks ... But Grace stiffened as she felt Mike's hard, erect penis on her leg. 'I ... I'm sorry,' said Grace, sitting bolt upright. 'I'm sorry, Mike. I'm sorry, Kyle ... I just ... I don't know what——' She was mortified.

'Cut,' said Kyle. 'Don't worry babe, take your time. No problems, hey, Mike?'

'None whatsoever, Grace,' said Mike gently.

A tear escaped down her cheek as she tried to regain her composure. 'It won't happen again, it's just that, I didn't think that ... I didn't expect ...' She looked down at Michael's now deflating penis.

'My fault Grace, sorry about that. It's a bit of an occupational hazard I'm afraid! I'll try and keep it under control,' mumbled Mike, embarrassed.

'OK guys, now let's go for another take. Positions please everyone. Make-up, quickly retouch Grace's face,' ordered Kyle.

Grace repeated the scene, removing Taylor's shirt as before, stroking and seducing his body. He rolled over and moved on top of her. At this point, Grace lost her nerve again.

'No, no, please, nooo,' she cried, jumping up and grabbing her wrap, running off the set to her dressing room. Locking the door, she sank to the floor, shaking and sobbing until she heard a gentle tapping at the door.

'Hey babe, it's me, Kyle. Let me in, please Grace.' She unlocked the door and threw herself into his arms.

'I've let you down, I'm so sorry, so sorry,' she cried.

'Do I look worried? Just relax. Mike and the crew have gone for coffee break ...'

'Kyle?' she hesitated. 'What was it you said about giving me something to ...'

'Oh, you mean valium? Sure, no problem.' Kyle reached into his pocket and produced a bottle of pills. 'A couple of glasses of wine with that should do the trick. Not exactly what the doctor would recommend, but it will help you get over today's hurdle,' he said, reaching into her fridge and opening a bottle. 'You know, Honey, don't take this the wrong way, but I wondered if you'd like to see my analyst – he might well be able to get to the bottom of this problem. Think about it,' he smiled, reassuringly. 'Now take your time, Gorgeous, just come out when you're good and ready.'

Grace appeared back on set within twenty minutes, her mouth and throat dry, and feeling as if she'd been hit by a freight train. All she wanted was to get this scene done and finished.

She went through the motions as before but Kyle was not happy with her. 'Babe, your eyes are staring and you're acting like a housebrick. Poor Mike's not into necrophilia – let's try and get some realism into this. Stand by ... rolling ... and ACTION.'

Take after take they persevered, but Grace became less and less able to function. 'Cut. It's a wrap,' said Kyle.

'I'm not at all happy with those close ups, Grace,' he said

later in her dressing room. 'I'm going to have to use your body and Mike's face. You became like a corpse after that valium, you probably drank too much with it. Where are they by the way?' he asked looking around.

Grace pointed to the bottle on her dressing table. Kyle picked it up and examined it. 'Did you take more than one?' he asked suspiciously.

'I ... er.. I took five,' she replied, dazed.

'You *what*? You took five valium and a glass of wine?'

Grace nodded forlornly.

'Do you have any idea how dangerous that is?' said Kyle angrily. 'Fortunately, it's not enough to be considered an overdose – all you'll suffer is a bit of a hangover, but you must never do this again.'

'I feel terrible, Kyle ... I want to die. It's not just the pills, it's the fact that I couldn't hack it. I couldn't get through that scene without help ... I was acting like a plank of wood,' cried Grace. 'Word will have got round, I won't be able to face Mike or the crew tomorrow, I've failed ...' she sobbed.

'Look don't worry. I really think you ought to go and see my analyst, though. I'll give you his number. Now C'mon, silly tits, let's get you home,' said Kyle, gently moving her rigid body toward the door.


The rest of the movie was shot successfully, and Grace soon regained her composure, though she couldn't quite forgive herself for what she saw as her failure.

With clever editing and a body double, Kyle had managed to put together an awesome sex scene. Nobody suspected that much of Grace's nude takes had ended up on the cutting room floor, nor that a body double had been used – that was the advantage of having a closed set.

The next ten weeks were spent in various locations in California, shooting from dawn till dusk. Filming had taken five months altogether, and *Temptation* ran over schedule by only three weeks. Now Kyle had to settle down to the real work – the editing.

Grace was absolutely exhausted after the filming was over;

she was a newcomer, and had yet to build up the stamina other Hollywood actors had acquired. The movie had sapped her of all her strength, and she went down with a debilitating virus, unable to leave her bed for days on end. She began to feel terribly depressed, unable to face the world feeling so feeble, vulnerable and confused – about what, she did not know.

Sybil and Poppy were perplexed, unable to understand what was wrong with Grace. It was Kyle who pointed out that her illness might not be entirely physical – he suspected she was suffering from some kind of emotional trauma, and with gentle persuasion he eventually convinced Grace that she should check herself into a clinic which he recommended.

# Chapter Fifteen

Entering the gates of the clinic, Grace nearly turned and fled when she saw the vacant, zombie-like faces of the other patients.

'Don't panic, Grace. This isn't a scene from *One Flew Over The Cuckoo's Nest* – these people are heavily sedated and quite ill. You're only here for a bit of therapy to help you understand yourself,' said Kyle.

Grace had agreed to stay there for the minimum two weeks, and as she forlornly unpacked her case in her sterile room she broke down again, wondering what on earth was wrong with her. Had fame affected her?

A knock at the door interrupted her thoughts. She wiped away the tears. 'Grace, I presume,' came a friendly voice. She nodded, attempting a smile.

Immediately, Grace felt at ease with her doctor. He was in his mid fifties, she guessed, with compassionate, gentle grey eyes. He had a warm, infectious smile and she was relieved to see that he didn't wear the white coat she'd been expecting. He held his hand out to her.

'Dr Warren Kline. Please call me Warren – may I call you Grace?' he asked politely.

'Please,' she mumbled.

'I'm afraid this isn't The Beverley Wilshire and the food here leaves a lot to be desired, but as I want you to undergo intense therapy sessions, it is better if you're resident here. I hope you're comfortable with that?'

Grace squirmed, not at all sure she'd done the right thing in booking in for a fortnight. He smiled comfortably noting her uneasiness.

'Two weeks certainly isn't enough time to get you better, but I'm sure we will get to the root of the problem and be able to begin treatment within that time.'

'Wh ... what sort of treatment are you thinking of?' she asked, nervously.

He smiled reassuringly. 'Don't worry, Grace, there'll be no drugs. Maybe a few hypnosis sessions, should the need arise. Kyle has told me a little about you, but I'm going to need to know absolutely everything, from your earliest childhood memories.'

'But I don't feel my problem stems from childhood – my insecurities are here and now, today,' she said, unwilling to go back over such painful ground.

'Well, I'm afraid we have to consider everything at this stage. Don't be frightened,' he said kindly. 'I'm here today to tell you a bit about how we run things here before we begin therapy. Firstly, you are not a patient here, you are my client, and everything we discuss is, of course, confidential. I think we should begin with the regressive work tomorrow, probably some hypno-therapy. Now please don't look so alarmed, it's completely safe,' he soothed.

Somehow, Warren Kline had immediately gained Grace's trust and put her mind at rest, and after their introductory conversation, she felt safe in the sanitary green room, sleeping soundly that night. She awoke refreshed that morning and, surprisingly enough, was almost looking forward to offloading her problems on to a complete stranger.

She dragged her hair back into a ponytail, pulled on a track suit and attended her first session with Warren. She warmed to him even more, and couldn't help wishing her own father had been like him. He had a comfortable disposition, and she found it easy to talk openly to him, though she did find she dried up when they got on to the subject of her childhood and parents. To her amazement, she seemed to have genuine difficulty in pin-pointing any specific details to give him – all she remembered was a blanket of loneliness and fear. She tried to explain to Warren that she wasn't holding out on him and he nodded understandingly, holding her hand as he explained how he was going to hypnotise her.

The big comfortable leather chair in which she'd been sitting, elongated into a comfortable bed. She lay back with her hands in the air, lowering them slowly as she counted down from thirty.

Coming to, over an hour later, she was surprised to find her cheeks wet with tears and her nails picked and chewed. Smiling kindly at her, Warren helped her up and reassured her that their session had been extremely valuable. They were far from resolving things but had made a good start, and were well on the road to discovering the fundamental problem.

They laughed over lunch in the canteen, as Warren took her mind off the session by talking about his own life. It was as they delivered their plastic trays back to the serving bay that Grace learned that Warren had lost his wife, Marcie, to breast cancer, six years previously. She had only been fifty-three.

'You see, Grace, Marcie had this crazy notion that by being married to a doctor, she was invincible, and that should she get ill I would know instinctively. She bore me three of the world's greatest kids and I have five grandchildren – she was some woman, Grace, and I still miss her very badly.' Grace was touched that he told her of his pain, and felt even easier about opening up to him the next day.

When she woke from her second hypnosis session Grace found again that she'd been crying and biting her nails. 'Every time during hypnosis, you've mentioned that you were on tiptoe. Why was that?' enquired Warren.

'So that Father wouldn't hear me in my bedroom – he always got angry if I made a noise. That's why I spent so much time in the attic,' explained Grace.

'Would he have been angry if he'd seen you peeping through the stable window on that summer's day?'

'Oh my God', Grace whispered, horrified. 'Who told you about that?'

'You described for me in great detail your father's violent sexual act with Petra,' he said carefully.

Grace winced as the memory flooded into her mind. 'Yes, he'd have been furious,' she replied, trying to regain her composure.

'Uh huh ...' said Warren scribbling in his note book. He was satisfied with his assessment and told her that the next day they'd embark on directive therapy.

Over a ghastly lasagne and tired green salad, Grace found herself telling Warren all about Beatrice, and surprised herself when she heard herself say that she was fond of her mother, but really didn't know her very well. It had never occurred to her that she'd never tried to talk to her about anything other than trivia – they'd never communicated about anything important in her life.

The next ten days proved to be painful and disturbing, yet somehow comforting, in as much as she realised there was a reason behind her insecurities and anxieties. Warren encouraged her to build bridges with her mother, convinced that this was where the answer lay. With her support and insight, she might be able to complete the complex jigsaw puzzle of her own mind and start to rebuild her life.

When her two weeks were up, Grace continued to consult Warren twice a week for therapy sessions, and began to feel happier and more centred than she ever had before. And his persuasion worked: she did eventually pluck up the courage to telephone her mother.

Thankfully her father wasn't there and Grace was delighted to hear how genuinely pleased her mother appeared to be on hearing from her daughter, once she got over the surprise. Grace got the impression that all was not well with Beatrice, but she didn't feel confident enough yet to ask her anything too personal. She felt shy as she made conversation with her, skating awkwardly around the subject of her father. It wasn't until Grace actually asked Beatrice if they could meet, as she needed to speak to her, that the ice broke.

'Oh darling, there's nothing I'd like more,' she said hesitantly. 'But there is your father to consider, and I'm afraid I don't think he'd ... well, you know your father ...' Grace's heart sank. Beatrice took a breath. 'Darling, you know how I feel about flying. But perhaps when you get back to England? Why don't you give me your telephone number in LA, at least let me give it some thought. I promise to call you back within the next couple of days.'

Grace put the phone down with mixed feelings, and immediately phoned Warren.

'Don't be impatient, Grace. Remember, it's more than ten years since you two last even spoke. Think about it – she's probably in slight shock. Give her a few days, after all she did promise to call you back,' he advised.

The next morning Grace sat at the breakfast table with Poppy, Sybil and a dog eared script of *Love All*. Grace had been trying to coax Sybil into helping her with Paige Jordan's character, but the older woman seemed to have lost interest in everything since her cruel ban from the film set of *Temptation*. Grace and Poppy were becoming really quite concerned about her.

The kitchen phone rang making all three of them jump. Poppy answered as usual, putting her hand over the mouthpiece as she whispered. 'It's a Mrs Seymour for you.'

Grace whooped. 'It's Mum, it's my mother.'

'Of course,' said Poppy, having forgotten that Seymour was Grace's real name.

'I'll take it upstairs, Pops,' Grace cried as she bounded up the stairs two at a time. Throwing herself on her bed and taking a deep breath she picked up the hand set. 'Mother?'

'Grace. I'm sorry if I was a little restrained yesterday, but I was a rather taken aback at your phone call. I've had twenty-four hours to think, and I've decided it's time to take control of my life at last.'

Grace made no comment, hearing her mother draw breath. 'I've always been here for you Grace, though you probably never knew it. The fact that you actually need me now fills me with great joy, and I feel terrible for having neglected you for so many years.' She paused. 'George – I mean your father – made it clear that I was not, well ... anyway, let's not discuss this on the telephone. When do you think you might be back in England?'

Grace's heart pounded with excitement. 'Oh Mother, I'm due to go to Florida within the week to start preparation for my next movie. But I ...'

'Well in that case I shall simply have to come to Florida. If Mohammed can't come to the mountain ...' Grace's eyes filled with tears.

'You ... you mean you'd come here, I mean to Florida ... to America to see me?' she stammered, amazed at her mother's eagerness, especially when her fear of flying was taken into consideration.

'I would walk the world bare foot to see my only daughter. You see Grace, you're not the only one who's been experiencing change. Now that James has left, and both dogs have died, I've had time to do an awful lot of thinking.' She took a deep breath. 'Anyway, I mustn't stay on the phone too long, I've got important things to do, such as consult my diary and arrange my flight,' she finished, warmly.

'Mum ... what about father?' asked Grace nervously.

'This has nothing to do with George. I will call you tomorrow to tell you when I'm coming,' she said, sharply. 'I have a few loose ends to tie up here then I'll join you in Miami for an indefinite period of time.'

'What do you mean "indefinite"?' enquired Grace.

'I'll explain all when I see you,' she said cryptically, 'and that will be as soon as I can possibly make it. Make sure you give me your new number in Florida – I think it best you don't call me here,' she added.

Grace hung up a few moments later, stunned by her mother's reaction. She'd always thought of her as distant and somehow servile, but the thought of seeing her soon went some way toward alleviating the fear she felt at the thought of leaving LA, and by association, Warren.

'You're a big girl Grace. Go with confidence, you don't need me as you think you do. Go make your picture, have fun with your mother,' he said kindly. 'You can't go getting too dependent on me. I'm just your therapist.'

'But you're *not* just my therapist, you're my friend. I need you ...' she said baffled.

'You don't need anyone, Grace. To be your friend outside the clinic boundaries would be unprofessional ...' he explained gently.

'Well in that case, I'm not paying you to be my therapist any more – I don't need your services,' laughed Grace. Warren grinned.

'Atta girl. With your permission, I'm going to recommend a colleague of mine in Miami who could continue your treatment. And remember I'm only a phone call away,' he said encouragingly.

'OK, but will you promise to come and stay with me in Florida if you get some time off?' Grace begged.

'Well, I'll certainly think on that,' he promised with a smile.

# Chapter Sixteen

Universal had allocated Grace a villa in Florida to prepare for the new film, a diamond smuggling thriller set within the tennis world. Grace and Poppy made the difficult decision to put the increasingly frail, fatigued and homesick Sybil on a flight to London before boarding their plane to Miami.

Grace was really very concerned about Sybil and her rapidly deteriorating health. Her arthritis and deafness were getting worse and worse and she found even the simplest task exhausting, but more worrying than all of this was her mental decline. She seemed to have lost her 'attitude', and was uncharacteristically withdrawn and apathetic. She no longer felt of use to Grace and mentioned on several occasions that she felt she ought to return to England, where she belonged.

Grace knew Sybil was homesick, and managed to arrange for her to stay at The Star and Garter Home for Retired Actors in Richmond on her return. It sounded a rather comic institution, she felt, but at least it was one she knew would suit Sybil. She would be re-united with many of her old friends, some of whom would have known Claude so she would have that important bond too.

Grace promised herself she would visit her as soon as she could, for she was well aware how much she owed the old lady who'd given up so much for her. As soon as *Love All* was completed she'd spend some quality time with her.

The villa, about thirty minutes drive from Fort Lauderdale, was a set of white buildings rambling across the many acres of lush green grass, with purple Bougainvillea climbing the white washed walls.

The two women explored the grounds, taking in the swimming pool and tennis court while they waited for someone to arrive with the keys. 'I've got just five weeks, Pops, to get myself fit, tanned and healthy, learn to play tennis like a professional and learn lines, so I can't exactly put my feet up for too long,' she sighed. 'Universal are sending a tennis pro next week to train me up and make me look the part,' she mused, feasting her eyes on the grapefruit trees. 'Well, the poor guy certainly has his work cut out for him – the last time I held a tennis racquet was when I was a kid.' They laughed in unison as they watched a car coming up the long and winding drive.

'Sorry to have kept you waiting Miss Madigan. My name's Jesse Clarke and I'm to make sure your stay here at Villa Retreat is as comfortable as possible. Here are the keys; let me take your bags inside for you.'

'Thank you,' they murmured as Jesse unlocked the Andalucian style doors with mini wrought iron port cullis. They gasped at the simplistic beauty of the mediterranean-style interior with its terracotta tiled floors and pastel soft furnishings.

The place was filled with Portuguese pottery, had hand carved wooden shutters, tables and chairs, and Casa Pupa scatter rugs added to the fresh, comfortable atmosphere.

The four double bedrooms were breathtaking – Grace's in particular, which was decorated in the palest of lemon, with white brocade curtains and lemon tie backs, and lemon water silk cushions piled high on the king sized bed. The kitchen was a gourmet's delight, with every mod con and beautiful, hand-painted tiles.

Jesse bade them farewell handing Grace his card and instructed them to call him should they need anything.

'Well, actually ...' started Grace, 'I was just curious about that strange-looking miniature table over there. What's it for?' she asked, pointing at the wooden rectangular table standing about a foot off the ground. Jesse looked surprised.

'Oh the maid should have removed that, sorry. When the Chairman of Universal was staying here in the Spring, he brought his dog from LA. He's a Great Dane, so isn't supposed to eat his food at floor level as it makes his head stoop, so we had the table made for him. Taboo, that was his name, a rather terrifying looking creature ... absolutely enormous. I'm looking after him at the moment, actually, while the Chairman is in London for three months.' He frowned. 'Not going down too well with the wife, I'm afraid – she's expecting our first child in three weeks ...'

Grace smiled delightedly. 'I'd absolutely love to have Taboo for you Jesse, I'm crazy about dogs and haven't had any contact with them since I was a child,' she said, her eyes shining with excitement.

'Well, it would sure get me off the hook with the wife, Miss Madigan, and it's real kind of you. But I understand you start shooting in three or four weeks ...' said Jesse thoughtfully.

'Yes, but that's no problem, I'll take Taboo with me. And when I'm on set, Poppy can look after him, can't you Pops?' said Grace enthusiastically.

'Mmm,' replied Poppy, none too enthralled by the idea.

' ... after all, I can hardly see Theo throwing the Chairman's dog off the shoot,' Grace added, manipulatively.

'I don't think you ladies realise what you're letting yourselves in for,' Jesse said, looking worried. 'You, see Taboo's absolutely enormous – probably almost double your weight.'

'Well, he'd be very good for security purposes,' said Grace, realising it was true as she said it. 'Well that settles it Jesse, I'll look after Taboo. I am scheduled to be here for four to five months overall you know, and I promise to walk him every day.'

It was love at first sight between Grace and Taboo, as soon

as he unfolded himself from the back seat of the car and bounded across the springy grass, his ears flapping, his nose all of a quiver as he galloped over to inspect his new mistress.

Poppy looked at Taboo apprehensively as he leapt up at Grace, licking her face and almost knocking her over.

'I can see that he's already settled in. After all the Villa's familiar to him. I'll leave you to it – call me if you need help,' said Jesse grinning over his shoulder.

Grace and Taboo were inseparable and although Taboo's attention span was limited, Grace trained him patiently and taught him silly tricks. Poppy watched them frolicking on the grass as she went over Grace's script, highlighting her lines in fluorescent green.

'You have the tolerance of an ant usually, yet with that dog you have all the patience in the world,' said Poppy in amazement.

'Ah, that's because animals love you unconditionally, Poppy. And they'll never let you down,' replied Grace, wistfully.

'Well whatever makes you happy,' said Poppy. 'Anyway, enough about that delinquent dog, Grace. It's time we went through your lines.' At that moment Taboo let out the most ferocious bark and ran past Poppy, knocking her to the ground.

'Darn dog ...' she muttered, getting to her feet. They followed Taboo to the drive where they saw a red pick-up truck approaching.

'You see Poppy? He's a brilliant guard dog,' exclaimed Grace. Poppy made no comment.

The tall blond muscular man looked vaguely familiar to Grace, as he climbed out of the truck and smiled at them both. He was wearing tennis whites, so Grace assumed him to be the tennis pro the studio were sending. His deep tan revealed a taut and well defined body, and seemed to emphasise his sun-bleached hair and penetrating dark blue eyes. He was, quite frankly, gorgeous.

A look of terror came over the man as he was faced with a growling Taboo, and Grace threw her head back and laughed. 'Good boy, Taboo. Lie down,' she commanded. Taboo duly rolled on the ground with his long gangly legs in the air, looking ridiculous.

'Quite an Adonis,' thought Grace as she switched her attention back to the man who was walking over to introduce himself. A sort of chemical attraction stirred within her, and she found it hard to drag her eyes away from him.

'Hi Grace,' he began. Grace bristled.

'Miss Madigan,' she corrected.

'Miss Madigan. We've met before, but that was when you were Grace Seymour,' he smiled. 'I'm Lloyd Davies – James's friend.'

Grace, blinked, recalling the shy lanky blond boy she'd thought a wimp when she'd last seen him years before. Could this really be the same person? 'Nice to see you again Lloyd,' she said, coolly, trying to control the attraction she felt for him.

'Likewise. I could hardly believe my good fortune when Universal approached me to put you through your paces. If you're half as good as your brother we'll have no problems,' he smiled playfully.

'Well I'm not. So you have got problems,' she replied, haughtily. Poppy smothered a laugh. They made a date for the next morning at 7.30 a.m., before the heat set in and Lloyd set off in the red pick-up.

'What the hell's got into you?' asked Poppy crossly. 'The poor guy's just doing his job, why did you have to be so curt with him?'

'Too familiar by far,' said Grace tossing her hair. 'Just because he happens to look like a Greek god, doesn't mean he can swan in here and act as if he's known me for years.'

'Ah, so that's what it's all about,' Poppy thought to herself, and smiled.

The next morning at 7.30 precisely Grace was woken by the sound of Taboo greeting Lloyd. His whites were now covered with grubby paw prints and he was dishevelled to say the least. Donning a bath robe, Grace ran outside. 'Down, Taboo. *Down!*'

She couldn't help but laugh unkindly at Lloyd's undignified arrival but he took it in good heart. 'I see you've met the welcoming committee,' she said smirking. Lloyd nodded as he got to his feet again, grinning wryly.

'So, shall we get down to business?' enquired Lloyd conscientiously. 'Probably not worth bothering with whites or anything because I'm more interested in your fitness level at the moment. I think we should start with some cardio vascular exercise first.'

'Some what?'

'Cardio vascular. It gets your heart rate up ... burn off some of that fat.'

'*Fat!*' said Grace, horrified.

'Come on, Grace, you know I don't mean that you're fat. I just mean we need to turn some body fat – which everybody has – into muscle.'

'Humph,' she grunted, turning to get changed. She reappeared twenty minutes later with a white Le Coq Sportif polo shirt and shorts.

'First of all a good stretch is important before any kind of exercise, so bend your left knee and ...'

'Are you going to teach me tennis or not?' said Grace, irritably.

'Grace,' Lloyd sighed. 'I have been appointed to turn your physique into something resembling Steffi Graf. I wouldn't dream of trying to show you how to act on stage, so please let me do my job as best I know,' he said, bravely.

This shut her up, and after stretching they set off down the drive walking at a fast pace, Taboo in tow. 'So how come you're doing this – coaching – I mean?' puffed Grace. 'Did you get knocked out of the Flushing Meadow Tournament?' she taunted.

''Fraid so, in the second round by Michael Chang. Was very close though . . but the real McCoy doesn't start till next week, here at Fort Lauderdale,' grinned Lloyd. The smirk slid off Grace's face.

'Won the Boca Raton Tournament last month, in straight sets to Lendl, which makes my sponsorship with Pounce look very promising. In fact James is working on the deal right now. He'll be here the day after tomorrow to discuss the ...'

'Tomorrow? You mean my brother's arriving here in Florida – how come I didn't know?' said Grace hotly.

'C'mon, Grace, longer strides. We're going into a jog now.'

Grace's T-shirt clung to her body and her hair was plastered to her head as perspiration poured down her beetroot red face. But she was determined to keep up with Lloyd.

'You need at least another fifteen minutes of this aerobic work before your body will benefit. I'll just step up the pace a little ...'

Determined not to give up, Grace gritted her teeth, tasting the salty droplets of steaming sweat that had formed on her upper lip. Her knees were shaking and her legs felt like jelly but she refused to give Lloyd the satisfaction of seeing her quit.

'Up ... up ... up, Grace, lift those feet *up*. C'mon now, nearly there...' coaxed Lloyd. Grace collapsed on the grass by the pool next to Poppy, gasping for air.

'Bloody stupid idea, running up hills,' grumbled Grace.

'Well, have a rest and drink plenty of water so as not to get dehydrated,' he said, 'then we'll start on some conditioning work,' he added, slyly.

'Conditioning work?' Grace was horrified again. 'Look Lloyd, can we just get down to the tennis? That *is* why you're here, isn't it?'

Lloyd sighed. 'I'm here to make you look like an athlete, Grace. We'll get on to the tennis court in due course. Trust me.'

Half an hour later Poppy appeared with some iced tea. 'Just some stretching and then we've finished,' cajoled Lloyd.

'Forget the sodding stretching, I'm off for a shower,' fumed Grace as she headed towards the villa.

'You'll regret it in the morning. Those muscles need——' he began, but the door had slammed. 'Quite the temperamental actress, I see,' said Lloyd quietly to Poppy.

'She can be, yes,' replied Poppy carefully.

'I feel like "public enemy number one,"' Lloyd muttered into his iced tea. 'I just hope she'll be in better humour when James arrives the day after tomorrow.'

'James? Grace's bother? Is he coming here?' Poppy demanded promptly.

'Yep, that's him – a real pal. An outrageous hell-raiser – but a real pal. He's got meetings with Pounce and Universal in Miami regarding sponsorship and advertising.'

Poppy was flushed. 'Excuse me Lloyd, I simply must help Grace with her script ...' and she left, abruptly.

'Don't worry about me,' Lloyd muttered. 'I'll just let myself out.' He watched Poppy's waifish figure stride into the villa, admiring her freckled legs in cut off denims. Finishing his iced tea, he boarded the pick-up and headed for the tennis club.

'Why didn't you tell me James was coming!' Poppy said marching into Grace's bedroom. She was sitting on the bed in a towel still wet fom the shower.

'I didn't know myself until an hour ago. God, I can't wait to see the pain in the arse!' Grace said gleefully as she combed the styling mousse through her thick glossy hair. 'Why are you looking so drippy?' grinned Grace observing Poppy's face.

'You're the one that's dripping,' said Poppy defensively.

'Take my advice, Pops, don't fall for that reprobate brother of mine. He may be a gorgeous hunk but he's a living nightmare on legs, and he has the most appalling taste in women. Stay well clear – he'll only break your heart. Anyway I think Mr Universe downstairs has the hots for you – he'd be a much better bet.'

'Don't be ridiculous!' said Poppy hotly, dodging the wet towel Grace threw at her as she left the bedroom.

# Chapter Seventeen

Taboo jumped off the bed to greet Lloyd's arrival the following morning, and Grace grimaced at the thought of a repeat performance of yesterday's workout. Wincing, she struggled to heave herself out of bed, but her legs were aching like they'd never ached before. Staggering across the bedroom's marbled floor and wrapping herself in her bathrobe, she limped out to meet Lloyd in the drive.

'Look Lloyd, I'm sorry you've had a wasted journey but ...'

'Yes, I'm sure that your legs are aching, that's why stretching those muscles out is so important. So we'll start with a very gentle stretch now,' said Lloyd, not unkindly. 'Just a track suit will be fine,' he continued, amused at her disgusted expression. 'We'll concentrate on toning the abdominals today and leave the cardio vascular for tomorrow.'

Nevertheless the workout was still strenuous, and Grace made little in the way of conversation. Poppy appeared with a jug of lemon barley water just as they were drawing to a close.

'So if it's all right with you guys, I'll bring James with me tomorrow morning, as he'd never find this place on his own,' said Lloyd as he prepared to leave. 'I must make tracks as I've got a practise match with Stefan Edberg,' he added, reaching for his car keys and heading for the truck.

'Wow, that guy has an amazing bod,' exclaimed Poppy as she watched him leave.

'Whatever turns you on,' said Grace dismissively.

'Just what is your problem, Grace?' demanded Poppy hotly. 'Why do you have to give the poor guy such a hard time. There's no need to act so snottily, he's only doing his job.'

'What am I supposed to do, fall on my knees and kiss his feet? He's just the tennis coach, Poppy, not the bloody Pope!' retorted Grace.

'He is an acclaimed professional tennis player, who's been on the international circuit for only three years and is seeded, I believe, nineteenth in the world,' cried Poppy defensively. 'He is also your brother's best friend.'

'Well since you're so fond of him, why don't you kiss his arse and massage his ego, after all that's what he wants. I think he'd do well to remember his place and have a little respect,' said Grace arrogantly.

'Look, Grace. This prima donna attitude of yours is becoming obnoxious, and I'm not going to hang about to listen to you,' Poppy blurted out, picking up the empty jug and glasses. 'Anway, I think I'd better start thinking of something for tomorrow's lunch – presumably James and Lloyd will stay for lunch?'

'There's no need to do anything,' said Grace sulkily. 'I've phoned Universal and told Theo that we need a cook and housekeeper, they'll be coming tomorrow.'

'Oh, I was rather enjoying the peace and tranquillity,' said Poppy disappointedly.

'It's only on a daily basis for a few hours, and I need you to help me with the script now Sybil isn't here. Anyway, I'll leave it to you to arrange times, I don't want to have to deal with staff whilst I'm in preparation for this movie. Bring me a nail file, Poppy, would you?'

Before Poppy could retort 'get it yourself', the phone rang and Grace raced to pick up the phone. 'Mother,' she cried delightedly when she heard the familiar voice.

That night Grace was rudely awoken by Taboo barking frantically as he raced off to the front door, howling and scratching at the beautifully carved antique wood. Both Grace and Poppy were at the door within seconds.

'Either he's catching fleas or he needs to go out badly,' said Grace mystified, opening the door to let him out. Outside, half hidden by a stone, sat an envelope. Grace bent down to pick it up.

'Someone's been here, Pops. Taboo was trying to tell us ...' Taboo was sniffing in the undergrowth, growling menacingly, then standing stock still with ears pricked and nose twitching.

Grace tore open the envelope, finding inside another piece of A4 paper with a child-like scribble in coloured wax crayons.

**TWINKLE TWINKLE HOLLYWOOD STAR
HOW I WONDER WHAT YOU ARE
UP ABOVE THE WORLD SO HIGH
WHAT A SHAME YOU'VE GOT TO DIE!**

Both girls stared wide-eyed at each other then looked back at the menacing message.

'Call the police,' Poppy instructed.

'What for? I'm not bothered,' Grace said trying to sound nonchalant. 'It's just like the other one I got in Los Angeles.'

'You didn't tell me about that,' protested Poppy, frowning.

'I didn't feel the need. I've still got it in my other handbag. Look, let's not get hysterical, it's just a crank. This is the sort of thing one has to endure being in the spotlight. I'm going back to bed,' Grace said dismissively. Poppy stared after her.

'We'll discuss this in the morning,' insisted Poppy to the closing door.

Neither Grace nor Poppy slept a wink that night and Taboo restlessly padded across the bedroom floor, his claws clicking on the marble. Grace lay awake worrying and puzzling over the two anonymous letters until the dawn.

\* \* \*

'Where is the old girl, then,' shouted the familiar voice. 'Sis,' he bellowed through the villa. They caught up with each other in the kitchen, throwing their arms around each other. 'So how's my superstar sister, then? Looking a bit rough I see,' he said playfully. Grace immediately cuffed him around the head and he laughed. 'No sense, no feeling.'

Poppy and Lloyd stood witnessing the touching reunion of brother and sister, and then they all sat down for breakfast, Taboo locked outside.

There was an ear piercing scream and they heard Taboo barking frantically. 'Oh shit, I forgot about Helga,' said James, rushing out to the garden to help his six foot new blonde girlfriend to her feet.

'Who the hell is Helga?' Grace demanded, directing her question at Lloyd.

'Well you know your brother ... er, she's a German player, seeded thirty-two. Very promising – one hell of a serve.' Poppy looked pained.

'Spare me the details ... dear God, look at the size of the woman!' exclaimed Grace, looking out of the window in disbelief. 'She's built like ... a weight lifter. I hope that's not what you want to turn me into, Lloyd.'

'Don't worry,' he laughed. 'You could never look like that – you're far too feminine.'

Grace picked up on the compliment but ignored it as James and Helga entered the kitchen. 'Er girls, this is Helga, my favourite fraulein. Helga, this is Grace, my sister and Poppy.'

Glad of the distraction from the threatening note, and feeling much safer now that her brother was here, Grace made everyone breakfast while the others caught up on news.

'I hate to be a bore,' said Lloyd. 'But let's get this training out of the way and we can all sit down and catch up with the gossip properly over lunch. Come on, Grace ...'

'Ya, I need za CV now, then very much protein,' said Helga as she stripped off her T shirt to expose rippling muscles underneath a skimpy singlet.

'You coming James? You could do with it. You're getting a bit of a paunch there, pal,' said Lloyd, jibing at his friend and poking his stomach.

'Er, no thanks old chap, I need every ounce of energy, if you know what I mean,' said the rakish James, lifting his eyebrows. 'Anyway, you know I specialise in indoor sports,' he added mischievously.

Lloyd laughed. 'What about you, Poppy?'

'I think I could live without it, Lloyd. The staff are arriving any minute and I've got a lot of organising to do,' said Poppy dismissively.

Grace, Helga and Lloyd disappeared leaving Poppy, James and Taboo in the kitchen. 'So how's life treating you, Pops?' said James towering over her as he squeezed her shoulders.

Poppy blushed at James's touch and busied herself loading the dishwasher. 'Oh much the same, James. I must say that I'm enjoying Florida, but Taboo does drive me mad.' The dog, hearing his name, jumped up at Poppy nearly knocking her over. 'See what I mean?' she said impatiently.

'I see only that you're a tiny little scrap of a thing that needs protection,' said James in his usual smooth style as he enveloped Poppy in a hug. She squirmed with embarrassment, her face flushing furiously. James lowered his handsome face to hers and burst out laughing.

'Dearest, darling Pops. You're such entertainment. Nothing amuses me more than to see your little face fevered and all of a dither,' James, frowning as he saw she looked upset. 'Forgive me, little one, I'm not making fun of you – I'm just mucking about. Anyway, I know you've got the balls to deal with me.'

'Has Helga got balls?' asked Poppy coquettishly.

'Ouch, such bitchiness from one so sweet,' grinned James, his eyes twinkling at her. 'Helga is ... well, Helga was a challenge, I suppose. No humour, that's for sure, but she's keeping me occupied.'

'You're incorrigible, James. I don't want to hear any more,' said Poppy, laughing to conceal the pain.

In all the years she'd worked with Grace, had James never noticed her? And why did he have to be so cruel? He'd always teased her like a little sister, but she didn't feel like his little sister. Why had he never considered her as a woman? She'd often asked herself these questions lying in her bed at night.

'So is Grace behaving herself then, Pops,' asked James, grabbing a beer from the fridge.

'I'm not one to tell tales,' said Poppy rolling her eyes. 'Isn't it a bit early for booze?'

'Never too early for me,' chuckled James.

'James, why do you have to go to such lengths to prove you're such a stud? Maybe we have an underlying problem here ... Me thinketh that this stallion doth protest his butchness too much,' pronounced Poppy, exasperated.

'Humour me Pops. It's the one thing I'm really good at – let me bask in my own glory,' he pleaded, laughing.

'Do you come with references then, James? I've never heard anyone else but you appraise your sexual performance,' she said, archly.

'Ouch. Touché.' He mopped his brow in defeat. 'Anyway, you were telling me about Grace,' he added, more seriously.

'Well to tell you the truth, James, she's been a bit difficult, if you know what I mean. She seems to take things out on Lloyd.'

'Probably fancies him rotten – it makes her insecure somehow, and then she gets her prima donna hat on,' said James.

At that moment the others arrived back together with the cook, housekeeper. James ushered everyone outside and left Poppy to instruct the staff.

After a delicious picnic lunch on the lawn of gazpacho, jumbo prawns, quiche and salad washed down with plenty of dry Californian white wine, they wiled away the afternoon laughing and chatting – the quick-witted jokes flying well above Helga's head as she feasted on her beef steak and two pints of milk.

'You want to play tennis now?' Helga asked James, wiping the milk off her top lip with her muscled forearm.

'Later, later. Have a swim and work off some energy,' suggested James, his mouth full of prawn. 'An army can't march on empty stomach.' Oblivious to the others' laughter, Helga stripped off her shorts and dived into the pool, proceeding to do length after length of front crawl.

'My God that is a big job,' said James as he put down his

napkin. 'But a man's got to do what a man's got to do. No rest for the wicked folks!' James climbed to his feet. 'Helga ... Helga, we play ball now.'

Everyone burst out laughing as they disappeared around the side of the villa, and Poppy bit her lip, pretending to be amused.

'He's not really as bad as he seems,' defended Grace. 'He's an old softie, really, just afraid of showing his own feelings and he avoids any emotional liaisons at all costs. This obnoxious act is just a cover up for his vulnerable side,' she said knowingly.

Poppy and Lloyd looked unconvinced.

But she didn't have time to expand her theme, for a commotion had broken out across the lawn and Grace ran to see what was ailing Taboo. She came back crying with laughter, for the dog had tried to join in Helga and James's frolicking and leapt on top of them, covering them with slobber.

James and Helga gave up their pursuits, and they all threw themselves in the pool, laughing and cavorting and very slightly inebriated. Sitting down on the grass afterwards, soaking up the sun, James said, 'Oh Grace, I need you to go to a film première with Lloyd. We need the publicity for him as I'm about to do the personal endorsement deal with Pounce.'

Grace stiffened. 'Why can't he take someone else?' she said sourly.

'Because, Thicko, it won't create quite the same impact as appearing with my superstar sister, the great Grace Madigan. Anyway, Lloyd's considered a heart throb. What's the problem?' he asked. Grace pouted and stared at the clear blue sky. 'Look, I've moved heaven and earth to get Lloyd assigned as your coach, he's giving up precious practice time for you, so just be grateful. The press coverage can only do you good too.'

'What, being associated with some crummy tennis player, seeded at nineteen,' she scoffed. James frowned at her, and she noticed that Lloyd had crept up and heard her last comment. She coloured.

'Look James, forget it!' said the offended Lloyd. 'Who

needs a bloody film première, anyway?'

'You do, and you're going – with Grace!' Silence fell on the group. 'And you can stop giving me all that "big time" bullshit right now. You've turned into the typical Hollyweird Actress and I'm not sure it suits you, Sis,' he frowned. 'Come on Lloyd, Helga, we're leaving,' and they headed off to the pick-up.

# Chapter Eighteen

The white stretch Cadillac, courtesy of Universal, arrived as planned at five-thirty to escort the party to the première. Dressed in a black Cerutti tuxedo with emerald green cummerbund and bow tie as per instructions, Lloyd looked magnificent as he emerged from the limmo. Wincing at the afternoon sun, his eyes crinkled and he appeared even more ruggedly handsome than usual. He pulled himself up to his full height and sauntered to the front door of Villa Retreat, trying to look relaxed in the 'monkey suit' that James had insisted he buy.

Poppy opened the door wearing a full-length, backless black satin evening dress, her golden corkscrew curls piled on top of her head. Her face glowing, she was transformed and Lloyd hardly recognised her – for he'd never seen her wear so much as a scrap of make up before.

Ready to pay compliment, his attention was diverted by the arrival of Grace, who quite took his breath away. Trying to regain his composure, he gazed in open admiration at the beautiful creature before him. Her hair was scraped from her face into a bun at the nape of her neck, jet black khol and black winged eyebrows enhanced her gorgeous green eyes, and her lips and nails were a bright, glossy red, matching the Poinsettia pinned behind her left ear.

Swallowing hard, Lloyd, trying his best to look unmoved, as his eyes took in her bare, creamy shoulders and cleavage covered by a gorgeous emerald green taffeta sheath dress. As he complimented her politely, he noted the minuscule waist and hips cinched in the fantastic fabric. The floor length dress was split up the front, and with the scarlet high heels that would have made Coco Chanel turn in her grave, Grace looked absolutely stunning. She almost looked like an exotic Mardi Gras queen, he thought – most people would see gaudy clashing colours for carnivals only, but Grace carried it off beautifully.

'Well Lloyd, what do you think?' enquired Poppy grinning. 'We'll have no shortage of press tonight – they'll go mad for the colours. You can guarantee most of the other female celebrities there will be wearing the usual black or white Lagerfeld, but this will give us maximum coverage, so stick to Grace's side like glue.'

'I must say ... ' started Lloyd.

'Shall we get this farce on the road?' said Grace yawning.

'We've got to wait for James. He's on his way from Pompano Beach, he's been ...' explained Lloyd, stifling his annoyance at Grace's attitude.

'Yeah, yeah, we know where he's been and what he ... don't tell me he's bringing Eva Braun.'

Lloyd laughed. 'No, not Helga. I think even our James has bitten off more than he can chew with that one.'

'So it will be just the four of us then?' asked Poppy animatedly.

'We've only got four tickets, so I assume so,' replied Lloyd feeling Poppy's excitement.

At that precise moment a taxi dropped James off. He made his way down the drive, and stopped when he caught sight of the three of them.

'My, my, don't we look the donkey's bollocks!' he exclaimed.

'Which is more than I can say for you James. Did you sleep in that suit? On second thoughts, don't answer that, I don't want to know,' said Grace sourly.

James's eyes fell on Poppy. 'Hell's bells, Pops, is that you?' he said admiringly. 'You look so ... so ...' Grace saw the driver looking at his watch.

'C'mon guys, let's hit the road. I'm sure Universal will have put a bottle of bubbly on ice for us in the limo,' she suggested.

As they drew up outside the cinema, James instructed the driver to wait for the limo in front to move off, and for the flashlights of the cameras to subside before they made their entrance onto the red carpet. Fans were peering in through the black windows, trying to capture a glance of the celebrities.

'Now, Grace, Lloyd, you two wait until Poppy and I are inside the doors, then I want you to milk it with the press. We want front page tomorrow, so give it plenty, Grace – hang on to Lloyd's arm, even give him a kiss if you can muster it,' James demanded over his shoulder as he got out of the car.

Poppy felt like a princess with James's arm around her. Of course the press paid little attention to them, but she positively purred with pleasure at the thought of being James's date.

Grace, the true actress, rose to the occasion and played her part to the full. The crowd surged and chanted her name, and she waved back at her audience, loving it. Remembering James's directions, she stood on tiptoe to give Lloyd a kiss, and he responded by pulling her close to him, far closer than was necessary. He was quite overwhelmed by the woman and knew that this was about as close as he'd ever get to her, so, uncharacteristically, he took full advantage of the situation.

The photographers snapped away, and CNN International's presenter commentated excitedly on the apparent liaison between internationally renowned actress Grace Madigan and up and coming tennis star Lloyd Davies.

Grace pulled away from Lloyd when their work was done, smiling sweetly and blowing kisses to her fans as they made their way inside. Behind them followed other stars.

'What the hell are you playing at?' she hissed through her

sugary smile, but Lloyd was saved from having to answer by the appearance of a TV reporter.

'Miss Madigan, Mr Davies. Could we have a quick interview with you?'

Grace shrugged off Lloyd and spoke briefly, answering questions about *Temptation* and *Love All*. When asked about her friendship with Lloyd Davies she replied 'No comment', knowing full well it would fuel speculation.

She was still irritated with Lloyd for taking liberties, but she also began to like the idea of the media thinking she was some kind of sex siren, unlike the cold fish she really was. And come to think of it Lloyd really looked quite a dish. No it certainly wouldn't do her image any harm.

Lloyd couldn't have described the film to anyone as he'd spent the entire performance watching Grace out of the corner of his eye. She was aware of his muscular shoulder touching hers, but was momentarily distracted by her wayward brother's sudden apparent interest in Poppy. And Poppy looked as if she was enjoying every minute of it. Not one of the four of them had any idea what they'd just watched, and Grace skilfully dodged the journalists afterwards in case they asked for her opinion.

At the reception at the Marlin Hotel on Miami Beach, celebrities mingled with the media, and James had a whale of a time, promising the press exclusive interviews with star tennis players in return for good coverage on 'tomorrow's tennis superstar' Lloyd Davies.

Grace flew straight over to Mike Russell and Theo Palaris, exchanging gossip and catching up with the news before being interrupted by a familiar tall blonde. Theo, remembering his manners, introduced the two women. 'Honey, this is Grace Madigan, she starred alongside Mike in *Temptation* – you've seen some of the editing ... ?' prompted Theo.

'I don't recall ...' said the blonde dismissively. 'I'm Violet Valentine – I think we met in London ...' she added, vaguely.

'I don't recall ...' said Grace even more dismissively before turning to talk to Mike, who laughed at the frosty expression on Grace's face.

'I *didn't* recognise her, it's true,' she protested.

'That'll be because Theo sent her to have her nose and teeth done, lips pumped up and chin rebuilt,' he whispered. 'As I understand it, the surgeon removes fat from the buttocks and implants it into the lips. Isn't it a horrible thought?' he grimaced.

'Well, that explains why she talks through her arse,' quipped Grace dryly, but her attention wandered as she caught sight of Lloyd across the room, surrounded by a gaggle of beautiful women. It annoyed her intensely that he was enjoying himself so obviously. He was supposed to be accompanying her, and he was making her look ridiculous.

James and Poppy made their way over to Grace hinting that it was time to leave. 'Always leave them wanting more Grace. Didn't Freddie teach you anything?' asked James with his arm around Poppy's waist.

'Oops. So sorry, Honey.' A glass of champagne knocked against Poppy's bare back, soaking the black satin dress. They turned around to see the very unrepentant face of Violet Valentine.

'James, darling! What are you doing here, such a long way from London's financial centre?' she smiled.

'I'm in the promotional business now, so I'm here in a professional capacity,' replied James.

'Really?' she exclaimed, showing genuine interest. 'I suppose it's who you know, rather than what you know. I must call you when I'm next in London, you obviously have a new number.' Grace noticed to her horror that Violet had already made a note of Lloyd's hotel number on the same piece of paper she was now writing on.

'This is Poppy. I think you two met at my sister's first night party at Blakes – after *Romeo and Juliet*?' said James.

'I don't recall..' Valentine mused looking down at the diminutive Poppy.

'Oh, well I certainly remember you. I believe you were with Luc Fontaine that evening – I hardly recognise you, you look so ... *different*,' quipped Poppy, having noticed that the actress was significantly larger in the chest than she had been since they last met, amongst other things. Grace grinned to herself.

'Of course!' she preened. 'How could I forget that evening. It was that night that I met Theo. It was a case of love at first sight, I'm afraid, and he hasn't had eyes for anyone else ever since,' she tittered, and Grace smiled to herself as she remembered her own experiences with the man. 'Theo's simply adorable – do you know, he's actually having a cameo role specially written for me in his new picture,' smirked Violet.

'Which picture is that?' enquired Grace curiously.

'Whoops, silly me ... nearly gave away confidential details of Universal's next box office phenomenon. Must dash, darlings, Theo will be getting jealous.' She kissed James exaggeratedly, totally ignoring Grace and Poppy, before sashaying across the floor towards the portly Theo.

Grace pursed her lips as she saw that Lloyd was still surrounded by starlets. His eyes twinkled as he paid court to the bevy of beauties, and the press seemed to be paying particular interest to the man they were hailing as the new Don Juan of the tennis court. James followed Grace's icy stare.

'The boy learns fast, you've got to admit, Grace,' he chortled. 'Let's leave him to get on with it – I'll get the driver to take us back to the Villa.'

'He's making a damned fool of me,' hissed Grace. 'We arrived together and we'll be leaving together,' she insisted.

'Hold your horses, Grace. What the hell is your problem? You treat him as if he's a nasty smell most of the time ...'

'Just who the hell do you think you're talking to? If you won't crowbar those limpets off him, then I will!' Poppy gasped as Grace strode across the room and elbowed her way through the throng of female admirers. Hiding her annoyance she slipped her arm through Lloyd's, taking him by surprise.

'We're leaving now, Lloyd,' she said firmly, conjuring up a smile.

'That's a shame, I would have liked to cadge a lift with you guys,' he said, waving at James and Poppy. 'Never mind, I'll make my own way home. See you tomorrow morning.'

'I meant we're leaving *together*,' said Grace insistently, still sustaining her smile. 'After all you do have to practise your serve tomorrow ...' Lloyd looked into Grace's thunderous eyes and recognised dangerous ground, resignedly bidding farewell to his newfound fans.

Descending the stairs with James and Poppy, Grace linked her arm through Lloyd's in a hammerlock hold. Once out of earshot, Grace launched into a vicious attack.

'How dare you publicly humiliate me in this way? Against my better judgement I allowed you to escort me to this farce tonight purely to boost your image and you repay me by embarrassing me – flirting with simpering silicone bimbos,' she hissed.

Lloyd clenched his teeth in silent fury and doubled his pace as the approached the waiting car, almost dragging Grace along with him. James and Poppy hurried after them and they all piled into the enormous stretch limo.

'Not very gracious behaviour if you ask me, my feet hardly touched the floor ...' started Grace.

'Now just you listen to me you spoiled brat! It's time you learned a little human decency and humility,' Lloyd exploded as he turned to face her. 'I've put up with your daily tantrums and abhorrent attitude for too long. You can bloody well find yourself a new fitness instructor and tennis coach, 'cos I won't put up with you and your snotty disposition any more.'

'How dare you speak to me like ... James, are you going to let him speak to ...' stuttered Grace, demanding that her brother intervene.

'There are times, dear sister, that I'd like to give you a clip around the ear, and this is one of them. You've been unbearable lately, especially to Lloyd and Poppy, and I for one have had enough of you,' retorted James.

Grace stuck her chin out indignantly. 'In that case, you'd better make your own way home,' she replied haughtily.

'Good idea, otherwise I won't be responsible for my actions. Maybe we should all go and have a nightcap and allow the high and mighty Grace Madigan to be driven home alone to simmer down and get her priorities sorted out,' said James climbing out of the car with Poppy.

'Coming Lloyd?' he called over his shoulder, before

slamming the door.

'What are you waiting for you wimp, get out!' Grace spat at Lloyd.

'Before I go, Grace, I'm going to give you something to remember me by. Something I've been itching to do for weeks.'

Grace screamed in surprise and fury as Lloyd threw her over his knees. Ignoring her cries of outrage and her thrashing legs, Lloyd calmly raised his right hand and smacked her bottom repeatedly. She shed tears of indignation as he overpowered her, bringing his right hand down on to her green taffeta-clad rear end again and again.

When he was done, he dropped his head in exhaustion, as Grace fell back into her seat, her dress slightly torn and her swollen red face a complete mess under her dishevelled hair. Realising that he'd gone too far and got carried away, Lloyd apologised.

'Grace. Look I'm sorry, I didn't mean to go so far ... but you deserved——'

'Just go away, I never want to see or hear from you again,' muttered Grace, appalled at what had happened.

'I'm afraid you can't dismiss me as easily as that, there are a few things you need to learn ...'

'*I* need to learn?' shrieked Grace sarcastically. 'You could do with a few lessons in basic etiquette yourself ... you're nothing but a thug and I want you out of my sight,' she thundered.

Aware of several pairs of eyes trying to peer through the tinted windows, Lloyd reluctantly got out of the car to join James and Poppy on the sidewalk, still simmering with anger.

'It's that bloody shrink,' said James in disbelief as he watched the limo disappear into the late night Miami traffic. 'She should have had her arse kicked years ago. C'mon Lloydie, lets have a drink,' said James, noticing his friend's brooding face.

'I'm not finished with your sister, there are things I have to say to her in private,' said Lloyd still furious. 'I'm going to race back to the villa in a cab – I'll take a rain check on that drink.'

'Calm down, mate. Remember, you're playing Todd Martin tomorrow. Why don't you go home and get some shut-eye. Leave our temperamental drama queen to stew in her own juice.' But Lloyd was determined to get things sorted out.

'I really feel that I should be with Grace – you know how she hates to be alone,' said a worried Poppy.

'It's about time she was accountable for her own actions. She can't always rely on people like you, Pops, waiting on her hand and foot and smoothing her ruffled feathers,' said James. 'You've done more than enough for her and received no thanks so don't give it a second thought.' He took Poppy's hand and they wandered aimlessly across the road, finding themselves on South Beach.

Kicking off their shoes they walked through the shingle and seaweed in comfortable silence, the moon dipping below the horizon. Within a matter of minutes they were in virtual darkness and James stopped, staring solemnly at Poppy for what seemed an eternity. She could hardly bear the suspense as she gazed up at him adoringly, and he slowly drew her to him, kissing her warmly.

She responded shyly, and returned the kiss, feeling a certain sincerity in James's behaviour. A warmth and vulnerability exuded from him that she never would have expected as he gently kissed the tip of her nose and eyelids, whispering her name over and over. She withdrew slightly to catch her breath, and examining James's face in the shadows, she was surprised to see him looking strangely pitiful. 'James, James, are you OK?' she asked with concern.

'I ... I'm not sure. I feel dizzy ... think I need to sit down ...' he muttered, leaning on Poppy as she led him on to the drier sand and helped him sit down. 'Probably eaten something dodgy,' he bluffed. 'My stomach's in terrible knots.'

'Maybe you had too much to drink ...?' suggested Poppy, looking concerned.

'I didn't ... dear God, I didn't have time to get pissed, I was too busy with the press, and watching you ... Poppy, you're so goddamned ...' he looked away into the darkness.

'I'm so goddamned what?' asked Poppy.

'So ... so ... well ... so damned comfortable,' he admitted staring at the sand disappearing between his toes.

'Comfortable! What is that supposed to mean?'

'I suppose you could call it a compliment,' he said shyly, burying his feet in the sand and kicking it over her evening dress.

'A compliment from James Seymour? Well there's a first time for everything, I suppose,' she joked.

'Don't take the piss, Pops – I'm really feeling ill. What have you done to me?' he whimpered boyishly.

Slowly it dawned upon Poppy that James might be feeling nervous. Could he really be nervous, she marvelled, of her? 'It's probably alcohol withdrawal. Let's find a bar and top you up – I'm not sure I recognise you sober,' she laughed, struggling to her feet.

James yanked her back down beside him almost dislocating her arm, and she yelped. 'I'm sorry Pops, I'm not very good at being gentle, am I? I am trying ...'

'Yes. Very trying,' she sighed, grinning. 'I guess you haven't had much experience of gentleness or tenderness, since you've always been pre-occupied with grabbing a quick snog, rugby tackling bimbos into your bed and notching up your latest score,' she teased. 'Mind you,' she added, 'when you kissed me, you were dangerously close to it yourself. Do you think you could do it again?' she asked coyly.

James was acutely embarrassed. 'I ... I'm not sure. I would need a trainer – maybe you could coach me?' A faint smirk appeared on his lips.

'Just promise I won't need the team physiotherapist after?' Poppy whispered bringing her face up to James, and brushing his lips with her own.

James groaned. 'Oh, God, my stomach's about to go through the floor. What on earth is wrong with me? All I need is to kiss you, to hold you, to learn how to be a gentle, sensitive and caring lover, but I don't seem to be able to move.' He looked at her tenderly. 'Oh Pops, tonight at the première when you had your arm through mine, I felt so comforta ... I mean ... great! Really great! It felt really like it belonged there, I wish it could always be there ... It's just, oh hell, I'm just no good at this mushy stuff. Pops, do you think there's a bar that will serve me a brandy? I think I need one,' wailed James.

'Just shut up and lie down.' Poppy instructed gently, laughing at him. She propped herself up on one elbow and stroked his brow, whispering. 'James, do you think you could be nervous?' she asked. He looked confused. 'You see, James, I think you may have what is commonly known as butterflies.'

'Don't be absurd, that's for wimps,' he said, offended. 'I've just eaten a dodgy prawn or something.'

'James, don't be ridiculous. Tell me what's really bothering you?'

'Well ... I ... well, if you really want to know, I think I've fallen in love with you. In fact I *know* I've fallen in love with you – probably have been for some time now. There, I've said it now ... I've made a right plonker of myself, haven't I?' Poppy said nothing, and James tried to read her expression through the shadows, talking nervously. 'I know I'm not very good at this kind of thing, but I do know that I've never felt this way about any woman before – *never!*' He paused. 'Say something, Pops, won't you? Am I making a complete bloody fool of myself?'

'Oh James, you've no idea how long I've waited to hear some kind of pledge of affection from you. But you'll always be a rogue, leopards don't change their spots ...'

'This leopard will,' James promised. 'This leopard is nearly thirty years old and fed up with roaming the jungle aimlessly. I've come to realise I need and want a mate – I want you, Pops. Give me this chance, Poppy, and I swear you won't regret it ... Poppy, I ...'

'Shhh,' hushed Poppy as she leant over him and kissed him tenderly, savouring his full, soft mouth on hers. James lay perfectly still, not wanting to break the spell, and allowed Poppy to lead him: he never wanted the moment to end. Poppy's finger tips sensually raked through his hair, as she touched and kissed him, stroking his ears, nuzzling his neck.

Although breathless with desire, he made up his mind there

and then on South Beach, Miami, that somehow, some day, he was going to marry Poppy Bates.

# Chapter Ninteen

Grace wearily climbed from the back of the limousine, her eyes red from crying. As she made her way to the front door, keys in hand, her eyes narrowed as she focused on the large male form sitting on her doorstep. With his bow tie untied and dress shirt unbuttoned he looked a forlorn and sorry sight.

'Grace, I need to talk to you ... I'm sorry ...'

'I think you've done enough talking tonight! I have nothing to say to you Lloyd Davies. Please leave these premises this minute, before I call the police,' retorted Grace.

'Grace, please. I just want ...' he begged.

'I can think of two charges already: assault and trespassing,' she said coldly.

'I couldn't go back to the Motel without explaining myself, so I raced ahead of you in a taxi ...'

'Well you can race straight back again,' she said, attempting to get her key in the lock.

'I'm not leaving until this is sorted out,' said Lloyd stubbornly. 'Just stop with all the "actress" baloney and listen to me,' he said impatiently.

'I don't have to listen to you or anyone I don't choose to,' she said imperiously.

'Well I've got news for you Grace Seymour – for once you're going to do as you're told,' Lloyd said taking her arm as he marched her into the kitchen and sat her down on a chair.

'How dare ...' she started.

'Just shut up and listen to me,' he barked. 'Look, I came here to apologise for my behaviour earlier on. I'm not condoning what I did, but you deserved a damned good hiding, the way you've been carrying on. I'm by no means a violent man and I'm deeply ashamed of my actions, but you've driven me temporarily insane. Please forgive me, Grace. I have no wish to fall out with you,' he tried to smile at her, but her face remained a frozen mask. 'God damnit, Grace. I'm not stupid ... I can feel the electricity from you ... between us ... don't deny it any more,' he cried, banging his fist against the wall.

'You're a mad, crazy deluded man,' she shouted back angrily, storming out to the garden to distance herself from him. But he followed her. 'I wouldn't go near you if you were the last man on earth,' she lied, as she turned to face him, trying to control her conflicting emotions. He was even more attractive when he was roused like this.

He said nothing, and the two stood there in silence, the only sound Grace's rapid breathing as she battled with herself. Buckling under a force that was stronger than her, she moved imperceptibly closer to Lloyd as he stared hungrily at her. What on earth was she doing? she thought vaguely as she felt his lips close on hers. And from that moment on, they were lost.

As the kiss deepened, erotic and sensual, Grace's hair stood up on her neck and her stomach churned uncontrollably. The disappointment she felt when he pulled away was acute, and she frantically pulled him closer to her, roughly dragging his head down to meet hers again.

Lloyd pulled his head away again moments later and, gasping for air, noted her beautiful green eyes glinting in the dark. Unable to keep away from her for more than a second, he gave himself up to her demanding mouth. Staggering under the force of their mutual passion, Lloyd stepped back and before they knew it they were floundering around in the swimming pool. The shock of their submersion made them move apart momentarily, but they reunited quickly – if anything, their passion heightened even more.

Steam was rising from their flushed faces as Grace and Lloyd found themselves voraciously returning each other's kisses. They were deluged with lust, literally drowning in their passion until Lloyd managed to get them out of the pool and on to the cool grass.

They tore at each other's clothes, caressing limbs and straining all the time to be closer to one another. The animal in Grace had escaped leaving her no time to panic or be frightened. Their sweaty, entangled bodies rolled over and over in the luxuriant turf, the steam from their bodies rising into the atmosphere of the humid Florida night.

There was no turning back for Grace, she wanted – she needed – every inch of this man, everything he could give her and more.

LLoyd could barely catch his breath – this certainly wasn't what he'd planned, but hunger and passion had completely consumed them both and he had lost control.

The shadows danced over their naked bodies as the moon flirted with the horizon, creating a golden glow on their fevered skins. Their writhing torsos slid longingly together, their limbs entwined and beads of perspiration trickling from their brows.

'I need you, Lloyd. I can't wait any longer,' Grace gasped.

'Grace, wait, I ... please——' started Lloyd. But she shook her head and pulled her to him. Being only human, Lloyd entered her gently and felt he'd pass out from the ecstasy. Moving slowly at first, the rhythm soon built up and before long they were thrusting away years of desire and passion. Whimpers of excitement escaped Grace – she didn't even have time to wonder at what she was experiencing, there was nothing she could do but give in to this overwhelming physical pleasure.

\*   \*   \*

Somehow she woke up in her own bed, sore, and feeling as if every bone in her body were bruised.

'Awake at last,' came Lloyd's soft voice as he appeared with two steaming cups. Grace tried to speak, but her mouth was dry and sore. 'Two much needed cups of coffee,' he added, setting them down as he perched on the side of the bed. Laughing, he removed pieces of grass entangled in her matted hair. 'This certainly is a day to remember.' Grace grunted and reached for the coffee.

'Today, I'm playing the most important match of my life – against Todd Martin, a tough cookie – and when I thrash him I'll be seeded right up there.' Lloyd pointed his index finger upwards. 'I've had no sleep, no protein, no stretch, no warm up and I'm about to step out on court with a top player. And do you know what? I'm invincible today, Grace. I'm a winner!'

Grace rubbed her eyes and groaned loudly as she tried to raise her aching body. Lloyd propped her up with a pillow and seeing her wince as she moved said, 'You think *you've* been in the wars. You should see what your nails have done to my back – unlike Agassi, I'll have to keep my tennis shirt on today,' he laughed, but then suddenly noticed Grace's rather nervous expression. 'Are you feeling all right – you're very quiet?'

Grace swallowed hard. 'You're right, Lloyd. I've probably been denying our mutual attraction for too long, and last night somehow managed to expel the sexual tension between us. So maybe now we can be civilised to each other,' she said, pertly. 'A physical magnetism, that's all it is. I enjoyed our night of passion but last night was a one off – you caught me off guard, off balance,' she announced as coolly as she could. For the truth was, she couldn't get her head around the fact that she'd actually *enjoyed* sex. Up until now she'd considered herself frigid. She had to get rid of him until she'd sorted out her feelings. 'Good luck in your tennis match today,' she added dismissively, heading off to the bathroom.

Once ensconced in the marble chamber behind the locked door, Grace involuntarily dropped the sheet she'd covered herself with and stared at her naked form in the mirror, weeping. For what and why, she wasn't sure.

Lloyd, still sitting on the bed, was baffled by Grace's sudden mood swing and off hand dismissal. What on earth was she doing? he wondered, his pride hurt. His thoughts were interrupted by the sound of a key in the door downstairs, and he welcomed the jovial voices of James and Poppy. He joined them in the kitchen and the three sat at the table, Lloyd running his large bronzed hands frustratedly through his sun bleached hair.

'Listen, Lloydie,' said James to his pal. 'Whatever has, or hasn't occurred between you and my silly sister is unimportant at this moment in time. In four hours time you are going to be playing one of the most important matches of your career. And look at yourself – you're a half starved emotional wreck! Pops, would you mind rustling up some scrambled eggs or something, darling? I'd do it myself, only I'm hopeless in the kitchen,' he smiled at her as she rose and went to the fridge.

'As soon as you've got some food inside you and you're showered and shaved, we'll pick up your kit and get you to Fort Lauderdale for your massage and warm up session,' instructed James, pacing the floor.

'I just don't get it, James. What makes her run so hot and cold?' asked Lloyd, bewildered. 'God ... how that woman drives me mad.'

'Forget Grace and her crazy head trip for now,' James thundered 'We'll discuss it when you've slaughtered Martin. Now, eat this!' Lloyd stared vacantly at the eggs in front of him, trying to muster up an appetite.

James sighed and took a gentler approach as Poppy went in search of Grace. 'Listen mate, my sister Grace is a law unto herself. She's been under immense stress since being here in America, just leave her to me and get this milk down you ... I promise you everything will be just fine,' he said, trying to sound convincing and crossing his fingers.

Poppy eventually persuaded Grace to unlock the bathroom door and went and sat on the cold marble floor with her. She tried to persuade Grace to reveal her problems in her usual kind and compassionate way but could get no reaction. For an hour Poppy did her best to comfort her desperate friend, holding her hand, drying her tears and making her endless cups of tea.

'Look Grace, please talk to me. James and Lloyd have gone to the tournament and we should be there too, to support Lloyd in his time of need,' Poppy urged.

Grace viciously turned on her. 'Go on then. I'm not stopping you! Just clear off and stop feeding off me – you're like all the others – leeches, all of them. Just leave me alone.'

Poppy was taken aback. 'Look, I know you hate being alone. I'm trying to help you!'

'You're here because you're paid to be,' Grace spat. Her friend swallowed hard and tried to remain calm, accustomed as she was to Grace's irrational mood swings. But this time she'd gone too far, and she was livid.

'Well in that case you can cancel my pay cheque because I'm not prepared to wipe your nose for you any more when you snivel about how life has dealt you such a bad hand. The only important thing in your life is *you* and your career. But what about me? What about me?' she cried, rising to her feet. 'I've had to put my life, and career, on hold, whilst I have to pander to all your insecurities and demands. We all have those nagging insecurities Grace, but us lesser mortals deal with them. But that's too much for the great actress, Grace Madigan, isn't it? She's different. Well, I tell you Grace, you've become insufferable,' she finished, hotly.

Grace was astonished at Poppy's outburst, but hit back immediately. 'Go on then, leave. Get out,' she yelled, hysterically.

'Fine,' Poppy retaliated. 'At last I'll have a life of my own and follow my own dreams. I've been loyal to you, Grace. I've loved you like a sister ... but you think everyone is here at your disposal. What about me? What about James – where do you think *we* were last night? Of course it didn't occur to you to think about us or anybody else. And what about Sybil? How many times have you bothered to phone or write to her since she left?' She paused to catch her breath. 'How often do you call Hannah, nowadays? Only when you want to be told how wonderful and talented you are, when you need your ego boosting. What about Freddie's wife Estelle who's just had a hysterectomy? Don't worry I sent her a card from you, oh, and I signed your name on Hannah's birthday card as well, after all that's what personal assistants are for, isn't it, Grace?'

Grace stiffened, shocked at Poppy's attack. But her friend hadn't finished yet.

'And last but not least on your list of victims is Lloyd Davies. Here is a warm and sincere man, with the patience of a saint, and you've gone and treated him as you do everyone who's good to you – you use and abuse and take for granted. But I know you inside out, Grace Madigan, and I know for sure that from the minute Lloyd got out of that red pick-up truck ... it was so damned obvious ... you fell for him. You may think you're the best actress to hit this planet, but I could see the chemistry between you. Will you never allow yourself to love and appreciate anyone without destroying them in the process?'

Poppy, breathless with emotion, stopped to regain her composure. 'I'll be out of here with James on the next flight – and in the meantime, I'm going to Fort Lauderdale.' Poppy turned on her heel and slammed the front door as she left, leaving Grace crying softly on the bathroom floor, getting what comfort she could from a bewildered Taboo.

The telephone call to Warren Kline lasted nearly two hours, but he did manage to calm her down and get her to relay the details of her interlude with Lloyd. Grace listened to his advice and put the phone down feeling more positive. She splashed cold water on her swollen eyes, and rushed to shower and dress – she needed to look her best. Going through her wardrobe, she chose in the end to wear a simple linen, mint-green shift dress with matching jacket. Warren was right, she thought as she hurriedly dried her hair, if she felt and looked confident, she would be!

Somehow she needed to put right the terrible wrong she'd inflicted on Lloyd. Poppy had been more correct than she'd liked to admit in her diagnosis – the minute Grace had laid eyes on Lloyd she'd felt an overwhelming attraction, one that had frightened her in its intensity. Warren had made her see that she shouldn't be so afraid of laying herself open, of risking being hurt. She could no longer deny herself or Lloyd the opportunity of potential happiness.

'Martin leads three sets to two,' the umpire announced. 'Davies to serve.'

Lloyd served a double fault. 'Love, fifteen.' And within what seemed like minutes came his cry, 'Game to Todd Martin!'

Lloyd Davies was getting a thrashing from Todd Martin. He sat under the umpire's chair cradling his head in his hands before wiping himself down with a towel. Grace's heart leapt to her mouth as she caught sight of the agonised expression on his face as he sipped from his Vitfizz paper cup. Crumpling it up he gave it to a ball boy and viciously picked at the strings in his racquet, his face distorted with anguish.

Grace couldn't bear to watch the threatened assassination of the man she had now acknowledged she cared for deeply, and on impulse she ran down the aisle to the boundary. 'Lloyd,' she cried. 'Lloyd!'

'Quiet, please.' came the umpire's expressionless voice. 'Martin to serve.'

'Win Lloyd, win. Win for me – win for *us*,' yelled Grace.

Astonished, Lloyd turned to see Grace with her fist in the air.

'Quiet please,' insisted the umpire, and Grace was grabbed from behind by her brother and roughly dragged along the seats to be plonked down between him and Poppy.

'How the hell did you get in here, there isn't a ticket to be had and security is ...' James whispered angrily.

'Being Grace Madigan does have *some* advantages,' she whispered, grinning. Poppy had not acknowledged her presence.

Lloyd's sweaty brow furrowed as he looked through the spectators at Grace's encouraging smile.

'Oh my God, that's going to completely blow it. He was playing like a retard before you arrived – now he might just as well throw the towel in,' James hissed. 'You'll have completely destroyed his concentration ... Oh my God, what a brilliant return!'

'Love, fifteen' came the announcement.

'Focus, Lloyd. Focus!' Grace yelled determinedly. James covered her mouth with his hand.

'For Pete's sake, shut up, you'll get us slung out of here,' he whispered, infuriated by his sister. The umpire turned in his high chair and glowered at them.

'Final request for silence,' his voice boomed threateningly.

The crowd roared at Lloyd's brilliant return of serve and Grace didn't take her eyes off him as he turned the match around.

For two and a half nail biting, agonising hours, the three of them sat on the edge of their uncomfortable seats, while the two players thrashed it out. Not once did Lloyd glance at Grace, but he kept his concentration on the game in hand, giving himself a serious pep talk. His career depended on this match, and there was no way he was going to allow Todd to win.

By pure determination and tenacity Lloyd managed to break Martin's serve, and in the blazing afternoon sun, he scored point after painful point, bringing their combat to a cliff-hanging fifth set.

The tie-breaker was excruciating and only James could bear to watch as Lloyd made to serve ... 'Ace,' he screamed at the top of his voice, leaping to his feet.

'Game, set and match to Lloyd Davies of Great Britain,' announced the umpire.

'Yes!' hollered James, stamping on Poppy's foot and crushing her with an over enthusiastic bear hug. The crowd cheered frenziedly as Grace elbowed her way through to get to the court. He saw her out of the corner of his eye, but avoided her gaze as he pulled a white windcheater jacket over his sweat-sodden body.

Grace called to him but Lloyd was busy putting the covers on his precious racquets and receiving congratulatory slaps on the back. She turned to James and Poppy but they'd gone. Of course, she thought to herself, they'll have gone to the changing rooms to wait for Lloyd there.

She tried to push her way up the steps through the gaggle of fans but it took her ages to get very far. Eventually she caught sight of the players' hospitality rooms, and Grace jostled through the autograph hunters to find Lloyd. A cry swept through the throng and she looked up to see James, Poppy and Lloyd getting into the official car to go to the press conference.

'Lloyd,' she cried out, but her voice was drowned out by the other devotees. She was swept along with the tennis disciples as they rushed towards the car, but it soared off and almost immediately the crowd dispersed, leaving Grace standing alone and forlorn next to the enclosure.

She retrieved a discarded game programme in despair, and stood staring at the small black and white photograph of Lloyd. This was the man who'd changed her life, who'd awoken the passion within her. She stood for ages in the dazzling sunshine, the hot tarmac almost tacky beneath her feet. Of course he was just teaching her a lesson and giving her her just desserts, she considered. But as soon as she explained her emotional problems, Lloyd would understand. She was sure of it. She knew it was time to come clean and open her heart.

# Chapter Twenty

Shooting for *Love All* was due to commence within the next three weeks and Grace was far from prepared. She'd had problems learning her lines alone now that Poppy had left, and although Theo had arranged for a live-in housekeeper and temporary personal assistant, it wasn't the same as having Poppy. She didn't really know where her friend had gone, only that wherever it was, she was with James.

Grace felt more alone than ever in the big house, and wandered sadly from room to room, with only Taboo to keep her company. She spent the majority of the day trying to call Lloyd, but all she could get was the receptionist at his motel informing her that Mr Lloyd was unavailable and that she could leave a message. She declined.

How she needed Lana. Lana would have known instinctively what to say and do. Grace blinked back a threatening tear at the thought of her friend. She needed to hear a friendly, familiar voice and for the first time in many months, Grace admitted to feeling homesick. She dialled the transatlantic code for England to speak to Hannah, and after a long conversation with her old nanny, decided to call Sybil too.

Though she felt guilty after Poppy's attack for not having spoken to them for so long, she was at least able to reassure herself that they were both well, and that they both still obviously cared for her. Feeling immensely more cheerful she picked up the phone again, intending to talk to her mother, but quickly realised that she couldn't really call her at home. She then tried Justin, then Warren, with no luck, and began to feel lonely and sorry for herself again.

It was then that she admitted to herself that she'd relied too heavily on other people to look after her in the past, and the next day she rose early, determined to make the best of things.

Taboo barked ferociously and for a moment her heart leapt as she thought that perhaps Lloyd had changed his mind and decided to carry on with the training. Dragging a natural lipstick across her lips she leapt to the door, but standing in front of her was a middle aged lady with a shock of red hair. 'I'm from Universal. My name's Vera,' she announced efficiently. Grace's heart sank, but she made her welcome and showed her around.

But ten minutes later Taboo barked excitedly again, running out of the back door. Following him, she turned the corner of the villa to come face to face with Lloyd.

'Lloyd!' She felt herself blushing. Taboo's welcoming ritual temporarily distracted them both.

'This situation is mutually unsatifactory, but Theo insists I continue to coach you and remain technical advisor for *Love All*,' he said coldly. 'Since I won the championship he's more than keen for my name to appear on the credits, so I'm afraid we're stuck with each other. I suggest we go back to where we left off ... your backhand.' He managed a smile, but it didn't reach his blue eyes, which remained cold, devoid of any trace of emotion.

'Lloyd, I'd hoped you'd come ...' Grace started.

'As I said,' he interrupted, 'I came because I'm contracted to do so.'

'But I want to apologise ... I need to tell you——'

'You want, *you* need – it's always you, isn't it Grace,'

Lloyd interrupted quietly, his anger palpable.

'Please don't be angry. I need to explain, I just couldn't deal with the attraction I felt between us – I put up barriers to protect myself ...' explained Grace with great difficulty.

'Well that's all water under the bridge now, a one-off as you called it. Shall we get on with this stretch?' he said, dismissively.

'But can't we at least be friends?' asked Grace, dismayed.

'Sure. It helps for a better working environment,' he grinned. 'But,' he added seriously, 'the minute I get wind of a temper tantrum, or that "star" act, I'm out of here, contract or no contract. I'm here purely to fulfil my professional obligations.'

'Please, Lloyd, can't we talk about this?' Grace begged, desperate not to let the opportunity pass.

'If it's to do with your muscle tone or your athletic performance, yes,' said Lloyd curtly, 'but I don't think there's anything to say about our so-called friendship. Let's just keep our relationship strictly business. Now, shall we get started?'

Grace gave up any hope of intimate dialogue and did her best to impress Lloyd with her fitness level. Things weren't progressing as she'd hoped but at least he'd turned up, even if out of duty. Just having him near brought comfort to her and she listened to his instructions attentively.

'Much better, Grace, much better. Remember to prepare earlier, I want to see your full swing ... again. Don't jab ... yes, another one ... good, and again ...'

Grace glowed under his praise as she wiped the sweat off her face with the back of her hand. 'See how well you can do when you concentrate?' Grace nodded as she watched Lloyd demonstrate a backhand, in exaggerated slow motion. She tried not to stare at his rippling thighs and forearms.

'You're not concentrating Grace,' he scolded gently. He repeated the movement, overstating his swing. 'Now ... I'm going to feed you a backhand and forehand alternately. I want to see you change your grip and footwork accordingly.' Grace took a deep breath, knowing that this combination had caused her problems in the past.

'Not bad ... not bad at all.' He delivered the last twenty-five balls and Grace worked hard, running around the court to send them back within the boundaries of the white lines.

She stood exhausted at the baseline trying to get her breath. 'Come to the net, I'm still concerned with that grip of yours.' Aware of her sodden polo shirt clinging to her body and what must by now be a ruddy face, she advanced trying not to look so desperately out of breath. Cool as a cucumber and without a bead of sweat on his brow, Lloyd swung his legs over the net. 'Let me show you, stand in front of me.'

Standing immediately behind and engulfing her, he shadowed her and, fitting together like spoons, they swung at invisible balls. His strong arms running alongside hers felt like an embrace, and Grace revelled in the sensation. The feel of his tall muscular body behind her made her think back to their night of passion by the pool, and her eyes wandered to the spot where she'd found her femininity.

'Concentrate Grace, follow the swing through like so.' Grace swallowed, finding it impossible to concentrate when he was standing this close to her. 'Yes ...' she muttered aware of the perspiration trickling down her neck.

As if reading her thoughts, he said. 'Enough, Grace. You're too tired to concentrate – it would be counter-productive to continue.' Grace dropped her head, humiliated, and saturated in sweat.

'Shall we pick up the balls?' he asked cheerfully. 'I've never seen you play as well. You're making splendid progress.' Lloyd complimented. Grace nodded appreciatively.

'Same time tomorrow, then,' Lloyd called over his shoulder as he let himself out of the wire surrounds. Grace looked at her watch. They'd been on court almost two hours and she felt wretched. Still panting she swigged from her bottle of water before slowly making her way into the villa with Taboo at her heels.

She showered, ate the lunch that Vera had prepared and attempted to study her script. It was a lonely afternoon and evening – as were many to come, for this became the pattern of her life over the next few days.

Then, one morning after her lesson Grace attempted to invite Lloyd to lunch with her. 'Thanks Grace, but I've got a

# Playing for Love

Sportsman's lunch to attend in Miami. In fact I'll be late if I don't get a move on.' He left in good spirits, leaving her feeling even more alone.

Grace's tennis game improved in leaps and bounds and Lloyd was very pleased with himself. Once in a while he'd stay and have iced tea with her, and she made the most of his company, lapping it up.

'So where is it that James and Poppy have gone?' she asked casually.

'I'm not altogether sure,' he replied carefully.

'But surely you must need to know, if he's looking after your career,' she said, puzzled.

'True. But the big tournament is over and there's nothing more for him to do here at the present time. He's having a well deserved break at a secret hideaway,' said Lloyd pleasantly.

'Why so secret?' probed Grace.

'They obviously don't want to be disturbed. Believe it or not our James is a completely changed man, totally devoted,' he replied.

'I find it hard to believe that my brother the rogue could change – it's a physical impossibility. And what you're really saying is that they don't want to be disturbed by me,' said Grace sadly.

'Well, you do seem to have a knack of dominating people's lives ... you're a full time job, Grace. No offence ...' he smiled ruefully. 'Anyway, see you tomorrow as usual.'


That evening Grace escorted Theo Palaris to a charity ball in Boca Raton. Universal had funded the glamorous evening, a function to raise money for Miami's underprivileged children. It was a flamboyant affair boasting many local celebrities, and Grace played her part, laughing and joking with all the appropriate people until she came to a standstill, having spotted the familiar, ruggedly handsome tennis player with the brilliant blue eyes.

On his arm was a gorgeous, tall, Titian-haired beauty of Hawaiian extract, and Grace's stomach went into orbit, her heart sinking to her knees. Theo noticed her staring, and laughed.

'He sure is a bit of a beau. Quite a catch, I suppose, now that he's won the tournament. Didn' seem too keen to honour his contract to coach you though Grace ... ' he drawled. 'Somethin' goin' on with you guys?' Grace shook her head sadly. 'I reckon he's got a bit too darned pleased with himself lately. Violet tells me he hangs out on South Beach and is quite a hit with the bikini babes ...' he continued, oblivious to Grace's forlorn expression.

She excused herself and fled to the ladies to try to calm her tortured nerves. Running her wrists under the cold tap she pulled herself together, telling herself she couldn't afford to go to pieces. Returning, to her horror she found Theo and Lloyd in conversation. She managed to smile dazzlingly.

'Hi Grace, Theo said you were here somewhere,' said Lloyd amiably.

'Lloyd's bin' giving me a progress report on your tennis game. Says you're looking pretty awesome on court,' said Theo.

Grace's fixed smiled widened as she took in the stunning girl standing next to Lloyd. 'Oh, Grace, this is Marsha.' She smiled shyly at Grace.

'Lloyd tells me he's been coaching you,' the beauty offered.

'Yes, he's a wonderful teacher,' Grace replied, pulling herself up to her full height. She rose to the occasion, performing brilliantly – she was witty and amusing as the four of them made pleasant conversation, and only when Lloyd and Marsh left in search of some friends, did Grace allow her smile to collapse. She'd never known such pain and was anxious to get back home. Feigning tiredness, she asked Theo to call for his driver so she could escape back to the villa.

In the back of the car, Grace leafed through *The Miami Tribune*. Coming to the celebrity and gossip pages, she stopped and stared at Lloyd's face yet again. She turned the light on and examined the photograph: he was pictured with the dreadful Violet Valentine at a restaurant opening. Grace continued to stare at the photo and accompanying article for a full ten minutes before she folded the paper up and put it on the seat beside her, her bottom lip trembling.

Looking out of the window she sadly admitted to herself that she'd lost the only man she might ever truly have loved, and that her chances of happiness were becoming more and more remote. Lloyd wasn't angry or even upset with her – he was simply indifferent. And worst of all, it was all her fault.

# Chapter Twenty-One

## London, 1997

George Seymour sat at his desk clutching a copy of the tacky tabloid, shaking with rage at the photograph of his daughter with Lloyd Davies. Almost beside himself, George tore out the relevant page and placed it with the other articles the press cutting service had been sending him over the years on his daughter.

He swallowed away the bile that had risen at the back of his throat at the sight of Lloyd's face and fought to regain control. He missed his daughter enormously – craved her, even – but knew it would be counter-productive to attempt to make contact with her.

George was not a man to be messed with, indeed his profile was one of staggering success and he was not without his share of media attention, but when it came to his only daughter, he was weakness itself. He *was* Texoil, renowned for his clever and ruthless business mind, but this same power that made him great had brought out the egocentric bully in him over the years. He had become something of a legend, and what with his handsome good looks, he had become a target for many a gold-digging female. George was not averse to the odd indiscretion, but his head and heart were out of bounds – not because of any sense of matrimonial fidelity, but because emotion just didn't come in to it. Money and power were his only interests.

George unclenched his fists and loosened his jaw as Bettina's voice on the intercom interrupted his chain of thought. 'Your wife is here to see you, Mr Seymour.'

George quickly put the manila file with the photographs, articles and investigative reports away in his top drawer and locked it, slipping the key into his inner jacket pocket. The heavy oak door opened and George raised his powerful, swarthy frame to greet Beatrice dutifully with a peck on the cheek. As usual Beatrice looked impeccable in a simple, but beautifully cut cream suit adorned with a three string pearl necklace and matching earrings.

'Bea, what a charming surprise. You should have let me know you were coming to London – we could have had lunch. I'm sorry I haven't got back home this week, it's been bedlam here with both the Texans and Arabs in town ... is there something wrong, Bea?' he asked, noting her cold, expressionless face.

'I was summoned by Annabell Thurlston to meet her for lunch at Daphne's today,' said Beatrice flatly.

'How nice. Don't tell me – she's still whining on about old Clive's golf addiction,' started George.

'No, actually. Apparently Sophie is pregnant and ...'

'Well I'll be jiggered, old Clive is going to be the first Grandad amongst us reprobates ... I don't remember the wedding. Who ...'

'There was no wedding,' sighed Beatrice, and before George could get a word in she added harshly, 'James is responsible – he's the father.'

'*What?* Am I hearing you correctly, Beatrice?'

She nodded solemnly.

'The bloody idiot,' roared George, his face colouring in rage.

'Don't shout, George,' said Beatrice wearily. 'It doesn't do any of us any good.'

'I'd like to get my hands on that little shit,' he raged, disregarding Bea's words. 'That boy has caused me nothing but embarrassment.' He paused for a second. 'But hang on, how do they know for sure that James is the father? I wasn't aware he and Sophie were an item?'

'You've never been aware of James, full stop,' replied Beatrice bitterly. 'The only time you've ever taken notice of your son is when you've taken it upon yourself to give him a good thrashing. You treated your horses and gun dogs better that you treated your family,' she added.

'But I needed to bring him into line,' thundered George, outraged at his wife's unaccustomed outburst. 'What the hell's got into you? Our son was rebellious and cocky, and deserved every punishment he got. By Jove, if I could get my hands on that little runt I'd skin him alive and decimate his wedding tackle to make sure he couldn't father any more little bastards.' George paced up and down his office, spit forming on his clipped moustache.

Beatrice stood quietly, then turned on her husband. 'You're a bully, George. You always have been, and I've had enough,' she said defiantly as she pulled herself up to her full five feet three inches. George stopped in his tracks. He'd hardly ever heard Beatrice even raise her voice, let alone challenge him.

'I'm sick to death of the way you treat people,' she continued, 'especially your own family. Your two children don't want to speak to you and I don't blame them. It's either your way, or no way – you've never contemplated a compromise, never discussed anything with us, just bulldozed your way through life. You've even managed to alienate me from my children and I'll never forgive you for that. Never!' Beatrice fought back years of stifled tears and stared at George with hatred in her eyes.

'After we were married and you'd got your hands on Texoil, everything changed almost immediately. You stopped talking to me, looking at me, touching me – how we ever managed to conceive Grace and James I'll never know. I was just an anonymous accessory, known as Mrs Seymour, accompanying you to your boring functions and shooting parties, always keeping my mouth conveniently shut. You've destroyed me, destroyed our family ...' She was silenced by a blow from George's familiarly cruel hand as he struck the side of her face. It momentarily knocked her off balance.

'Get a grip of yourself, woman!' he shouted. 'How *dare* you waltz into my office, unannounced, and hysterically accuse *me* of creating *your* shortcomings. You show absolutely no gratitude for what I've done for you, you're lucky I'm still here, goddamnit. Let's face it, Beatrice, you don't exactly have a lot going for you, do you? What do you have to say for yourself? What have you contributed to this marriage? *Nothing!* Absolutely nothing.'

'Is it any wonder I have no self-esteem? You've beaten every little bit of personality and confidence out of me,' she raged, dabbing at her tear-stained face. 'Well, you've hit and humiliated me for the last time, George ... the last time! You will never lay another finger on me – I'm taking control of my life, and the first thing I'll be doing is flying to Florida to see my children,' she said, composing herself.

'I particularly need to spend time with Grace, who you seem to have done an even better job of destroying than you did me.' George raised his eyes to heaven. 'She's called me a few times, needing to talk ...'

'She called?' George stopped Beatrice in her tracks. 'She called and you didn't tell me?' he yelled.

'She wanted to speak to *me*, not you! We have a lot of catching up to do and having wasted so many years, I'm not about to waste another day. I'm leaving as soon as my fund raising commitments will allow. I don't know how long I'll be gone, and I certainly don't know what the future holds for us ...' She paused, glaring at him. 'Oh, and when I do return, it will be in a different capacity – Uncle Freddie's assistant at his art gallery is leaving, so I've been offered the job. Funny how life works out – it's the same position he offered me over thirty years ago. Better late than never.'

George was stunned and stood staring at his wife. He hardly recognised the woman he'd been married to for three and a half decades. What was going on? Beatrice straightened her pearls, picked up her handbag and made for the door.

'Bea ... are you actually blaming me for the way our

children have turned out?' asked George incredulously.

'Yes, George, I am,' she replied coldly. 'I'm sorry I can't stop, but my son has got himself into a mess, my daughter needs me, and I need to get over to see them.'

George stood with his mouth gaping as Beatrice strode past him. 'Goodbye George,' she said quietly before leaving, closing the door quietly behind her.

Incensed, he punched the wall with his fist and cried out in pain, indignation and fury. He couldn't give a toss about his wife and son, not really, but as for Grace, his only daughter, she would always be his and his alone. Nursing his hand, he staggered to his chair and pressed his intercom. 'I'm not to be disturbed under any circumstances,' he barked at Bettina.

He collapsed over his desk and cried like a baby, taking the key from his pocket and unlocking the top drawer again. He needed to get another look at this Lloyd Davies ...

# Chapter Twenty-Two

**Florida, 1997**

Lloyd arrived as usual for his lesson with Grace, but neither of them made reference to the previous evening. The atmosphere between them was tense but they both tried to ignore it and focus on the job in hand.

'Let me check that grip of yours,' said Lloyd, taking her hand to place the racquet in it. As their skin made contact she felt a bolt of electricity shoot through her and felt certain that Lloyd had experienced it too. Turning his back immediately he walked back to the base line talking over his shoulder so that Grace couldn't see his expression.

That day he stayed for lunch. They made pleasant conversation, avoiding all personal topics but eyed each other warily, treading on egg shells with one another. When it was time to leave, Lloyd lingered a few minutes before heading off. At times Grace wondered if that electricity she felt was all in her mind. Was Lloyd punishing her, or was he genuinely indifferent to her?

The telephone rang in the villa and Grace ran to catch it.

'Can I speak to Lloyd please?' asked a familiar voice.

'No I'm sorry, he's just left,' replied Grace. 'James ... is that you?' she asked, hesitantly.

'Yes,' he replied crisply. 'Tell him I need to speak to him urgently tomorrow if I don't manage to catch him today.'

'James ... James I need to speak to you. I have to apologise to you – I realise I've been unbearable ...' started Grace.

'I think it's Poppy you need to apologise to,' said James distantly.

'I need to make peace with a lot of people, James. I hope it's not too late to put right all the hurt and pain I've caused,' she pleaded.

'We're all extremely weary of being passengers on your rollercoaster, Grace. You can apologise if you wish but quite frankly it'll take more than that.'

'I've made the biggest mistake of my life and I'm paying the price ... I've got nobody to turn to, James,' said Grace biting her lip. 'Please can I speak to Poppy?' she said trying not to get upset.

'Grace?' Poppy's hesitant voice came on the telephone.

'Poppy ... Poppy – I don't know what to say. Please forgive me for my dreadful behaviour. You're so special to me, you and James – I didn't appreciate how much I'd put you through. Will you come back, please ...' begged Grace.

'Well, my priorities have changed quite a bit, but I will come back to help you through the shooting of *Love All*,' she said, kindly. 'After that, well who knows ...' She added calmly, 'Listen, we're in a bit of a hurry right now so I'll have to go, but we will come back soon, I promise.'

'Wait, Poppy, where are you?' cried Grace. But it was too late – she heard the dialling tone and slowly replaced the hand set.

The next day during their warm up, Grace relayed her conversation with James and Poppy to Lloyd. 'You see Lloyd, I realise that I got carried away with the "fame game" but I'm going to change, I promise. I've learned my lesson, and I just want to be given another chance.' She looked up at him shyly.

'Well, you sound genuine enough and I'm pleased for you,

but it doesn't change anything between us except for the fact that we can now indulge in civilised conversation – so let's be friends and leave it at that for now.' He smiled, patted her arm and turned his attentions to correcting the level of the net.

Her lesson went well and Grace felt more and more confident with her performance on court and that afternoon made great progress with her script. Although Vera and Taboo were constantly there, her loneliness was more than evident as she wandered from room to room reciting her lines from the manuscript. But she was learning to cope with the solitude.

The ring of the telephone summoned her attention, and she picked up the hand set.

'Mother! At last! I was beginning to think you'd changed your mind about coming! Let me get a pen to write down the flight details.'

She rose early next morning with enthusiasm and immediately started her warm up in readiness for Lloyd's lesson.

'Such enthusiasm heartens me!' he called grinning, as he walked up to her, squinting through the morning sun.

'Let's go straight into a game, I'm feeling formidable today,' she laughed.

'So I can see,' he laughed back, unzipping his racquet.

Grace returned Lloyd's serve with confidence and determination. The ball skimmed the net at great speed, landing in the confines of the corner base line.

Lloyd stood impotently staring at the place of ball contact. Turning his head slowly to her he said, 'What the hell was that?'

'My return, what do you think?' she replied laughing out loud.

Lloyd threw back his head and guffawed. 'Well I'll be damned. That was absolutely spectacular. Show me it wasn't a fluke,' he demanded and served her another ball. Grace brilliantly returned it again, this time slamming it on the other side of the court. 'Good grief woman, what did you have for breakfast. Steroids?' he shouted jovially.

Lloyd bantered humorously with her as they continued their lesson and Grace felt she'd never been so happy. Bewildered, she realised she'd never had much cause to laugh or have fun before, but Lloyd brought out the playful side in her.

'I can't help but feel a great sense of achievement when I see you playing like that,' said Lloyd when they'd finished. 'What happened to that spoiled sulky female I used to coach?' he asked playfully.

'Gone,' she jibed back. 'She was a bit of a pain, wasn't she?' she laughed.

'Would you warn me when she's about to return? Only I owe it to mankind to send out a red alert for immediate evacuation should she reappear,' he said with mock seriousness.

'Don't worry, I got her a one way ticket out of here,' she smiled, and asked him shyly if he could stay for lunch.

'I'm sorry, no can do. Got a retirement lunch to attend in Fort Lauderdale – Max Rendall, a sports commentator. He's fantastic, covered all the major matches for television, so I'd best be getting along,' he said excitedly as he stood up.

Grace nodded and attempted a smile as the glow went off her enthusiasm.

'If you're not doing anything, I'm sure you'd be more than welcome,' he grinned, seeing her despondency.

'Really?' asked Grace, her face lighting up again.

'Sure, if you can be ready in under five minutes,' he replied casually. Grace tore off to the shower and washed her hair in record time, pulling on a pair of white slacks and navy T-shirt.

'Am I too casual?' she asked, breathlessly as she reappeared downstairs, her hair still wet.

'Couldn't be more appropriate,' he replied, as he led her to the car.

They headed toward the freeway and Grace attempted to make herself presentable by powdering down her flushed face. As Lloyd turned the steering wheel to link up to the freeway, Grace's lipstick almost disappeared up her nose. Lloyd looked at her and laughed. Grace looked in her mirror to see the comical sight and joined him in his amusement.

'I give up,' she laughed as she wiped off the scarlet smear.

'You don't need any of that stuff – you look beautiful as

you are,' he said spontaneously, looking out of the corner of his eye at her natural features and nearly ebony locks wildly flying about her face. Embarrassed, he looked away, focusing on the road ahead.

Grace was incredibly pleased, but also too embarrassed to look at him or acknowledge the compliment.

The party was a jolly affair, and Grace realised just how lonely she'd been over the last couple of weeks. Lloyd was busy talking tennis to his colleagues and Grace amiably joined in. Many people spoke to her and were curious about *Temptation* which was due to be released, but she was amongst the tennis fraternity and more than aware that the various players were the stars in this particular show. She wasn't calling the shots here, or holding court, but she didn't feel insecure or even bothered. Grace was content.

The sun had lost its warmth and Grace pulled her white cardigan around her shoulders as they trundled along the dirt track back towards Villa Retreat.

'Your family must be incredibly proud of you, having achieved so much,' Grace said, smiling up at him.

'I think they are. Mum sacrificed everything to get me a good start in life and I mean to make sure she benefits by reaping the rewards,' said Lloyd sincerely.

'It's something I've always wanted – to make my parents proud of me ...' started Grace. 'But somehow it all went wrong,' she said, sadly. He smiled at her, squeezing her hand. He knew from James what a difficult childhood they'd both suffered.

Grace was feeling brave, and decided to confide in Lloyd about her mother's imminent arrival. 'We've had no contact in the last ten years and I have to confess I'm more than a little nervous,' she explained, pausing to gauge his reaction. 'I ... I don't suppose. Well, you wouldn't come with me to meet her at the airport, would you? I had hoped James would be back by now, and I'd really appreciate a little moral support.'

Lloyd was surprised, but pleased that she'd asked him. 'Sure, no problem. Let me know exactly when she's due, as my diary's pretty crammed,' he said amiably. Grace's face fell, as she immediately assumed he was referring to Marsha or Violet, or one of the 'bikini babes' from South Beach.

'Well actually, it's tomorrow afternoon,' said Grace. 'I only heard yesterday, myself. If you can't make it don't——'

'No don't worry, I do have a previous appointment but I'm sure I can juggle that around,' he replied thoughtfully. 'We could go straight after our lesson if you like.'

Grace thanked him and got out of the car, not wanting to push her luck any further than she already had. As she walked up to the villa she could feel Lloyd's eyes on her, but as soon as she let herself in, the red truck turned around and roared off into the distance.

Beatrice checked her lipstick and rushed through the passport control at Miami airport, anxiously keeping an eye out for her much-missed daughter. She focused on the strikingly handsome but strangely familiar blond, bronzed man, but before she had a chance to wonder where she knew him from, she spotted Grace standing beside him, barely reaching his shoulder.

Beatrice stood in her tracks, surveying her beautiful daughter. How could she have allowed George to banish her own flesh and blood from her life for so many years. Emotion overcame her and she rushed into Grace's receptive arms. They clung together, unable to speak for several minutes as they let the tears flow.

Lloyd looked on, surprised but touched by the display of emotion. Wanting to give them a few minutes alone, he got the luggage in to the trunk of the car, and waited for them there.

'Of course ...' mumbled Beatrice incoherently as they drove off. 'You're Lloyd, James's friend – you used to come and stay with us during school exeats.

'Oh Mother, I'm sorry ... I forgot to introduce you,' said Grace accepting the lace handkerchief Beatrice proffered to wipe her tears of emotion. But before long she was chattering animatedly, attempting to fill her mother in on the life she and James had been leading. She rarely paused for breath on the hour long journey to Villa Retreat, and Lloyd smiled to himself as he listened.

Beatrice couldn't help wondering exactly what the relationship was between Lloyd and her daughter, and even once Grace had explained that he was training her, she was still not convinced that there wasn't more to it.

As the car drew up outside the villa, Taboo came hurtling across the lawn, his face quivering with anticipation, his wet nose snuffled up against the car window.

'What an adorable Dane,' exclaimed Beatrice, a dog devotee, and then, to her joy, she caught sight of James and Poppy, who'd appeared from the side of the villa. Behind them was Warren.

Grace gave a whoop of delight and rushed to give them all a hug. 'Poppy, James. You're back – what brilliant timing. Look who's here!'

James rushed over to his Mum, sweeping her off her feet in a bear hug. Grace laughed, and turned to Warren. 'I'm so pleased to see you, but what are you doing here?' demanded Grace, overcome with joy.

'Well, it just so happens to be my granddaughter's third birthday and as my son and daughter-in-law live nearby I thought I'd drop by ...' Warren's eyes rested on Lloyd and Beatrice. Remembering her manners Grace introduced the unfamiliar parties whilst James shuffled impatiently in the background.

Unable to stifle the enthusiasm at seeing his mother, he jumped in, demanding her attention. 'Now, Mother,' he grinned boyishly. 'I want you to meet someone very special ... she's, well, she's ...' he stammered.

Grace laughed at her brother's sudden unusual shyness. 'James is trying to introduce you to Poppy, Mum,' interrupted Grace impatiently.

'Er, yes. Poppy, I'd like you to meet my Mother, Beatrice ... and Mum, I'd like you to introduce you to the very recent Mrs Seymour – Mrs James Seymour.' His voice tremored as he pushed Poppy toward his dazed mother.

Beatrice and Grace stood stunned as James explained how he and Poppy had flown to Las Vegas, the minute Lloyd had won his match against Todd Martin, and married.

'We didn't see the point in waiting, you see ... will one of you please say something?' demanded James.

Warren, unfamiliar with James's reputation, stepped forward to congratulate him, and Lloyd, who'd suspected what they were up to, followed him, grinning as he gave them both a hug.

Grace was still struggling to come to terms with the fact that her wayward brother had actually got married. She'd never thought he would, but groped for the right words, happy tears filling her eyes and racing down her cheeks.

'I'm so happy for you both!' she cried and turned to Lloyd. 'You knew, didn't you?' He nodded and smiled.

'I guessed as much. I knew they'd gone to Vegas.'

Beatrice was left gaping at her son in disbelief. It had been an emotionally charged day, what with flying across the Atlantic to meet with her daughter whom she'd not seen for over ten years, and then being confronted by James and his bombshell. She was knocked for six, delighted for her son. But how on earth was she going to break the news about Sophie Thurlston now? Beatrice managed to pull herself together and hugged her son and new daughter-in-law warmly, keeping her worries to herself for now.

The six of them sat in the shade of the tree drinking Pimm's and gossiping. Grace couldn't believe she'd finally got her mum by her side, and revelled in Beatrice's new found confidence and good humour. Never had she seen her mother so extrovert and lively.

George's name had not once been mentioned thankfully and she pushed that unhappy thought to the back of her mind. Warren gazed at Beatrice, and was delighted to find that she was nothing like Grace's description of her. Obviously some major change had occurred that he knew nothing of, but it had obviously done her the world of good. Feeling slightly out of place at the family reunion, he drove back to his son's house to complete his family weekend, promising to come back and see them all the following weekend. Lloyd reluctantly returned to his motel in Miami.

That night Beatrice, Grace, Poppy and James sat up until the early hours before eventually departing for their rooms.

They were awoken in the morning by Taboo's welcoming ceremony for Lloyd. Although a little jet-lagged, Beatrice watched her daughter being put through her paces on the tennis court and was more convinced that Lloyd's role was not simply as tennis instructor. He sure as hell didn't need the experience, nor the money, so why would he have agreed to do it? She noticed that her daughter positively bloomed in his presence.

But that day they had to cut the lesson short as an urgent telephone call came through from Universal. It was Theo, informing Grace that the shoot dates had been moved forward – she was to stand by for a fax with the new schedule.

'Oh God,' exclaimed Poppy as she read it. 'Because of some weather report for Key Biscayne, Theo wants to shoot the crowd scenes and action footage on Thursday!

'Apparently, a storm is forecast in and around the Florida Keys so he needs to shoot certain scenes ahead of the original schedule.' She paused and then read on. 'He says he wants you to rest as much as possible ahead of the main shooting, and keep learning your lines, so ... Oh, Lord, he wants me to stand in for you for the day.' She looked up at Grace.

'But how can you stand in for me? We might be the same height and build but we're hardly identical!' she fretted.

'Apparently it'll only be back views of you he's shooting that day – he wants to get the close-ups later in the week, and he's going to get me a dark wig.' She giggled at the thought. 'He did tell me before I went off to Las Vegas that I might have to stand in for you occasionally when I made the mistake of telling him I'd played county tennis when I was younger.' She brushed the tendrils from her eyes and read on.

'The camera will be shooting from behind – over my shoulder and through the net capturing the crowd and concentrating on your opponent, played by ... I don't believe it.' She looked up. 'Played by Violet Valentine.' Grace grabbed the fax from Poppy to see Theo's instructions with her own eyes.

'This is ridiculous. She's not an actress – she ... she's a prize bitch. What the hell is Theo playing at? This is supposed to be a big production with big names,' protested Grace.

Grace continued to air her grievances to the rest of the clan who were now seated around the kitchen table. 'God, I can't bear it. Do I really have to play alongside some bimbo who's only got a part in a picture because she's fucked the producer?' Beatrice winced and Lloyd frowned.

'I'm sure her role is tiny, Grace,' reassured Poppy. 'She's probably only booked for the one day, so he'll need to concentrate on her,' she added.

'She's no threat to you, for goodness' sake, Grace. Stop bitching,' said Lloyd, beginning to show irritation.

'The voice of authority,' Grace shot back at Lloyd. 'Well she's obviously good in the sack, you should know, James,' she exploded, turning to her brother. Silence fell on the group. Beatrice, obviously embarrassed at her daughter's language, fumbled with a piece of croissant for Taboo who sat drooling by her side. Poppy's humiliated cheeks burned as she stared blindly out of the window and James stiffened in his chair, his mouth tight. Only Lloyd broke the silence.

'OK, Grace, that's quite enough,' he said firmly. 'Go and get a fresh towel. We've got to complete today's lesson.' He rose from his chair, looking angry as Grace flounced out of the room.

There was an air of awkwardness as Grace reappeared outside with a towel, looking sheepish. 'Listen, I'm really sorry ... I know I promised not to behave like that any more, but it's just ...' began Grace.

'Look Grace, when you're working, I can understand how you can get worked up and volatile,' he said patiently. 'But in this room are the people who love you most, so please, no more temper tantrums!'

Grace cast her eyes down like a child, feeling genuinely shamed. 'I know, I really *am* sorry. The next time my behaviour becomes unbearable, please kick my arse,' she said, trying to lighten the atmosphere. 'And Poppy, thank you for doubling for me on Thursday. Theo's right, I really *do* need more preparation time, and if you don't mind I'd really appreciate it.'

Poppy smiled graciously, and as Grace and Lloyd left to finish their training, she looked over in amazement at James.

How well Lloyd seemed to understand Grace – how well he dealt with her! She started clearing the lunch things away, trying to carry on as normal.

'I'd like to have a word with you, James,' Beatrice said as Poppy left the kitchen.

'Of course, Mum, just let me get a couple of phone calls out of the way first, then I'll be right with you.' He left the room, distracted, and Beatrice sighed. When was she going to get a chance to talk to him?

That afternoon James drove to Miami for a meeting with Pounce executives and Grace, Poppy and Beatrice sat in the garden helping Grace with her script whilst Lloyd practised his serve on the tennis court. Grace found herself missing Sybil, and told her mother all about the old woman – though Beatrice felt uncomfortable with the thought that someone else had been more of a mother to her than she had been.

Grace found herself telling her mother all about Lana, too, and she wept as she told her about the murder, which was still unsolved. The worst thing was that Lana still could not be buried, because of the murder investigation, and so hadn't yet been laid to rest. Mother and daughter became even closer that afternoon.

The next day after breakfast, Beatrice finally got her chance to talk to James alone, as Lloyd was putting Poppy through her paces on the tennis court, in preparation for her day on set.

Grasping the moment, Beatrice approached her love-struck son. 'We must talk, James,' started Beatrice. 'I have to——'

'Just as soon as I've drafted a letter to Wilson, Mum ... we'll talk then.' James cut her short, heading for the office. But Beatrice was not missing her chance, and followed him into the office, carefully closing the door behind her.

'This simply can't wait another minute, James,' she said firmly.

'OK, Mum, spit it out. What's on your mind?' he said, switching on the word processor and sitting down at the desk. Beatrice bravely stepped forward, turning the computer off at the mains. James looked at her in astonishment.

'Sophie Thurlston, that's whats on my mind,' she announced.

'Sophie? What about Sophie?' he said mystified.

'You really don't know do you James?' said Beatrice. James shook his head. 'She's pregnant.'

'Really?' said James grinning.

'Yes really, and you're the father,' replied Beatrice, incensed at his flippant attitude.

This brought him up short. 'Sophie Thurlston's pregnant and I'm the father,' he repeated slowly, allowing the fact to sink in. 'You're saying I made Sophie pregnant?' he restated incredulously.

'Oh for goodness' sake, James. I know perfectly well that you've been seeing her on and off, amongst hundreds of other girls no doubt ...' Beatrice stopped abruptly in mid-sentence, noticing for the first time the desperately unhappy face of Poppy through the open French windows. James, following his mother's gaze, turned to see his wife staring at him.

'Pops, darling, please let me explain,' he faltered. But she didn't want to hear his excuses or explanations, and cried out angrily.

'I've been such a mug ... I should have listened to Grace. We've not even been married one week and already I feel plagued by your past,' she said bitterly, through the beginnings of tears.

'Poppy, please. Let's talk about this?' pleaded James, distraught. But Poppy was already marching through the villa to their bedroom, throwing some of her belongings into a bag. 'Pops, you're not leaving me – listen ... I ...' he begged.

'I should have been more realistic. I don't have a problem with Sophie Thingamajig or Violet Valentine as individuals, it's simply the fact that just they're just a fraction of the vast number of women you've gone to bed with. I ... I just really don't think I can cope with the constant flow of females that would keep haunting me and reminding me of your past.' She then burst into tears.

James attempted to approach her, but Poppy held her arms in front of her gesturing to him to keep his distance. 'I feel a fool and I'm certainly not hanging around here so that everyone can feel sorry for me,' she cried heading for the double doors at the front of the villa.

'Poppy, you can't leave me. I didn't do it ... I swear!' he protested.

But she wouldn't listen. 'I'm going to Key Biscayne – after all, I'm shooting there tomorrow and I need time to think all this over.' She paused to wipe the tears from her face and turned to glare at him. 'It's obvious this marriage wasn't meant to be – there are simply too many female ghosts in your closet for me to deal with.' She pushed past James and walked out the front doors to Lloyd's red pick-up truck. He ran after her pleading with her to stay, genuinely worried about her driving in a distressed state, and reminding her that Lloyd needed his car anyway.

'Do you know what James? I don't give a damn – I'm sick and tired of taking care of everyone else.' Poppy crunched the gears and eventually got into reverse, and with wheels spinning in the gravel she took off.

James stood, bereft, in the drive with the dust settling around him. Deeply unhappy, he turned to see Breatrice standing in the doorway fidgeting with her handkerchief, and his pain turned to anger.

'Who the hell do you think you are, breezing back into my life and destroying my marriage? I knew it was too good to last ... you're just as much of a pain in the backside as you've always been. The sooner you bugger off on that plane back to London and the old man, the happier I'll be.'

Oblivious to the deep pain he was causing her, he strode past her through the wooden doors into the kitchen where he grabbed a bottle of beer, clipped the top off on the side of the table and sat down. He banged his fist on the table with fury at his interfering mother.

# Chapter Twenty-Three

The tight white sweat band securing Poppy's black wig was already making her hot and uncomfortable and shooting hadn't even begun. The make-up lady knelt in front of her, coating her legs with pan-stick and a damp sponge to camouflage her freckles and darken her skin tone. She was dressed in Grace's character's clothes: a white tennis skirt with red trim, matching knickers, a white short sleeved shirt with red polo collar, white socks and tennis shoes.

Poppy sighed listlessly, pushing unwelcome thoughts of James firmly to the back of her mind. The one thing she knew was that she had to get away from the Seymour camp – far away. In all the years she'd worked for Grace, her own life had come to a complete halt, personally and professionally. Being a stand-in for Grace was by no means her life ambition, and she knew she had to get her own career back on track. She knew she'd have to break away to make it, and to come to terms with the fact that her marriage to the man she'd loved for years had fallen apart within a matter of days.

'Poppy,' boomed Theo. She turned to see the rotund

producer swaying towards the make-up trailer, flanked by a very tall blonde, an even taller, heavily built male and a smaller, rather weedy, bespectacled man. 'Hi, doll! How ya doin?' he greeted, taking the large cigar from his mouth. The trailer groaned and lurched to one side as he stepped into the portal.

'Yer lookin' good kid. Shame we only need the back of your head and legs ... come and meet Albert Marks, my new director, he's a specialist in fast action movies. Violet you already know, I think, and this is Gregg Chappell, head of Vitfizz, our sponsors.' Poppy took a deep breath, determined not to be intimidated by Violet, and stepped out to greet them. What had happened to Kyle, she wondered?

'I'm mighty grateful to you for doubling for Grace today. Paige Jordan's role is action packed and I don't need Grace to be burned out before she starts.' Poppy smiled and acknowledged his thanks. 'So how is young Grace? Working on those backhands I hope,' he enquired.

'Absolutely – she's in splendid shape. Lloyd Davies has been worth his weight in gold,' replied Poppy, truthfully.

'Gold my arse! I'm glad we clinched the deal with Lloyd to be trainer and technical advisor before he hit the big time and got himself seeded sixth – he'd be mega bucks to hire now! Ya know the crazy guy was so desperate for the job we got him for expenses only? What a schmuck,' he laughed drawing on the reeking cigar. Poppy managed a smile, trying to share his enthusiasm.

'OK Poppy, so let's have the run-down on the Madigan Davies saga – are they getting it on or not? Rumour says it's a sure thing. Of course we all know about you and her brother. Congratulations, by the way,' he gushed. Poppy smiled sadly and looked the other way. Theo, for once showing some sensitivity, changed the subject.

'Well, I'd better go and check on the cameras and position. Just to warn you Poppy, we've got fifteen hundred extras hanging around for the crowd scenes, so don't be fazed. See ya in ten.' Theo reeled away like a ship in full sail.

'He's quite a character, isn't he?' said Gregg, who'd returned to her side. 'I wanted to take the opportunity to congratulate you,' he added. 'I only heard the news from James a few days ago, but he was like a dog with two tails after your trip to Vegas,' he smiled, holding out his hand. Poppy stared at it and swallowed hard, brushing away a defiant tear with the back of her hand. Gregg was pained to see her looking so upset, and concerned that all was clearly not well. But he tactfully declined to pursue the conversation further and squeezed her arm gently.

He chaperoned Poppy toward the court, where there were hundreds of extras hanging around wearing Vitfizz sunshields and holding paper cups displaying the company logo. Albert turned up with Violet, and gave the two actresses a quick briefing.

'OK, girls, as you know, we need to get some long shots and close ups of Violet, and the crowd's reaction – atmosphere and tension, that's what we need. Poppy, be careful of the tracks behind you at the base line, that camera will be permanently on the move shooting between and around your legs. As you can see there is another camera above you on the hoist, and a third back in the spectators seats, so try not to turn around – we mustn't see your face.' Poppy professionally acknowledged his direction.

'Violet, we'll be concentrating less on your tennis playing, and more on your expression – I want to see anxiety, concentration, aggression and plenty of stress, please. Paige is giving you a very hard time, so make sure it shows. I'd like some shots of you wiping your face on your wrist band, retying laces and rearranging your racquet strings occasionally, just to make it all look authentic.

'I'm going to keep you girls playing as long as possible, so that you look the part and so I get plenty of material. Any questions?'

'Look, about my make-up ...' started Violet.

'Violet, I've specifically briefed Make-up that you're a fresh faced natural Danish beauty. Absolutely no more eyeliner or lipstick, we're making an action movie here, not a fashion shoot,' he said, exasperated. 'Towards the end of the shoot we're going to need to see you a bit red faced and sweaty,' he said cautiously. 'But you know you never look anything other than gorgeous, babe. Positions, please, everyone ...' he yelled through his megaphone.

Violet, frowning, walked around to the other side of the court, and Poppy miserably prepared to serve to her. Although she'd not played for some time, Poppy's brilliant form instinctively returned and she grinned to herself at her supreme competence on the court. Violet galloped ungracefully around the court and there was no need for the make-up artist's spray 'sweat'.

'Cut!' yelled Albert Marks. 'Take five, girls, while I talk to the extras.' He strode around the net with his megaphone, while Poppy and Violet sat under the umpire's chair, helping themselves to a drink. Poppy could hear Violet gasping as she wiped herself down with a towel.

'Not too strenuous for you, I hope?' said Poppy, noting Violet's blood red cheeks.

'Nope,' she shook her head determinedly through laboured breaths.

'That was great, girls,' interrupted Albert, returning from his spectators. 'Let's step up the pace a little, now. The extras are going to interact more with Paige, so give me plenty of hot stuff! Positions please, every one ... rolling, and ... ACTION!'

As Violet and Poppy started up again, the crowd went mad, jumping up from their seats shouting for Paige. No call came from Albert so they carried on playing. As she was attempting to smash a serve at Poppy, Violet's bandanna fell off her head on to the court – still no call from Albert. They played on, both actresses now completely drenched with sweat. Albert must really want us to look exhausted, thought Poppy, laughing to herself as she saw that Violet's hair had fallen loose and that her whites were stained from falling over.

Albert, clearly delighted, eventually called 'CUT' about ten minutes later, by which time both girls were utterly exhausted. The make-up artist and hairdresser ran on court to repair the damage.

'No, leave them,' shouted Albert. 'They're perfect – just how I want them.' He walked up to the girls. 'Sorry to have to make you work so hard, but I need to see some real exhaustion from Violet. Gimme some more takes like that and we'll have some pretty spectacular footage in the can!' Theo waddled on court and slapped Albert on the back.

'Shit hot, Bertie – I've been watching on the monitor – you're doin' great girls, great.'

Violet continued to moan about her hair and make-up, but Theo managed to soothe and calm her down, knowing that if she blew this chance it would be the last time he could persuade Universal to cast her in anything. 'Here's your chance, doll, don't blow it – I warned you that the movie business wasn't as glamorous as it appears,' he said, firmly, making his way back to the viewing monitor.

Albert went to brief the extras again. 'Right, you lot. After the winning shot from Paige, and on my cue, I want you to spill out on to the court. I know it's unconventional, but you're to surround Paige, clamouring at her as if you're English football fans. We'll be on camera two for that to get an ariel view. Violet, don't stop acting at that point, stay in character. We need to see real disappointment from you.'

Both girls wearily made their way back to their base lines to begin battle again and Albert ran back to his watch. As they started up play again, the extras almost made themselves hoarse shouting out their encouragement to Paige. Both girls played and acted their hearts out, despite their exhaustion, and Bertie and Theo were absolutely delighted with them.

Poppy took great pleasure in destroying Violet's game and image and silently thanked the story line that allowed her to do so. There was no way she could have allowed herself to lose to Violet Valentine, even in a film.

The crowd leapt to their feet again roaring their approval and at the cue from Albert cascaded on to the clay court. Poppy looked over to see the tortured face of Violet as she dramatically dropped to her knees in despair. Violet milked the scene of wretchedness for all it was worth, crying genuine tears of humiliation. As directed, Poppy began to make her way forward to the net to shake hands with her opponent, hindered by the swarms of back slapping well-wishers.

It was at this point that she felt an almighty blow below her right shoulder blade. The impact made her knees buckle and she fell down heavily on to the court, dazed and winded, feeling as if she'd been hit by a hundred weight brick. The searing pain in her back was indescribable, and her vision began to blur.

Somewhere in the distance Albert shouted 'Cut ... clear the set immediately,' but that was all she heard before she lost consciousness.

# Chapter Twenty-Four

James sat in the sun-lounger feeling very sorry for himself, planning his drive later that day to meet Poppy after the shoot and explain everything. He'd had a long and heated discussion with Sophie Thurlston that morning on the telephone and was left fuming. Why had she found it necessary to tell his parents? Why was she so determined to ruin his life, his marriage? For the first time in his life James felt out of control – as far as women were concerned he'd always been the one to call the shots, but having lost his heart to Poppy, he now knew what it was like to be on the other side.

He could hear Lloyd and Grace, working out on the tennis court and irritably headed for the villa to take a shower and prepare for his trip to Key Biscayne. Discarding his clothes he turned on the radio before stepping into the shower. But as he vaguely listened to a local news report, he stopped in his tracks, his blood running cold.

' ... the actress standing in for Grace Madigan on the shoot of *Love All*, Theo Palaris's latest movie, has been rushed to Miami General Hospital after suffering what looks like a

Monica Seles copycat stabbing. We'll have a fuller report later ... There's been a drug related shooting in downtown Miami ...'

James pulled himself together, threw his clothes back on, grabbed the keys to Lloyd's new car and ran out to the court.

'Poppy's in the hospital – she's been stabbed!' he yelled hysterically, and without waiting for a response he dashed out to the car. Grace and Lloyd were hot on his heels, shaken by the news.

'James, wait for us...' shouted Lloyd through the open car window.

'Sorry mate ... gotta leave now,' gasped the panic-stricken James, putting the car into gear.

'OK, we'll follow on. Which hospital?' hollered Lloyd, running alongside the car.

'Miami General!' he shouted and shot off in a cloud of dust.

James broke all speed restrictions on his frenzied drive to the hospital. His mind was in turmoil at the thought of losing Poppy – his wife, best friend and love.

He rushed through the double doors, following the emergency room signs, and found himself face to face with a stern faced receptionist. He fought hard to control his emotion and to regain composure as he gave Poppy's name.

'Poppy Bates – she's been stabbed ... where is she? ... She's my wife ...' he cried, anguished.

'Please sit down, I'll get the doctor in charge,' the receptionist said casually. James bit his lip anxiously knowing that to hustle the receptionist would only make for further delay, so he paced around the desk as she called out for a Dr Brett.

Luckily, he didn't have to wait long, for within minutes, Dr Brett was by his side, leading him briskly down the corridor. The kindly man quickly filled James in on his wife's condition.

'We've been very lucky. The paramedics got to her in record time and patched her up pretty good, but by the time she'd gotten here, she was pretty short of breath, and I'm afaid I do think she's suffered a punctured lung.' James looked alarmed, but the doctor reassured him quickly. 'I've performed a pneumothorax, that's creating a hole in the the chest cavity to release the trapped air, so she should be fine.'

'But a collapsed lung, that's serious, isn't it?' snapped James, impatiently.

'Well, Mr Seymour, it's definitely no day at the beach, but she's stable now. We're still a little concerned about the internal bleeding, but we're going to keep a close eye on her ...' he soothed.

'Oh my God!' wailed James. 'Is she awake? I mean is she——'

'She's been drifting in and out of consciousness, but why don't you come in and take a look,' he said gently. 'Please don't be alarmed by all the medical paraphernalia that's surrounding your wife, we're just taking precautions. That reminds me,' he said, looking awkward. 'I'm presuming you have medical insurance?'

'Yes, yes,' replied James, agitated. Money was no object when it came to saving Poppy's life. As they rounded the corner James saw a police guard and Gregg Chappell standing white-faced by the door.

'James, James I'm so sorry ... very sorry,' said Gregg, carefully.

'Get out of my way,' said James, uncharacteristically aggressive as he stormed past him into the intensive care unit. There were four beds, three of them occupied by faceless people hooked up to life supporting machinery. He only recognised Poppy by her petite frame and golden hair still tightly bound in tiny pincurls. He dashed to her side and gazed lovingly at her tiny, beautiful face covered by a plastic oxygen mask. She was deathly pale – even her freckles seemed to have faded, and James turned desolately to Dr Brett.

'Please do something, Doctor, she looks so ...' James was lost for words as he peered at all the apparatus around Poppy.

'Try not to worry too much,' the doctor soothed. 'She's a healthy young woman, she'll make it through. We've simply got to wait for the drainage to finish,' he explained. James's eyes followed the rubber tube which led into a bottle of water on the floor. Putting his hand on James's arm, Dr Brett smiled reassuringly. 'See, she's doing the work on her own. Watch the bubbles escaping into the water – that means she's exhaling, breathing unaided.'

'What about the internal bleeding?' demanded James.

'I've got my eye on that ... and I'm as sure as I can be that no major organs are affected, otherwise we'd certainly know about it by now,' he assured him.

'She looks so, so ...'

'I don't think you'd look too hot if you'd had a maniac knife you in the back, Mr Seymour,' he said gently. 'Give her time, Mr Seymour, and just be thankful her injuries weren't any more serious.

A nurse bustled towards them. 'Dr Brett, there are quite a few people outside in the waiting room, wanting to know how the patient is ...'

'Tell them they'll just have to wait. Now, Mr Seymour, you sit here with Poppy, and if you need anything call the nurse here, her name is Jenny.' Jenny smiled at James as Dr Brett's bleeper sounded and he rushed off.

James sat holding Poppy's pathetic little hand, gazing at her face. Somehow, it seemed to James, her very life seemed to be draining out of that rubber tube.

'Pops,' he whispered in a strangled tone. 'Pops, you're going to be OK, I promise,' he said, convincing himself. 'As soon as you're well enough I'm taking you away on honeymoon, wherever you want. Grace will just have to get by without you, 'cos I can't.' He pulled his chair closer to the bed.

'Darling, listen to me if you can. All this rubbish about Sophie Thurlston being pregnant is total fabrication ... I haven't even laid eyes on her in five months, let alone anything else, I swear.' He gulped, stroking her arm gently. 'I spoke to her on the phone yesterday and eventually got her to admit she'd invented the whole story out of revenge. You see, Pops, I treated her like I did most women – very badly – and I didn't even tell her I was coming to the States. Hell hath no fury, as they say, so she conjured up the pregnancy story as a way of getting even.' He paused, his eyes wet with tears.

'I've been such a chauvinistic shit, I know, Pops, but I swear to you that I'm a changed man since falling in love with you. You're my life,' he said desperately. He felt her hand stir and looked down in wonder to see her warm amber eyes focused on him.

'Poppy!' James had to restrain himself from grabbing her to his chest. 'How do you feel?' he demanded.

'I've been better,' she muttered attempting a smile.

'I've got so much to tell you, Pops ...' blurted James.

'I know ... I heard,' Poppy said fatigued 'Why didn't you tell me before?'

'I tried,' he cried, exasperated. 'You and Mum had me convicted before I could get the chance to get to the bottom of it,' he protested.

Poppy smiled sleepily. 'What happened ... my back ... something hit me,' she muttered.

'You were stabbed, my darling,' he said gently. Her eyes widened with astonishment.

'Stabbed?' she repeated incredulously. 'But who ...'

'We don't know yet, some lunatic most likely,' replied James through gritted teeth.

Seeing her conscious, Jenny came and took Poppy's pulse, taking notes. 'I'll let Dr Brett know you're awake,' she smiled. 'Mr Seymour, the waiting room is now at bursting point, could you possibly deal with the relatives and press?'

As soon as he left the room he was bombarded with questions from a Lieutenant Rodrigeuz and his two detectives from the Miami Police Department, reporters from local television and radio stations, Theo Palaris and Gregg Chappell, not to mention Grace, Lloyd and Beatrice. They surged forward like a tidal wave, firing questions.

He patiently answered the questions to the best of his ability, though he wasn't able to give them any answers as to who might have stabbed her.

The next twenty-four hours were mayhem as the Miami Police thoroughly questioned anybody who had been close to Poppy. Inspector Rodriguez's hunch was that it had been an opportunist attack, and he hastily acquired all the names of the extras and crew from the set.

Poppy, now out of immediate danger, was moved to a private room courtesy of Universal, and James was slowly coming to believe that she'd make a full recovery.

Leaving the others at the Villa, Lloyd reluctantly had to head off for Fort Lauderdale, for a practise match with Michael Chang. For all his efforts to keep his distance from Grace, he was finding it more and more difficult – particularly now that he was so heavily involved with the family's problems. Driving down the freeway he thought happily how Grace had clung desperately to him on hearing of the attack on Poppy. It was a very nice feeling, despite the terrible circumstances. But who on earth would want to cause harm to Poppy? She had no enemies, and anyway she was merely standing in for Grace ... Lloyd almost crashed the car and gripped the steering wheel when the truth hit him. Of course, she was wearing Grace's clothes, Poppy was supposed to *be* Grace. Grace must have been the real target! His scalp tightened and the hair prickled on the back of his neck as thoughts raced through his head.

Lloyd accelerated into the first gas station he saw, and raced to a payphone. Fumbling in his pocket, he found the card Lieutenant Rodriguez had handed him.

'Yes indeed, Mr Davies, I understand your concern,' said the policeman. 'But believe me, I really don't think Ms Madigan is at risk. Of course I'll follow this up, but I'm still very much inclined to think that we're looking for a crazy screw ball who fancies himself on the front page of the Miami Tribune rather than someone with an active grudge against Ms Madigan or Ms Bates.'

'Lieutenant,' said Lloyd impatiently. 'I am absolutely convinced that the attacker was after Grace. It's obvious that ...'

'With all due respect, Mr Davies, we don't all sit around on our rear ends shooting the breeze all day here at the MPD. What you suspect is definitely a possibility, and I won't rule it out, but ... OK, look, I'll put another black and white on patrol around Villa Retreat. I suppose it is pretty remote 'round them parts ... Ms Madigan has my hotline, and she's not alone, so I don't think you've any reason to worry.'

'But ...' started Lloyd.

'Guts an' nose is what you need in this business – take my word for it, and my guts tell me we're looking for a nutcase who decided to copy the Monica Seles stabbing,' he said firmly.

'Well, Lieutenant, *my* guts tell me that the assailant could well have been aiming consciously at Grace. Couldn't it have been an obsessed fan of hers? Or someone she has upset?' asked Lloyd, equally firmly.

'Yeah, yeah, sure. I know where you're coming from ... don't you worry none, Sir. I guarantee Ms Madigan won't come to no harm.'

Only minimally relieved, Lloyd continued his journey to Fort Lauderdale, though he did console himself with the thought that James and Beatrice would be with her, at least. He desperately wanted to go back and protect her himself; his instinct was to pick her up and whisk her out of all this mess. He had to pull himself up short at this thought – he was getting too involved again, could feel himself being drawn to Grace like a magnet and recognised that this was dangerous ground. He couldn't risk being hurt by her again. He had to get her out of his system.

Poppy regained strength daily and James rarely left her side. Rodriguez had stepped up security by arranging for a full time guard outside the hospital room, and Grace was constantly aware of the police vehicles regularly patrolling around Villa Retreat.

They all managed to get back to some semblance of normality, and Grace reluctantly had to turn her mind to work, as shooting was due to continue in a few days. She was rather thrown by the arrival of Warren – she'd completely forgotten about her invitation to him – but was glad of the company in the circumstances, and he happily settled in to the chaotic household. He soon struck up a warm friendship with Beatrice, and good-naturedly mucked in with all the family.

After only a week in hospital, Poppy was escorted home from hospital by a devoted James, and they were all delighted to have her back amongst them.

'Where's Lloyd?' asked Poppy, noticing immediately that

his was the only face missing.

'He's playing in some tournament at Flushing Meadow, but he'll be back this evening to see you,' replied Grace.

'Don't you mean to see you?' said Poppy, smiling mischievously at Grace, who rapidly looked away.

'I doubt it. Tennis is his priority.' She sighed.

They spent a very pleasant day together celebrating Poppy's return, though she was still very tired, and Grace found she was missing Lloyd more than ever. At last she heard an engine in the drive, and leapt off her chair to greet him at the door. He was equally pleased to see her; their few days' separation had, if anything, added to the sexual tension between them once again, and they greeted each other awkwardly.

'How's Poppy?' he ventured.

'Pretty good ... considering,' replied Grace.

Lloyd nodded, pleased as he the saw the patrol car go by, and he retrieved a bouquet of flowers from the back seat of his car. Grace led him into the kitchen where he duly made a fuss of Poppy and gave her the flowers. Everyone was talking animatedly and James asked Lloyd how the match had gone.

'Damn,' thought Grace. I should have asked that.

'Where's the Greeting Commissionaire?' enquired Lloyd looking around him for Taboo.' It's unlike the monster not to give me a hero's welcome by knocking me over and slobbering all over me,' he added, smiling.

'He didn't greet us either, did he, James?' said Poppy, frowning. 'I wonder where he has got to.'

'Maybe he's got himself locked inside the tennis court again. Don't worry, I'll find him,' said James, rising from his chair.

'No, no, James, you stay here and catch up on the scuttlebutt. I'll find Taboo,' said Warren amiably as he went off to search the garden.

Nobody realised just how long he'd been gone until they heard a rather strange cry. 'Lloyd ... Lloyd, could you come here a minute?' requested Warren, his voice strangely sinister.

Grace rose and rushed outside, wondering what was up. Warren was standing outside the pool house looking upset.

'No Grace, go back inside. Get Lloyd for me please,' he appealed, closing the pool house door, his face grim.

Sensing something untoward, Grace rushed across the lawn and wrenched the door open, only to be faced with a sight which almost made her pass out.

Taboo was lying on the floor in a pool of blood. His beautiful black body had been stabbed and mutilated, his throat slashed.

A wave of nausea ran over Grace and she slumped into Warren's arms gagging, unable to take in what she'd seen. James and Lloyd appeared and they, too, were rendered speechless by what they saw. Lloyd wrapped his arms around Grace, hauling her away from the gruesome sight into the kitchen where he briefly explained to Poppy and Beatrice what had happened, holding Grace all the while.

'My beautiful boy, my darling dog ... Who could do such a thing?' cried Grace as she sobbed into Lloyd's chest. Soothing her as best he could, Lloyd reluctantly left her in the care of Beatrice and Poppy and went back to the pool house to find out what had happened.

He found Warren and James examining a bloodstained note left beside Taboo's lifeless body, their faces showing alarm. Lloyd went to pick it up. 'Don't touch it Lloyd,' ordered Warren. 'We're going to have to call in the police.' Lloyd bent down to read the crayon scrawled note.

## ONE, TWO, THREE, FOUR, FIVE.
## HOW COME MADIGAN'S STILL ALIVE?
## SIX, SEVEN, EIGHT, NINE, TEN.
## I GUESS I'LL HAVE TO TRY AGAIN!

Lloyd reeled as he read the note again. Well, that settled it. There was no way he was going to let Grace out of his sight until this maniac was caught. 'I'm going to get straight on to Lieutenant Rodriguez,' he thundered. 'So much for his gut instinct and his poxy patrol car!'

# Chapter Twenty-Five

Later that day Danny Rodriguez and his two rookies sat at the kitchen table while the forensic and fingerprint specialists went to work. After they'd tried to lift prints from the menacing note, they brought it into the kitchen. Poppy and Grace looked at each other in horror.

Grace leapt from her chair, ran into her bedroom and returned clutching the other two notes she'd managed to put to the back of her mind. She nervously handed them over to Rodriguez, who looked at her with irritation.

''Scuse me Mam, but why the hell didn't you show these to me earlier when we were investigating Poppy's stabbing?'

'I didn't feel that there was any connection ... I didn't think——' stammered Grace.

'It's my job to do the thinking, Ms Madigan, and it would have been very useful to have known about these. As you know, we initially thought Ms Bates had been attacked by a psycho imitating the Seles attack, but obviously this is not the case.' He looked at his notes. 'We've interviewed and taken statements from all the extras and crew who were on set that day, but they're all bona fide union members, and we've not come up with anything yet. It now looks as if this was actually a premeditated attempt on your life, Ms Madigan. Whoever it is, probably a lunatic or an obsessed fan, has intimate knowledge of your every move. It also seems as if he harbours a deep grudge – why else go to the trouble of killing the dog?' Rodriguez ignored Lloyd's scornful eyes, knowing that he should have taken more notice of the man's suspicions when he first voiced them.

'I need you to draw up a list of people who might have motives for wanting you outa the way. Try and make the list as broad as you can ... maybe an admirer you've brushed aside? A groupie you've been dismissive of? Perhaps even an old boyfriend?' he said.

'Well at last you're taking this seriously,' said Lloyd, angrily. 'Perhaps now you'll provide some proper protection – not just some lousy patrol car ...' He stopped when he noticed how pale Grace had turned.

'But there's no one ... nobody,' she said, visibly shaken. 'Why would anybody want to do me any harm?'

'Think long and hard, Ms Madigan, 'cos there sure as hell *is* someone out there who wants to harm you. It may not be someone you know personally, but we need to take precautions. I'm going to go back over my tracks at Universal to get the run down on all the people on the set the day Ms Bates was stabbed.'

Grace's mind ran riot as she tried to think back over the years, coming up with names of people who might have held a grudge: right back to Abe Cohen, her first agent; Luc Fontaine, her co star in *Romeo and Juliet*; the lighting specialist on *Temptation* she'd fought with constantly; Violet Valentine; Hugo, what about Hugo ...?

'Well ... there is my ex husband,' she said, hesitantly. 'But I can't think he's a real possibility, nobody's seen or heard of him in over six years now.'

Nevertheless, Rodriguez took down his name and particulars, and pressed her to come up with more names. Lloyd looked away in shock – he hadn't known Grace had been married before. James was the only one who noticed his expression.

'Wasn't worth mentioning mate,' he mumbled defensively. Beatrice also stared at James realising she'd never got around to asking her daughter about her failed marriage. He shrugged his shoulders dismissively as Grace continued to talk to Rodriguez. 'One of those arty farty types – too precious for my liking.' James turned to stare out of the window.

'Lieutenant Rodriguez, there's something else I'd like you to see,' said Grace, suddenly thinking of something. Wiping her eyes on her mother's handkerchief, she rushed off to her room to get the tatty old copy of the *Daily Mail* she'd brought with her from London. She gave it quickly to the policeman.

'Lana Logan was my oldest friend. She was murdered, you see – stabbed to death – and it's bothered me ever since that they didn't manage to track down the killer. I don't suppose,' she began doubtfully. 'I don't suppose there could there be a link could there? I'm probably letting my imagination get the better of me.'

'Have the cops really not charged anyone?' he enquired, reading the article carefully.

'Not as far as I know. I spoke to another friend, Justin quite recently, and they'd still made no progress,' she volunteered.

'OK, I'll get on to homicide in London and check it out. As of now Ms Madigan, you are under twenty-four hour police protection ... in fact you all are,' he said firmly. 'If there is a connection between all these attacks, then you're all in danger. I'm leaving my boys here with you now, plus I'll have a coupla black 'n whites stationed directly outside the house and in the lane.'

Grace stared at him blankly.

'I'll need your new schedule so we can arrange for protection when you're on set, too. Here's my bleeper and phone number, and you already have the homicide hot line. Call me with anything at all that happens, or if anything else comes to mind. Gimme the rundown on the staff here before I leave, will you?' he demanded.

'Universal supplied a housekeeper and cook. Presumably they'll have taken references,' replied Grace, knowing that the two old domestic women couldn't possibly pose any threat.

'Now guys,' Rodriguez turned to Lloyd, James and Warren. 'I don't want no heroics. Don't take no chances. Don't go anywhere or do anything without the boys here.' He gestured at the two burly bodies in uniforms. 'I gotta run. See you guys later,' he declared, making his exit.

Nobody spoke for several minutes, the dripping tap in the kitchen the only noise. Grace's eyes filled with tears as she fingered her beloved dog's lead, and Beatrice put an arm around her.

'How could anyone could be so cruel?' she said shaking her head disbelievingly. 'And who would want to harm Grace ... it's all so unbelievable, too fantastic for words!' She looked anxiously at her daughter. 'Grace, I really feel I should phone your father – I haven't called him since I arrived and I feel it's only fair that he should know what's been going on. Whatever you think of him, he does love you, and he'd never forgive me if something happened to you and I hadn't told him,' she faltered, seeing her daughter's expression.

'I don't see any need to contact him,' Grace said coldly.

Beatrice looked away embarrassed, the deeply ingrained loyalty in her coming to the fore. 'Look, I know your father's treated you badly, but he does have his own problems.'

'*He* has problems? Well, I'm glad to hear it, 'cos he's certainly succeeded in screwing up my personal life!' stated Grace hotly.

'I don't think there's any need to be so, so vindictive, Grace. Whatever you say, I feel I must call him. What time is it back home ... I mean what is the time difference?' she asked nervously turning to Grace, her eyes begging for her daughter's acquiescence.

Grace looked at her watch. 'He'll still be at the office, I should think,' she replied stiffly.

'Come with me?' said Beatrice taking Grace's hand.

'OK ... as long as I don't have to speak to him,' replied Grace, reluctantly.

They went into the study and Beatrice got straight through to the Texoil switchboard, who kept her waiting some minutes. Eventually she was put through to Bettina.

'Hello, Mrs Seymour,' she answered courteously. 'I'm

afraid Mr Seymour is out of the country ...'

'Oh God, where? I need to get hold of him urgently,' she cried.

'Well it's a bit of a mystery I'm afraid. He's been at meetings at the Fort Worth, Dallas and Oklahoma City offices, but he apparently failed to turn up at Tuscon, Cuba or Mexico City. It's been over a week now that he's been missing and we've been terribly worried ...'

'You mean he's been in America this week?' stammered Beatrice, her blood running cold.

'Yes, Mrs Seymour, but we've not heard from him in all that time, and you know how unlike him that is.' She paused. 'But I must admit, he's been acting very strangely recently, he seems to have been very unhappy. I do hope he's all right ...'

Bettina was in full flow when Beatrice ungraciously put the receiver down, her face white. She turned around slowly to face Grace, her mind racing. Where the hell was George?

'Grace, darling,' she said as gently as she could. 'He's here, he's in America. Apparently he's gone missing——'

'Oh my God!' exclaimed Grace her eyes wide. 'It's him, isn't it?' she cried hysterically. 'It's him that's after me – why didn't I think of him? He hates me more than anyone else in the world.' Her mother stared her, horrified to hear her own sub-conscious suspicions voiced openly.

'Good grief, Grace, don't be so ridiculous. Whatever your father was, he's no killer – I think you've read one too many fanciful scripts for your own good,' she said, trying to persuade herself as well as her daughter. 'A bully and tyrant he may have been, but I really can't believe he is connected to any of this ghastly business. Be realistic,' she said, attempting to leave the room. Grace stood in front of the door blocking her way.

'I *am* being realistic, Mum. I'd obviously blanked him out as a possibility, but of course it's him. He used to love terrorising me like this when I was a child, Warren made me see that – he's just taking it one stage further.' She shook her head angrily, glaring at her mother. 'You of all people know how angry he was at me for leaving,' she croaked through a dry mouth.

Beatrice wouldn't look at her daughter, and tried again to leave the room. It was impossible to think her husband may be responsible. Her mind refused to admit the possibility.

'Look, whatever you say, I'm not wasting any more time talking, I'm calling Rodriguez. Pass me the phone,' Grace said resolutely, taking no notice of Beatrice's anguished face.

'I'll be there within twenty minutes,' he barked when she got through to him. He arrived almost an hour later, looking exhausted.

'OK, Ms Madigan, this time, do ya think you could give me the whole story? I need to know about this guy, George Seymour. Every quirk, every idiosyncracy ... right down to what he likes for breakfast and what time he moves his bowels. You can't hold out on me no more!' he said firmly.

Beatrice could not stay and witness the scene, so Warren took her off for a walk while the others sat around the kitchen table, Danny Rodriquez taking rigorous notes.

'This son of a bitch may look the respectable business tycoon but he sure as hell has a few loose screws,' he exclaimed pointing to his head. 'Before I leave I'm gonna put out an APB, an' I wanna ask you for the last time if there's anything else I should know – however insignificant or irrelevant it may seem to you.'

James, in total shock, shook his head, and Grace, too, looked dazed as she told Rodriguez she really couldn't think of anything else. Poppy and Lloyd simply sat in awed silence. The policeman left, promising to let them know as soon as they heard anything, and assuring them of extra security around the clock.

James was speechless, and clutched Poppy's hand as he struggled to come to terms with the evening's revelations. True, George had displayed plenty of cruelty and violence towards him as a child, and he knew Grace had come off even worse on an emotional level, but even so, coming to terms with the fact that he might have committed murder was going to take quite some getting used to. Lloyd, reluctant to leave, and wanting desperately to stay and comfort Grace, eventually took himself off back to his motel, promising to be back first thing in the morning.

Beatrice would not speak to Grace for several hours, lost in her own thoughts. Destructive though she knew her husband to be, she could not accept that he could be capable of this kind of behaviour. Warren had talked through the situation with her as gently as he could, but she would never forget the expression on his face or the way he'd shuddered when he told her what Grace's hypnosis sessions had revealed. Things so terrible, apparently, that he couldn't repeat them. Just as well, she thought ruefully. I think I'd rather not know.

When Beatrice did finally pluck up the courage to approach Grace, Warren joined them, doing his best to heal the breach, and the three of them stayed up until well into the early hours. Many tears were shed, and Beatrice was horrified to learn just how much damage Grace had sustained as a child at the hands of her husband. She felt horribly guilty, and winced as her only daughter recounted the many childhood traumas she'd suffered. Warren was a huge support to them both, and held Beatrice's hand as she sat, devastated, listening to them talk.

'I have to say I'm afraid I think Grace is right to suspect he might have been involved in these attacks,' he said carefully. 'From all that I've heard, he sounds as if he might well suffer from schizophrenia.' Beatrice looked up sharply, and he stopped, wondering if he'd gone too far.

Grace studied her mother's pained expression and tried to read her thoughts as Beatrice crossed the room to gaze blindly out of the open French windows. Suddenly her once rigid back bone slumped and her shoulders began to heave, as she gripped the edge of the desk and howled in agony.

Grace watched helplessly, wondering how on earth she could comfort her. She waited, looking questioningly at Warren, before crossing the room to give her mother a hug. And then it all came out. All Beatrice's own painful memories of the hurt she'd suffered over the years. They came flooding out accompanied by many tears.

'If I'd only listened to my heart ... my female intuition ... Oh Grace, I should have known. I've failed you ... ' Beatrice sobbed.

Grace hugged and kissed her mother, trying to reassure her that she was in no way to blame, wiping the tears from her ravaged face, as Warren looked on. Though deeply upsetting for them both, he'd known that this process was necessary before they could even begin to put the past behind them and move on. What a lot of damage one man has managed to cause, he thought sadly.

Eventually, there were no more tears to come, as both mother and daughter reached the point where they were too drained and exhausted even to think any more. After giving both of them a large whiskey, Warren sent them off to bed, assuring them that they'd both feel better in the morning.

# Chapter Twenty-Six

The next morning, James was up early and greeted Lloyd with relief when he arrived.

'Lloydie, I need your help. Grace starts shooting for the film again today, and though Rodriguez seems pretty clued up on protection and all, I'd feel a hell of a lot better if you went with her.' He looked up at his closest friend in anguish. 'I'd go, but I don't want to leave Poppy even for a minute and she's not really well enough to leave the house yet.'

'No problem mate. Consider it done,' replied Lloyd gently, glad to feel he could help. He didn't confess that he'd already made the decision not to let Grace out of his sight for the foreseeable future. At least until they got hold of George.

An hour or so later, he left with Grace and two body guards and they headed for Key Biscayne. Two more armed guards were positioned at the Villa as a precaution – the police weren't taking any chances.

Grace spent the morning filming the first scenes in the female locker room. Despite the pressure on her, and the fact that her nerves were shot to pieces, she performed superbly.

She couldn't help feeling that her father would still be able to get to her, somehow, despite all the protection. She would never feel safe from him, she thought ruefully.

But in some ways the nervous energy seemed only to improve her performance. And it certainly took her mind off any reservations she had had about the nude shower scene.

Lloyd didn't take his eyes off Grace and refused to leave the set – after all, he'd promised James not to let her out of his sight.

Grace thought she'd find the shower scene a real struggle, but somehow her newly defined body and improved muscle tone gave her added confidence and she silently thanked Lloyd's training programme when she noted the appreciative eyes of the crew as she peeled off her tennis whites in front of the cameras.

For the first time, Grace was proud of her body. Lloyd had done more than re-build her anatomy to a lean, sinewy form; much more importantly he'd made her feel like a woman, and her new found confidence shone from within.

Lloyd averted his eyes, knowing that the sight of Grace naked would only loosen the tenuous grip he had on his emotions further. He told himself firmly that he was only here as a favour to James, though he couldn't help but admire her gorgeous body.

They filmed her first heat in the tournament with a Hispanic actress who was playing an Argentinian player, and Grace felt very vulnerable standing on court surrounded by so many unfamiliar faces. She knew all too well that she was in exactly the same situation as Poppy had been when she'd been attacked. She gained some comfort from the fact that Lloyd was here, and looked at him hauntedly. He immediately ran over to join her, putting his arm around her and walking her around the court, pointing out all the specialist security to her.

The feeling of Lloyd's arm around her was immensely soothing, and somehow the anxiety seemed to drift away. All she wanted was to burrow her face into his shoulder and pretend everything had been a bad dream.

Lloyd acknowledged Albert's signal from the side of the camera and alerted Grace to prepare and take her position.

She clung to him like a child, but Lloyd gently pushed her forward, placing the racquet in her hand.

'I'm here, Grace, just a few feet away,' he said gently as he took his position off set. She returned a bleak smile.

'ACTION!' called Albert. And Grace Madigan instantly became the professional actress, transforming herself in to tennis champion, Paige Jordan.

'Shit hot performance, Gracie girl!' enthused Theo when they'd finished, billowing cigar smoke. 'Bertie 'an I agree that we should re-schedule a couple of the interiors, which we were gonna shoot down the road at West Palm Beach tomorrow, and carry on working here on the tennis court action. So your call tomorrow is the same time, same location.' He patted her on the back. 'Thanks for taking care of her, Lloyd. Will you be around for the rest of the week?'

'Definitely, though I do have a tournament at Flushing Meadow at the end of the week. I'm afraid I can't possibly miss that,' he said, looking worried. Grace, too, looked alarmed.

'I completely forgot ... I've been so preoccupied with the movie and the fact my Father's out there somewhere gunning for me ...' she said anxiously. 'How long will you be gone for?'

'Only a few days, and that's if I get through to the final,' Lloyd said soothingly. 'You mustn't worry, we'll make sure Rodriguez knows exactly where you are at all times, so he can arrange protection.'

'I wish I could go to Flushing Meadow with you,' said Grace mournfully. 'And of course you'll get to the final.'

'Sorry babe,' said Theo. 'It's out of the question for you to go to with Lloyd, you're shooting every day 'cept Sunday. Don't worry, we'll double security while Lloyd's away. By the way, how's Rodriguez doin' on tracking down that flake? He's been driving my administrative staff nuts, checking and double checking the credentials of every extra, actor and crew member — he's like a goddamn sniffer dog!'

Grace knew she had to behave like a professional, and that she couldn't possibly go with Lloyd, but she knew she'd miss him enormously.

Grace and Lloyd returned to the villa to find that Beatrice had taken the liberty of dismissing the cook and cleaner. Grace protested but Beatrice would hear none of it.

'Lieutenant Rodriguez agrees with me and anyway I'll enjoy running this house myself,' she said firmly.

'Mum, you don't know the first thing about running a house. You of all people are used to having help,' exclaimed Grace.

Her mother looked sheepish. 'Well to tell you the truth, I'm rather enjoying myself. You see, I've never had a kitchen to myself before, and I've managed to make your favourite, macaroni cheese – with a little help from Warren – for your supper.'

'Mum, you'll exhaust yourself,' said Grace, though she was enormously pleased. 'You're supposed to be having a break!'

'Nonsense! I've never enjoyed myself more. Anyway, it takes my mind off things ...' she said remotely.

Grace acknowledged this quietly, and they all sat down to sample Beatrice's delicious dinner. Grace was particularly pleased to note Poppy's sparkling eyes and flushed cheeks and to see that she really was well on the road to recovery, though still very tired. James was acting the archetypal devoted husband, fetching and carrying for his injured wife, and Grace was delighted to see them so happy.

She'd also begun to notice a rather special bond developing between her mother and Warren – they seemed to radiate happiness in each other's company, and Grace couldn't be happier for them both. And as for Lloyd, well, she loved having him around, even knowing it was just at James's request.

Somehow they all managed to put their worries behind them, and the subject of George was left well alone.


The next day's shooting went just as well for Grace, and she found she enjoyed working on the action-packed film, getting on well with many of her co-stars. It was certainly the best vehicle for taking her mind off things at home, and Lloyd was pleased to see her coming out of her shell more.

As she was taking a break at lunchtime, chatting away, she caught sight of Danny Rodriguez out of the corner of her eye. He was holding a manilla folder and pushing his way through the shield of security. Grace stiffened as she watched him approach, a severe expression on his face.

'Ms Madigan, could I have a word with you?' Grace and Lloyd followed him to the trailer. Looking distinctly uncomfortable, Rodriguez broke the latest news to her.

'Ms Madigan, I'm here to inform you that we found what we think is the body of your father this morning on West Palm Beach.'

Grace was horrified. 'But that's where we're supposed to be shooting today. How did ... what happened?' she asked, frantically. Lloyd put a consoling arm around her, as the Lieutenant continued. 'He died from knife wounds – it looks like suicide ...'

Grace's mind reeled with shock at the news. Was her father really dead? There'd been so many times in her life that she'd wished him dead, and now it seemed he was, she felt numb, unable to express any emotion whatsoever. She found it almost impossible to comprehend fully what Rodriguez was telling her. Could her father really have taken his own life?

Slowly it dawned on her that her Father could never abuse her again, physically or mentally. He was gone.

'Are you sure that it is my Father?' she asked coldly, staring out of the window.

'As sure as we can be at this stage. He had ID in his wallet, plus three hundred dollars in cash. Also, he was in possession of your shooting schedule.' Grace gasped in horror. 'And there was a note ...'

'A note? What did it say?' Grace demanded.

'Just two words – "I'm sorry"' said Rodriguez trying his best to be sensitive.

'Are you satisfied that it was suicide?' asked Lloyd, unwilling to leave anything unsettled.

'Yep, unless forensic come up with anything, it doesn't look as if it could have been anything else.' He frowned. 'I mean, what with the position of the body and the angle of the wound, and the fact that the knife was in his hand ... it all looks pretty clean cut to me.'

Lloyd winced at his choice of words.

'Pretty messy way to go, if you ask me,' Rodriguez added. 'Would have made it a lot prettier if he'd just swallowed a bottle of pills like everyone else.'

'And by the way' said Rodriguez going through his file. 'Thought you might like to know, though it doesn't seem to be relevant any more, this Hugo Finlay character you mention don't seem to exist no more – the last record of him was for a GBH charge at Bow Street Court in London over six years ago and there's no paperwork to indicate he could be here in the US. So he's been eliminated from the file.'

'I told you he'd disappeared, but anyway, I suppose it's a relief to know you've checked him out,' Grace said.

'So does this mean she's off the hook?' asked Lloyd. 'No more body guards?'

'Yep. The case is just about closed. I think we've got enough here to convince a jury that Seymour was the guilty party.' He paused, looking preoccupied.

'Is there something on your mind, Lieutenant,' asked Lloyd, his eyes fixed on Rodriguez.

'Yeah, well, there is something else you ought to know,' he said producing the folder and slapping it down on the table. Grace stared at it blankly.

'I got all the forensic and police reports from London this morning on the Lana Logan murder, and sure enough ...' he rummaged around in the folder and produced several documents. 'It was the same blade that was used to kill the dog, and the same knife as the one used to stab Poppy. It's a very unusual kind of knife, apparently – historic or antique or something, so we just need to make sure that it is indeed the knife that was found by your father's body.'

'Well it's obvious, it must be,' Grace declared, her lips trembling. 'My God, I can't believe he'd do that,' she sobbed. 'I'm sorry ... I'm sorry ... is that all he could say? What a pathetic apology!' And she broke down, leaning heavily on Lloyd.

'Yes, Ms Madigan, it does appear to be obvious, but I do need to wait for the forensics before I can close the case and remove your security. It shouldn't take more than a few days, and I'm not in any doubt as to what the conclusions will be.' He looked at his watch.

'Now, if you guys'll excuse me, I gotta get my arse up to West Palm Beach again. I'm going to need a formal identification ...' Lloyd frowned, indicating that now was not the time, and Rodriguez obediently departed in mid sentence, leaving Grace and Lloyd alone in the trailer.

Grace leaned her head on Lloyd's chest wearily, as he held her close. 'I'll go and tell Theo the news. You're not working in this state – you're in shock, Grace.'

'I ... I'm fine, I think ... Yes, I'm absolutely fine and what's more, I'm a professional.' She attempted a smile. 'And you know what they say ...?'

'Yeah, yeah. The show must go on!' quoted Lloyd. 'But in this case it doesn't, I'm afraid. I'm directing this very unfortunate drama and I'm telling you now – it's a wrap.'

# Chapter Twenty-Seven

The squalid, filthy room in downtown Miami contained a small, rickety wardrobe, a battered television, and a load of videos and magazines scattered over the linoleum floor. Sunlight flooded through the threadbare curtains filthy from the soot and fumes of the busy street below.

Hugo lay on the grubby candlewick bedspread, legs crossed and arms stretched behind his head. Covering the yellow stained walls were endless photographs of Grace, and a single light bulb swung from the movements of the tenants above.

He swigged the remains of a half bottle of vodka and laughed his maniacal laugh as he relived his crusade of the last four months. Dropping the empty bottle on the floor, he vowed he'd show them that he was nobody to be fucked with – it was time the world recognised his talent and gave him some respect.

It was too bad that Lana couldn't have treated him with a little more respect. Could she, a cheap stripper, really have thought she was better than him? It was unfortunate that he'd had to kill her, but she needed to learn a little reverence and be taught a lesson. He picked up the dog-eared newspaper and cackled at Lana's photograph staring back at him. Yes she certainly got what she deserved, filthy bitch.

His top lip curled as he recalled her scathing and insulting attitude toward him. How dare she laugh at him? And who was she to call him a failure? He leapt off the bed infuriated, pacing the room as he thought back gleefully to the moment when he'd butchered her. What a feeling of power he'd felt as he'd plunged the knife into her chest ... then thrust it into her neck. The look on her face was something he'd never forget.

He sat down at the small formica table and chopped up the white powder using a razor blade with his right hand. His left wrist was heavily bandaged and was oozing with pus and blood from the savage dog bite. He was living in squalor – the smell of stale bread, sour milk and rancid butter filling the air. But all this was about to change.

He stared gleefully at the huge stash of one hundred dollar bills on the table. He'd relieved George of the majority of his cash that morning on the sand at West Palm Beach, just leaving him a little for authenticity. What amazing luck that he'd been carrying so much!

Oh yes, George Seymour was another individual who needed to be taught a lesson. Furiously chopping at the powder, he recalled George's hangdog expression as he'd loitered around Grace's trailer. Hugo couldn't believe his luck when he'd seen him, though it took him a minute or two to recognise who it was. The security guard was barking at him to move on and, looking ridiculous in his Savile Row suit, he had done as he was asked. What a sucker Seymour was, thought Hugo, laughing to himself. He'd swallowed the story hook line and sinker when he'd told him he was a member of the crew, and prepared to take him to the location where Grace would be shooting the next day. The stupid man wanted to have a family reunion ... wanted a private little peep at his darling daughter before laying his soul bare to his family.

He'd been bigger and stronger than Hugo had anticipated and in the end it was quite a battle to overcome and kill him whilst still making it look like suicide. He smiled an evil smile to himself as he recalled George's expression when he'd thrust the knife neatly into his belly, being careful to make sure the angle of the knife entry fitted the suicide theory.

And what a stroke of genius that he'd thought to invent a suicide note. It seemed 'I'm sorry' was sufficient to convince those imbecile cops. Yes, he'd done the world a favour and should be held in high esteem for a job well done.

He ostentatiously rolled up a hundred dollar bill and snorted the white powder, the caustic substance deliciously assaulting his right nostril, causing him to splutter and his eyes to water. With his new found wealth, he could afford to buy the real thing – he deserved the best. He'd go upstairs later and score himself some pure Bolivian flake, then go and buy some smart new clothes and a bottle of Stolichnaya. Looking in the mottled mirror he thought a shave and a shower wouldn't go amiss either ...

Leaning forward he snorted the other line of sulphate which made him gag slightly and the hairs stood up on his neck as he felt the rush of adrenalin hit him. Pacing up and down cradling his left hand he remembered with irritation his blunder over Poppy Bates.

He'd sat for hours as an extra – *him* an *extra* – waiting and waiting to teach Grace Madigan the lesson she so badly deserved. It had been a piece of cake to get a union ticket, and he recalled how his stomach had lurched at the sight of Grace's tiny frame on court.

He paced the room angrily, thinking how he'd humbled himself to queue with the other extras, inventing a pseudonym and false union number, just to kill Grace. And he'd got the wrong woman! Well, her time would come, just as Georgie Porgie's had. All good things come to those that wait ... and wait he would.

He switched on the television to await news of his most recent conquest and kicked the set impatiently, making the free standing ariel topple from the box. He threw himself onto the single bed as he concentrated on Lloyd Davies, his next victim. He was going to revel in slicing up his Welsh flesh!

He rubbed his burning, stinging eyelids, unable to remember when he'd last slept or eaten. Sleep was a luxury he could ill afford when he was on such an important mission –

he needed to have his wits about him. He leapt off the bed and sat at the table again, rolling up a fresh one hundred dollar bill and snorting another line of cocaine.

Everything he was doing was for the best, he knew that. Someone up above was sending him messages that he had to teach Grace a lesson, to save herself ... yes, he was her saviour indeed. He'd tried to steer her away from this life of vulgar commercialism before, but now it seemed there was no other way. All this bloodshed could have been avoided had she listened to him, stayed with him and obeyed him ... But Grace had blown it! She'd blown their future – thought she had known better by becoming the queen of celluloid.

He knew their Big Break had been just around the corner when she left. But it wasn't good enough for her – she'd become impatient and decided, because of one little indiscretion, to belittle and outshine him.

The only option left to him was to kill her, and though half of him was loath to lay a harmful finger on her – he loved her, after all – the other half couldn't wait.

# Chapter Twenty-Eight

'You're not fast enough at the net Lloydie ... you're just not sharp enough,' insisted James as he sat with Lloyd and Poppy on the plane, en route for Flushing Meadow. 'Get some aggression back into your game, for God's sake, or you won't even get through the first round!'

'It was only a warm up, mate ... I'm saving myself,' defended Lloyd.

'Always play to win,' admonished James. 'Get focused – put any other thoughts out of your mind.'

Dr Brett had given his consent for Poppy to accompany her husband with the proviso that she rest and take things easy, and she was thrilled to be going with the boys.

'I can't help but worry about Grace,' she said concerned.

'Listen Poppy,' said James soothingly, addressing his comments to Lloyd too, knowing that he was just as worried. 'Rodriguez is about to close the case, and in the meantime Grace couldn't be in better hands. She's in the Delano Hotel with the very best twenty-four hour security – there's no chance anyone could get anywhere near close enough to her to take a pop.'

'That's exactly what I don't understand,' said Lloyd. 'If the case is virtually closed, then why the need for so much protection? Do you think Rodgriguez knows something we don't?' he quizzed.

'Nah, he's just a perfectionist, anyway, he can't close the case officially until he gets the forensic reports in on George. So we'll just have to wait.'

Lloyd still was not satisfied. 'I do think it's a shame Beatrice couldn't have stayed with her.'

'Look, pal, you know as well as I do that she needed a break after having to go through the trauma of identifying Dad's body. I think it's bloody good of Warren to take her off to Jupiter for a few days,' retaliated James.

Lloyd let it rest for now. He put on his headphones and attempted to flick through a magazine to take his mind off his worries.

Grace sat cross legged on the bed trying to study her script. She'd just put the telephone down from talking to Beatrice who still sounded upset, but she was confident that Warren would take very good care of her.

Grace, too, was finding it painful to come to terms with the latest developments. She couldn't get Lana out of her mind, and couldn't quite believe her own father could have committed such a vicious murder – not to mention the attacks on Poppy and Taboo.

The telephone shrilled again, interrupting her negative thoughts. 'How are you feeling?' came Lloyd's soothing voice.

'Lonely,' she replied, but she smiled, delighted to hear from him.

'Your brother roped me in to a practise match before we'd even checked into the hotel,' he complained. 'But do you promise me you feel safe at The Delano?'

'Perfectly safe. In fact I think it's ludicrous to provide quite this much security – these uniformed gorillas are so intrusive.' She remembered that she'd promised herself not to complain so much. 'But apart from that, yes, I'm feeling great. So how did the practise match go?' she asked breathlessly.

'If you must know, Edberg wiped the floor with me,' said Lloyd forlornly.

'Well it's only a practise, remember,' soothed Grace. 'I'm sure you'll be fantastic tomorrow – you've thrashed Lendl before, and I know you'll destroy him in the first two sets.'

'I wish I had your confidence,' he laughed.

They chatted on well into the night, both aware that as well as the spark that had always existed between them, they'd also now developed a close and caring bond. Lloyd made Grace laugh and relax like no one else could, and she didn't ever want to put the phone down.

The next day, Grace set off for filming accompanied by the usual armed guard. Bertie was snappy with the cast and Theo, too, was irritable, concerned that the obstructive security and police presence would cause them to get even further behind schedule. Grace felt guilty about this, and self-conscious too, for by now it was common knowledge among the cast and crew that her father had been found dead in suspicious circumstances.

As soon as the make-up artist and hairdresser had left her trailer, Grace telephoned Lloyd to wish him luck. She was concerned to hear him sound much more nervous than he usually was, and again she tried to boost his confidence and soothe his nerves. He sounded deeply uneasy about something, that was for sure.

Grace put the phone down and tried to get herself in the mood for the day's activities. It wasn't easy – how was she supposed to behave when she'd lost the father she'd hated throughout her life? Would things ever really be the same again? And then there was Lloyd. She loved him to distraction, but she'd managed to drive him away quite effectively, she thought, ruefully. At least they were friends now, but she couldn't help wanting more ... so much more.

The sudden knock on the trailer door indicated that Bertie was ready to start filming with her. She stood up, put her wrist bands on and made for the court. At least if she made a mistake, it was easy enough to retake the scene, she thought. With Lloyd it wasn't so easy. She crossed her fingers and silently wished him luck again.

Grace pushed all thoughts of Lloyd away, and made to take direction from Bertie. It was a long arduous day and Grace was vastly relieved when she reached the hotel that night, accompanied as always by the guard. They stopped at reception so that she could retrieve her key.

'Oh, Miss Madigan, there are some messages for you,' the friendly receptionist said, smiling warmly as she handed her three sealed envelopes. Had Grace imagined a certain twinkle in her eye?

'Thank you, Sonja,' she replied, looking curiously at the envelopes. Waiting for the elevator she ripped them open, the body guard closed on her.

'All right, all right ...' She held her hands up in resignation. 'There's no message from Jack the Ripper, not that it's any of your business. They're just from Sybil, Rodriguez, and ... this last one's from Lloyd,' she said delightedly.

'Sorry, Mam, we're under orders to ...'

'I know, I'm sorry ...' she started apologetically, as she hurriedly tried to read Lloyd's message. Her heart almost stopped with excitement when she read the message written in Sonja's neat hand-writing. *Lloyd called, will be back at 8.30 tonight and wants to see you alone. Says to give the guards the slip and meet him at the villa for a romantic supper.*

Grace almost passed out with happiness, and anxious to keep her little secret from the guard, she stuffed the messages into her large tote bag and distractedly looked at her watch. It was 7.30 – how was she going to get away, she wondered, desperately?

''Scuse me while I pop to the ladies room,' she said casually as she made for the bathroom. The guard followed her to the door and stood outside, his vacant eyes staring straight ahead.

Inside the bathroom, Grace managed to escape through the maintenance door which was always left unlocked.

Following the long, dimly lit passage she found herself inside a sort of staff room. Without thinking twice she peeled off her T-shirt and jeans and pulled on a freshly laundered turquoise maid's uniform, complete with cap, and furtively pushed open the door. After trying several doors, she eventually found her way to the back entrance of the hotel, and trembled with relief and anticipation. She almost blew it when she noticed a large laundry van backing up to the maintenance area, but she pulled herself together, walking confidently towards the road where she managed to hail a taxi.

Grace sat in the back of the rusty cab as they headed north up the freeway. Taking off her maid's hat she brushed her hair and retouched her lipstick – Lloyd would die laughing when he saw her turn up looking like this, she thought, grinning to herself.

She looked at Sybil's note fondly, and made a mental note to give her a call if she had time before Lloyd got there. Lieutenant Rodriguez's message said to call urgently, but she wasn't so inclined to return that call in any hurry. He was probably only calling to inform her that the case was officially closed.

She wondered how long it would have taken the guard to realise she was missing – he'll be breathing fire, she grinned to herself. Right now, she could think of nothing else but Lloyd's message. What was his sudden request to see her alone all about? Could he have forgiven her for her dreadful behaviour and come round to the idea that they might have a future together? Grace hardly dared hope, but was beside herself with excitement at the thought of seeing him, happiness shining from her gorgeous green eyes.

She looked at her watch to see that it was almost eight-fifteen, and fidgeted impatiently in the back of the car until they reached Villa Retreat. Grace paid the driver and ran up the driveway to the front door, swinging her bag. Rushing in toward the kitchen, she called out Lloyd's name.

Almost immediately her nostrils twitched at the strangely familiar smell, and the hair stood up on the back of her neck as she recognised the deadly aroma of frankincense and myrrh.

The front door slammed behind her and she spun around to be confronted by Hugo.

# Chapter Twenty-Nine

It had been over six years since Grace had last seen Hugo and every second seemed to be cruelly etched on his tortured face. The dark, familiar features were on the surface freshly cleansed but beneath they were ravaged with alcohol, drugs and unhappiness. Oh my God, thought Grace, every drop of blood in her body turning to ice. What on earth does he want?

"'Ill met by moonlight, fair Titania ...'" he greeted, stepping toward her out of the shadows.

Grace had never known such terror as this moment when confronted by his unhinged, mocking expression and those peculiar, staring eyes. She stepped backwards, her back against the wall.

'One would think you were not pleased to see me,' he grinned menacingly, his eyes roaming her body.

'I, er ... it's a surprise!' she managed to stammer finally, knowing instinctively that she should humour him.

'I thought you'd be expecting me, Grace ... I've been watching you, you know,' he said creepily moving forward again and trying to touch her. Grace looked away, unable to meet his evil gaze. She desperately tried to control the fear and think straight, to work out what to do and what Hugo could be doing there.

Of course. She almost slapped herself. She should have known it had been Hugo who'd been terrorising her all these months. He was as irrational as they come ... But hang on, where did that leave George? Grace quickly gathered her wits, telling herself not to panic.

'I'll make us a cup of tea, shall I? We can catch up on old times ...' she said bravely, forcing her voice to sound normal.

'I don't think so ...' He smiled that ghastly smile and pushed her further against the wall.

'So Hugo ... why are you ... how come you ...' she stammered, annoyed with herself for not being able to hide her fear.

'I've come to save you, Grace,' he said menacingly. 'To save you from yourself. You've taken the wrong path in life, Grace, and I've been sent to put that right. I'm sorry, but it's really out of my hands now, I'm following orders from my spiritual guide.'

'Oh my God,' Grace thought, petrified. 'He's completely insane. What on earth am I going to do?' But somehow she managed to look as if she was listening intently to what he said. 'How can you save me, Hugo?' she asked softly.

'Later, Grace, later ...' he said with another evil smile, taking her hand.

Grace's impulse was to pull her hand away, but she calmly allowed herself to be led slowly into the lounge. She recognised the music playing very gently in the background – it was Tchaikovsky's Fantasy Overture from *Romeo and Juliet*.

'I must say I prefer this original version rather than Prokofiev's, don't you?' said Hugo pompously. Grace nodded, bewildered.

The incense was really very over-powering as they entered the room and there were hundreds of candles all over the place. Hugo smiled at her and her heart thudded frantically in her ears as he closed the door behind them. Through the gloom of the candle light she saw a long, flowing cream dress draped over the settee. Hugo positioned himself at the fire place. 'Yes, Grace. It's your costume from the last scene in *Romeo and Juliet*. And here ...' he reached behind him ' ... is the dagger you used to kill yourself by your lover's tomb.'

Grace stood dumbstruck and swallowed hard, staring at the ceremonial knife, her mind working furiously. Could that have been the knife that killed Lana and Taboo? The knife that was used to attack Poppy? Her face paled and she could feel tiny goose bumps breaking out all over her body. She fought to keep her composure. But what about George? The question persisted. Oh God, or had he killed him too?

She was vaguely aware of Hugo's voice ranting in the background, as she desperately tried to think up a way to distract this animal in front of her.

'Just imagine that this is the National Theatre and I'm playing opposite you as Romeo ... You've no idea how many performances I watched, Grace. That should have been *my* part, *my* role,' he raged. 'It should have been me up there with you on that stage.' Hugo paced the lounge shaking with anger and grabbed the bottle of Stolichnaya off the desk, swigging from it violently. 'So I thought tonight we'd have our very own performance, on our own private stage.'

'You want to play Romeo, here, now, with me?' she said, tentatively.

'Yes, Grace, the last scene,' he said, quietly replacing the bottle and regaining control of his temper.

'I ... I don't think I can remember my lines,' she said in panic. Hugo turned around, his face distorted in fury.

'Don't be so unprofessional!' he shouted at her. 'Get your costume on *now*!' Grace fumbled at the plastic buttons of her maid's uniform and self-consciously wriggled into her costume, aware of Hugo's eyes on her all the time.

'Don't flatter yourself, Grace. I have no interest in your physical being since you've shamed yourself so much. It's your mental and psychological attitude to life that concerns me.' Hugo reached into the pocket of his jeans to retrieve a limp and tattered nude photograph of Grace from the earlier days of their marriage. Grace winced with embarrassment.

'Cheap, so cheap ... so sad,' he said as he held the photo over the flame of a candle. The heat made the image melt and distort. Hugo discarded it distastefully. 'Let's try to forget your mistakes in this life and concentrate on your rebirth into the next.'

Grace pulled on the long dress she'd worn hundreds of times, trying not to shake. 'I want the last lines to be *real*, Grace. Make me believe you ... "This is thy sheath; and therefore let me die,"' he called out softly.

'Actually, Hugo, it's "This is thy sheath; there rust, and let me die,"' she corrected, but realised she'd said the wrong thing when she saw his face turn purple with rage.

'This is *my* script, and you're to play it *my* way,' he thundered. 'How *dare* you correct me! I'm the real actor here – all you know is celluloid. Have some fucking respect!'

Hugo then started to impersonate Douglas Crane, stage manager on *Romeo and Juliet*, sounding unnervingly like him. 'This is your final call, Miss Madigan. Miss Madigan, your final call. Lights, sound and beginners, please ... stand by. Beginners to the stage.'

Grace arranged her dress, trying to hide her terror and play for time. 'I ... I'd feel more in character if I could have Juliets' ringlets,' she said, hesitantly. 'It won't take me long ...'

'Forget about your bloody hair. Here is the tomb of the Capulets ...' he said, pointing to the coffee table. 'Now get in position and I'll feed you Friar Lawrences's cue ...' he said, almost pushing her forwards.

'Hugo, you know I need more than one line ... Could we have a rehearsal please? The balcony scene – I would have loved to played that, with you as my Romeo. Look, here's the balcony,' she said, jumping up on the settee, her knees trembling.

'"Romeo, Romeo, wherefore art thou ...?"' she tried to deliver the well rehearsed line to her tormentor.

'The *final* scene – I said the *final* scene,' roared Hugo, his face purple again, and Grace almost fell off the sofa in fright.

The shrill ring of the telephone came as a welcome distraction, and they both scrambled to get to the receiver. But Hugo brought his jewelled blade heavily down on the desk, severing the connecting cord in half and missing Grace's hand by a whisker. She slumped back on to the settee despondently, the fear taking root in her chest as the realisation hit her that she really was fighting for her life. She battled to remain calm and collected, trying to think of a way to get the better of Hugo.

'*Don't look at me as if I'm some kind of lunatic!*' he raged. '*I'm here to* save *you, Grace,*' he ranted. '*Get in position!*'

'OK, Hugo, if that's what you really want. But would you do one thing for me first? Would you play Romeo's death scene? I never had the privilege of seeing you perform that spectacular piece of drama ... it would really mean a lot to me ...'

'Don't bullshit me Grace ...' he snapped, and any last hope that she might be able to outwit him left Grace.

'I promise you, I'm not bullshitting ... every night I'd stand in the wings and watch Luc Fontaine deliver those immortal lines, and I always wished it could have been you. I wanted you to be my Romeo, I knew you would have given it more, well ... more——'

'*Depth*, Grace, I'd have given more *depth* to the character and given that incredible scene more meaning,' he said haughtily, his eyes growing distant momentarily.

'Show me how, Hugo. Show me how,' suggested Grace coaxingly.

'I'm ... I'm not sure of the text, it's been a long time ...' he said gruffly, but she had diverted his attention now.

'Hugo, I know you better than that. I don't believe for a minute ...'

'Let me just block the scene. Here is the tomb of Capulets, here stands Balthasar, here Paris and his page are positioned with the flowers ...' he said, reverting instantly back to the old Hugo, preoccupied with his performance.

'And here is the poison,' exclaimed Grace, handing him the bottle of Stolichnaya. Hugo paced the room blocking and memorising the famous scene, as Grace searched furtively for a possible means of escape. Her gaze fixed on the dagger but she eliminated the idea of trying to challenge Hugo with it as she knew he'd overpower her. The candles flickered in the dark room and Grace despaired as she watched Hugo set the scene.

He drank some vodka and took out a small packet of

cocaine, emptying it on to the desk and chopping at the white powder with a credit card he'd found lying on the table. He glanced at Grace warily. 'Just a little lifter for my performance ... join me?' he invited.

'Er, not right now, thanks Hugo ... later maybe.'

'*Now!*' Hugo screamed as he strode across the room and dragged her by her hair. Terrified, she watched him snort the drug before he handed it to her. She knew better than to refuse and she leant over, trying to make it look as if she was snorting more than she actually was. The little bit she did take in flew to the back of her neck, making her splutter and choke. 'Wash it down with this!' he demanded, handing her the bottle of Stolichnaya. 'It's good for us to be on the same wavelength ...' He flamboyantly held his hands up indicating he was about to perform.

Grace sat down on the settee again with relief as Hugo sat on the floor preparing his speech. Taking a breath he began.

'"Here's to my love ..."' He drank the vodka. '"Oh, true apothecary, thy drugs are quick."' Hugo dramatically stared past her into his audience. '"Thus, with a kiss ..."'

Hugo lay down and closed his eyes before delivering the final phrase and Grace took her chance, bolting around the desk to the French windows. He immediately leapt from the floor and went in pursuit, screaming abuse.

Grace had managed only to unlock the glass panelled door before Hugo was on top of her, punching her hard in the side of her head.

Dazed and semi-concussed she was dragged back and laid roughly on the 'tomb'. 'Fucking bitch! How *dare* you walk out in the middle of my scene.' He cursed and abused her in rancid tones, his foul spittle assaulting her face as he sat astride her. Grabbing the dagger, he held it to her neck and lowered his face to hers, whispering viciously.

'You don't deserve my concern ... I should deal with you as I did that stripper, the whore, and slit your throat from ear to ear.' He smiled as he ran the blade slowly across her neck, oblivious to Grace's pained expression. 'You should have seen her face as I rammed the knife in her chest ... I carved up the dog pretty good too, didn't I Grace?' Grace lay helpless, tears running furiously down her face. '*Didn't* I Grace?' he shouted. She nodded frantically as he laughed. 'I don't mind admitting that Lloyd Davies will be a tough one, probably as tough as old Seymour,' he continued.

'So you did kill my father,' Grace whispered. 'But why? You of all people knew we weren't close.'

'Why not? You're from his very loins, Grace. I was smart there – too smart for these yankee police. After I spilled his guts over West Palm Beach, all I had to do was plant another knife and that note ... well it threw them off the scent pretty easily, giving me enough time to concentrate on you.' He glared evilly at her. 'I had orginally planned to serve up Davies first, but he'll just have to wait his turn,' he whispered menacingly.

'No ...' cried Grace, her hand fluttering to her throat.

'How very touching!' Hugo grinned fiendishly. 'Now get up and prepare for your last scene. This is your last chance to redeem yourself before you die.'

But Grace was not acquiescing any further. She kicked and punched him wildly in a last attempt to escape. But he had her pinned down with his knees and raising both arms, he clasped the knife, and brought it slowly down towards her. She managed somehow to scramble her head and torso to one side as the dagger came down quickly at the last, cruelly piercing her shoulder.

Grace cried out in pain and Hugo triumphantly pulled the knife out, revelling in the blood seeping from the open wound all over the beautiful cream dress. In his deranged state, he seemed not to have realised that it was her shoulder, not her heart, that he'd pierced, and he had no idea that Grace was still fully conscious. She kept her eyes closed and remained motionless, desperately trying to control her breathing and to stop her ribcage from moving too obviously. Somehow, she managed to still her quivering nerves and ignore the searing pain in the shoulder, and not a muscle moved as Hugo studied her peaceful face through the candle light.

Hugo seemed almost disappointed that the fight was over so easily and wiping the blood from the blade on his jeans, he got up to kneel once more by the 'tomb'. 'I so wanted to play the last scene with you Grace, but you cheated me of that as you cheated me of everything else. At last you're at peace, my darling Grace, you've been saved.' Hugo closed his eyes, smiling a satisfied smile.

At that minute the glass from the french window shattered, covering them with tiny splinters. Lloyd had kicked in the doors and was now leaping over the desk and throwing himself bodily onto the dazed Hugo who, caught off guard, thrust the dagger wildly at Lloyd's leg. Lloyd winced in pain as Hugo nicked his thigh, but he didn't lose concentration for a second, and the two wrestled on the rug, thrashing around madly.

Lloyd managed to knock the knife from Hugo's grip by slamming his hand down on the terracotta tiles, and at this point Grace leapt off the coffee table and grabbed it, watching with terror as the two men wrestled on the floor. The fight became more and more intense and Grace, still feeling shaky from the loss of blood, hovered precariously nearby, the knife in her hands. For too many moments all she could see in the shadows was Lloyd's white tennis shirt, but at last an opportunity presented itself and she lunged forward with all her might, driving the knife into Hugo's belly.

Her hands flew to her face as she watched Hugo collapse on to the floor. Rolling over onto his back, he looked at her, astonished, and gasped, '"Thus with a kiss ... I die ..."'

Lloyd and Grace watched helplessly as moments later, Hugo's eyes rolled back into his head and he let out his last rasping breath.

Seconds later Lieutenant Rodriguez and his men came rampaging through the shattered frames whilst two other officers attempted to break down the front door. They stared disbelievingly at the bloody corpse on the floor.

'The paramedics are on their way,' said Rodriguez breathlessly, as he led the others into the kitchen, away from the distressing sight. 'Your injury looks nasty, Ms Madigan, and Lloyd, you appear to have done yourself some harm too, but I'm sure the doc will be able to fix you up good as new. Now listen you two, I'm not gonna bellyache for too long about the information you held back from me, but I have to say that your co-operation on this case has been about as useful as a letter box on a tomb stone!' He said, pacing the room.

'Apart from my boys informing me that you'd legged it from the hotel, all I got was a lousy message from some broad on reception telling me to get to Villa Retreat ...' he grumbled.

'And 'scuse me for asking, Ms Madigan, but why the hell didn't you return my call? I had important new evidence from forensic. Seems that the knife George Seymour held in his hands wasn't the knife that killed him – nor the knife that killed Lana and the dog ... This sleazeball here – I presume he's the guilty party?' Grace nodded, shivering. 'He put us off the scent by covering a kitchen knife in Seymour's blood and planting it in his hand.'

Grace nodded numbly, as Lloyd held her close. 'I ... I'm sorry. I wanted to get back here to meet Lloyd. I was going to phone you ...'

But he ignored her. 'Anyway, it transpires that MPD narcotics in downtown Miami pulled a drugs bust on a crack dealer. The enforcer took down the wrong door, and hey presto, they find photos, newspaper and magazine articles of the attempted murder of Poppy Bates and old press cuttings of Ms Madigan from some English newspapers. On further investigation, we turn up a false passport, cocaine and plenty of dough. All this mess coulda been avoided if ...'

'Yes, I know Lieutenant.' said Lloyd patiently. 'But we didn't know Hugo was on the scene until just now, and there wasn't time to call you personally – I knew I just had to get here.' He paused for breath and turned to Grace. 'After I blew my match with Lendl, I decided to get on the first plane back to Miami. Can you imagine my horror when I got to The Delano and the desk clerk told me of my supposed message to you?' he exclaimed.

Rodriguez looked puzzled again, but before he could open his mouth, Grace rummaged around in her bag and produced the piece of paper.

'Of course I immediately suspected something was up, so I stole a taxi from the hotel, I'm afraid,' continued Lloyd. 'I had to get here as soon as possible, and I told Sonja to get a message to you,' he explained.

'Well, I shoulda been in on it, Mr Davies, but we'll leave this for now until we've got you two seen to.'

'What I still don't understand,' said Lloyd puzzled, 'is that Sonja should know my voice well – I phone often enough. How come she didn't recognise ...'

'Whatever else Hugo was, he was a great actor, Lloyd,' Grace interrupted. 'He'd only need to hear your voice once in order to imitate it, and he's been spying on us for months,' she said tiredly. She was suddenly feeling cold and rather ill and she started to tremble.

'That'll be the shock setting in,' said Rodriguez gently. 'Someone get a blanket for Ms Madigan,' he shouted. As he spoke, a siren wailed in the distance, getting closer by the second. The paramedics were on the scene, and having temporarily dressed the wounds, Grace and Lloyd were rushed off to hospital. Hugo's body remained where it was for the forensic team.

# Chapter Thirty

Grace and Lloyd were under the care of the doctors and nurses at Miami General Hospital for three days. Grace's condition was reported as stable; she had suffered shock and significant loss of blood. Her doctor had assured her that within six months, and following a touch of cosmetic surgery, she would be back in low cut, off the shoulder numbers. The stitches looked ugly now, but she had faith in the doctors words and constantly reassured herself that things could most definitely have been worse.

Lloyd had needed a minor operation on his leg, and the main worry for all concerned was how long it would take before he could get back on the tennis circuit. Grace was frantic with worry until she knew he was OK, but the surgeon reassured her by announcing that the operation had been a complete success. It would be a little longer before he was fully recovered, and he would need extensive physiotherapy, but he was confident that Lloyd could be back on court in six weeks, and able to play professionally within three months. Not ideal, certainly, but Lloyd was so relieved that Grace was all right that he didn't mind.

Grace sat by his bed the next day, her arm in a sling to take the weight off her shoulder. 'Thank God you're going to be all right, I couldn't bear it if you ... well I feel so responsible. It seems I've brought you nothing but trouble,' she said apologetically.

'Between you and your brother, life is never boring,' he laughed, but his eyes were serious as he searched her face, wanting to say more.

At that moment Beatrice, James and Theo came through the door and they smiled ruefully at one another.

'They say laughter is the the best medicine. Share the joke with us mate,' said James as Beatrice went to kiss Grace.

'We can all afford to joke,' said Theo. 'The insurers have given us two weeks' grace, which means our budget is covered and you guys can take yourselves off to Key West for a bit of rest and recuperation.'

'Key West?' questioned Grace.

'Yep. The most southern island on the Keys,' he winked at Lloyd. 'There's the most wonderful hotel – a real honeymooners' paradise. I discovered it recently when ... anyway, you kids enjoy yourselves. Take advantage of the time off ...'

'I don't think ... I mean, thank you, but ...' said Grace, embarrassed and worried that Lloyd mightn't want to spend time with her alone.

'I think it sounds brilliant, Theo. I'd definitely like to take advantage of your kind offer,' said Lloyd. 'Okay with you, Grace?' he grinned warmly at her.

'I, well ... yes, of course I'd like to go with you.' She smiled nervously.

'Great,' said James. 'I've fixed up for you to see a local physio while you're there, Lloyd. As long as you work at it, six months from now, there's no reason you shouldn't be back up there with the big boys on the circuit.'

Lloyd grinned at him, everything seeming suddenly full of hope. 'Believe me, I'll be back with a vengeance,' he said firmly.

\* \* \*

Grace awoke from a blissfull and fortifying sleep. She lifted the muscular, tanned arm that weighed her down and turned over in the crisp white sheets to face the most handsome and sensitive man she'd ever known. She lay gazing at Lloyd's rugged face, barely able to breathe as she basked in the afterglow of their previous evening of passion. Her life was complete now. With Lloyd's gentle perception he'd converted her into a sensual and enthusiastic lover and all her former inhibitions seemed to have disappeared for good.

The morning light peeped through the white voile curtains which billowed gently in the sea breeze. She sighed contentedly as Lloyd dragged his eyelids open and smiled lazily at her. He grunted contentedly and pulled her closer to him, the soft hairs on his chest tickling her face. They lay entwined for what seemed like an eternity, as if everything around them had ground to a halt.

Stirring eventually, Lloyd rose to look appreciatively out at the turquoise ocean. 'Do you realise we've been here in paradise for three days and we haven't yet left the beach house?' he chuckled. 'Let's go and frolic in the surf before my physio appointment – sea water is supposed to be good for healing.' He turned, distracted as she nibbled at his ear. 'Grace ... Grace, if you carry on doing that we'll never get to sample the delights of the Straits of Florida,' he laughed, turning to stroke her back.

'The only delight you're going to sample is me,' she whispered. 'I want this time with you to last for ever. I've never been so happy in my entire life ... I'm frightened that I might be dreaming and that if I wake up the spell will be broken,' she said, looking up at him nervously.

'This *is* real, Grace, and I'm here, for good. I'll always be here ...' Lloyd said earnestly, stroking her cheek as he gazed adoringly into her eyes. 'In fact I think I've always loved you ... certainly always wanted you. My feelings almost scared me in their intensity, I never dared hope for one minute when James managed to get me the position of trainer and technical adviser that it would lead to this. Only in my wildest dreams did I allow myself to fantasise of this moment,' he said with emotion. He stroked her face gently and leant forward to kiss her.

'This is how I love you most of all – sleepy eyes, tousled hair, my very own "Amazing Grace." He kissed her gently but with a mounting passion. 'I want to make love to you again. I need to make love to you now, and every day for the rest of my life, Grace ...' His voice trailed off as he felt her stir beneath him and quiver with anticipation.

Their kisses became more ardent and urgent to the point where Grace thought she might expire from ecstasy. She pulled his body down onto her petite frame, wanting to feel him crushing her, possessing her ... here she felt safe, at last. He whispered her name as his lips travelled down her neck, giving her goose bumps. 'Grace. God, how I need you, Grace darling.' His face found the swell of her full bosom and he shuddered, moaning involuntarily.

His mouth searched for her nipple, gently flicking with his tongue at the dark brown areola, and he sighed with pleasure as he felt Grace arch her back. Sucking at her, he heard a cry escape her as she offered up her body wantonly. How he loved this dainty creature beneath him. How he loved the knowledge that she enjoyed him as much as he enjoyed her.

He lowered his head on to her abdomen, toned and taut from his training, and revelled in the feeling of the soft down of her belly on his face. Grace's hands ran through his sun-bleached hair, watching the ends curl around her finger tips as she gently pushed his head down to the core of her being. As he nuzzled at her, the musky scent almost drove him out of his mind and he revelled in her wetness. Lifting her buttocks gently with both hands, he heard her take a sharp intake of breath as he caressed her with his tongue.

Lloyd felt her body stiffen, quiver then relax time and time again as he brought her repeatedly to the point of no return. At last, feeling she would surely go mad with the pleasure, she cried out. 'I need you, I need you now ...'

Lloyd lifted his head and gazed down at her glazed green eyes in wonder. Kissing her deeply, he entered her very, very slowly, his eyes never leaving hers as she eagerly wrapped her legs around him. He ventured into her as far as his manhood would allow, savouring every nuance of her, and slowly began to move in a slow, sensuous rhythm. She murmured his name over and over as she felt the heat of fire ignite in the pit of her stomach and slowly travel through her body, flushing up to her face.

Grace felt she must be dreaming she was so happy. That night by the swimming pool had been her first experience of uninhibited sex, but this ... this was indescribable. She belonged with Lloyd, loved him with every ounce of her being, and the feeling of him inside her was the most wonderful thing she'd ever known. 'Don't ever stop ...' she demanded breathlessly. 'Don't ever stop loving me ...'

'Just try and stop me,' he responded gruffly. The gentle rhythm of their bodies was so natural, so exquisite, it was as if they'd been perfecting their art for years – like poetry in motion.

Their relationship had to be unique, no other woman could have ever felt like this before, and certainly no other man could ever make her feel this way, she thought. Reality was so far away. Was it possible to become addicted to making love? Could one die from ecstasy? She wallowed in their languid but passionate lovemaking, revelling in Lloyd's glorious smell, wanting to bury her nose into his every crevice, taste every inch of his skin, hold him, touch him ...

Lloyd's breathing laboured as he gained momentum and with each long thrust came perilously close to ejaculation. He slowed down his pace as he fought his body for control. Half of him wanting to explode inside her filling her with his love, and the other half wanted to prolong this moment of passion for ever. Had he died and gone to heaven? It was all too wonderful, too fantastic for reality.

Grace's legs clamped harder around his waist and she deliriously called out his name as the fire spread through her body. Her face crimson, she cried out in ecstasy, unable to hold back the blaze within her any longer. Lloyd, totally lost now, thrust away for all he was worth, emptying his heart and soul into her as he reached his own climax.

His heart pounded violently in his ears as he gradually returned to planet earth. Their moist, spent bodies lay limp on the bed, and neither spoke as they waited for their heart beats to regain their regular pattern.

The rest of their break at Key West was like a dream. They made glorious love as often as they possibly could, eating, laughing and sleeping together, neither one ever wanting to be out of sight of the other for more than a moment, neither wanting ever to end their time alone together and leave the place where they had finally succumbed to their love for each other.

# Epilogue

Four weeks after Grace and Lloyd returned from Key West, Bertie duly thanked all the actors and crew as they wrapped after the last day's shoot for *Love All*. Grace and Lloyd were glad to be returning home to the villa and were looking forward to the party Theo had decided to throw in honour of the première for *Temptation*, which was to be screened in Los Angeles the following week. Both of them were recovering amazingly well from their injuries, and those close to them couldn't help but wonder if the healing power of love might have more than a little to do with it.

They were greeted by Kyle, various Universal executives and Mike Russell as they gathered in the garden for a luscious feast of lobster, poached salmon and exotic salads, and Theo beamed from ear to ear as he toasted Grace. 'You're looking at one very happy man, Grace Madigan. You're our "bums on seats" passport, ain't that right Bertie?' he enthused. 'This is your year, Grace ... Enjoy!'

Grace couldn't imagine feeling happier, surrounded as she was by Lloyd and her family, all toasting the success she'd craved for so long. She couldn't wait to go to the première with Lloyd next week, so that the world could see how happy they were together, celebrating her first major film. She had, indeed, taken America by storm.

She looked happily over at Poppy who was chatting animatedly with James. A small part of her couldn't help wishing that Sybil and Hannah could be there to share her big moment, but she knew that the thought was a selfish one, and settled on planning a long phone call afterwards to tell them all about it. She spotted Warren, his eyes fixed – as always – on Beatrice.

'Warren, weren't you supposed to be back at the clinic ages ago?' asked Grace cheekily as she sidled up to him, champagne bottle in hand.

'Hmm, well that's something I've been wanting to talk to you about for some time, but there never seems to be a right time – these last few weeks have been so frantic.' He paused, trying to guage her reaction, and was relieved to see her smiling warmly.

'You and Mum seem to be getting on like a house on fire,' she said, her eyes twinkling. 'You're part of the furniture now.'

He smiled, embarrassed. 'Well, I never would have believed I could find happiness again after Marcie died. Now that I've met Beatrice, work suddenly doesn't seem so important to me ... So that's why the clinic has been taking a back seat. In fact,' he paused again, his smile widening, 'I think I might give it up altogether and retire.'

Grace laughed delightedly and looked over at her mother, thinking that she couldn't think of any two people more perfect for one another – apart from her and Lloyd of course!

'We will have to take things slowly,' he cautioned. 'Beatrice has to come to terms with George's death and I certainly don't want to rush her. But I have my hopes ...'

'Of course you do, and rightly so,' said Grace warmly, squeezing his arm.

'It's nice to see you looking so happy, Grace,' said Beatrice as she approached, placing a kiss on her daughter's forehead.

'I *am* happy – happier than I've ever been,' she beamed,

enfolding them both in a hug. 'And happy for you both.'

'Now enough of this soppiness,' laughed Beatrice. 'You should be circulating and talking with all your guests, Grace, and looking after that gorgeous young man of yours. Oh, and by the way, there might just be a surprise for you coming later on.' But she and Warren were off before Grace had a chance to quiz her further.

Obeying part of her mother's instructions, she walked over to Lloyd and sat next to him on the lounger, reaching for his hand and examining his palm. Looking up at her he smiled contentedly.

'Will you take a look at Mum and Warren?' she said.

'They look like a couple of teenagers, don't they?' he grinned. Grace watched the laughter lines on his face crinkle up in the sunshine as he observed James and Poppy sitting on the grass under the tree. How she loved this man.

'You know, Grace, I've known that brother of yours since we were at school together, and he's always been incorrigible. But just take a look at him now – he's a regular pussy cat,' he said, still unused to the transformation.

'If I wasn't witnessing this with my own eyes, I wouldn't believe it either,' Grace agreed, watching her little brother stroking Poppy's hair.

Aware that they were being discussed, Poppy and James climbed to their feet and wandered over to join them.

'How goes it Hop-a-long Cassidy?' said James cheekily, and the four of them continued to banter happily as a stretch limo with blacked out windows pulled up outside the front of the villa.

Grace's curiosity aroused, she noticed her mother look at her watch and start to make her way over. Taking her daughter by the arm, she smiled warmly at her. 'Remember that surprise I was telling you about? Well, come and see who's in that car.' Beatrice jerked her head toward the stationary vehicle.

'Who is it? Oh my God, Freddie,' she cried delightedly as she saw him climb out of the limo. She raced across the lawn to greet him, almost knocking him over with the force of her hug. 'Why didn't you tell me you were coming?' she exclaimed through her laughter.

'And spoil the surprise Beatrice and Poppy have gone to so much trouble to arrange?' He grinned at her and then patted his brief case. 'I had to come, Grace, this new script here, it's pure dynamite, and I wanted to see your face after you'd read it! But let's talk shop later. There's someone else here to see you.' He stood aside to help the second passenger out of the car.

'Well don't just stand there, my girl. Give this old baggage a hand,' came Sybil's unmistakable, gruff voice.

'Sybil, I don't believe it,' cried Grace, tears of joy streaming down her face as she helped the old lady out of the car. 'You came all this way to see me?'

'Well, it wasn't to have afternoon tea with Hillary Clinton,' said Sybil flippantly. 'Now stop all that nonsense and get me out of this damned car,' she demanded. 'I'm desperate for a drink.'

Grace laughed as the rest of the crowd gathered to witness the tearful reunion. She was almost irritated when Freddie interrupted.

'Stand back while I present another VIP,' he announced. Puzzled, Grace turned towards the car again, and and slowly but surely she recognised the large bottom and swollen ankles of Hannah as she emerged, undignified, from the large car. At this point, she really was overcome.

'Hannah ... Hannah! I'm so glad to see you.' And she wept uncontrollably on her old nanny's shoulder.

'There, there, ma wee bairn, blow your nose like a good girl. That's better now. It's been a bit of a shock for the poor lass,' she explained to the others. Recognising Lloyd, she smiled warmly at him. She'd been so pleased to hear from Beatrice how close the pair had become.

He came over to Grace and tenderly put an arm around her. 'Come on, darling. This is like a scene from one of those awful, nauseating American day-time shows,' he teased, providing a very necessary handkerchief. 'Poppy and Beatrice have been planning this for ages, you really ought to thank them.'

She readily did so, and dragged her new guests off to have a drink, eagerly introducing them to everybody. They all sat cheerfully on the grass, sharing happy times, and consumed many glasses of champagne.

'All right, folks,' said Theo finally, clearing his throat. 'I think it's fitting that I announce a toast.' He pulled himself up to his full height, his large belly protruding over his trousers. 'I want you all to raise your glasses to Mike, Sally and Grace, the stars of *Temptation* ... one hell of a production.' Everyone murmured their agreement and raised their glasses happily.

'Well ... I have something to toast also, if I may,' piped up James, for once, looking nervous. 'Theo's toast brings me on to news of another forthcoming production,' he said, looking over at Poppy.

'Not now,' she hissed. 'It's not the right time.'

'Yes now,' he hissed back, as the other guests strained to hear what was being said. 'The thing is ... Poppy and I are going to have a baby.' His announcement was met initially with a stunned silence.

'Oh my God, a baby!' whispered Beatrice. 'I'm going to be a grandmother ...' she laughed, smiling happily at Warren before rushing over to hug Poppy.

'Crikey, mate. That was quick work wasn't it?' said Lloyd, laughing as he dragged a shocked Grace over with him. She hugged them both, wiping away yet more tears.

'More champagne, Theo,' she demanded. 'We need to make another toast – to the rapidly growing Seymour family!'

Champagne corks flew, and everyone started speaking at once, the mood of excitement and celebration taking over, as guests clamoured towards Poppy and James. Grace was touched to see Lloyd looking so happy, and he smiled as he caught her eye, seeing the look of devotion in her eyes. He beckoned her over, and feeling like a teenager, she approached.

'Not a bad evening, eh?' he teased, his eyes roaming her face as if for the first time. Dusk was threatening to fall, and the moonlight had begun to reflect on the swimming pool. Leaving the other guests to their own devices, Grace led Lloyd over to a lounger and sat, gazing intently at him. He looked back at her quizzically.

'What is it, Grace?'

She looked away, unable to put her feelings into words, and he took her hand instinctively. 'Tell me what's on your mind,' he said gently, kissing the palm of her hand. 'Or have you lost articulation after today's excitement,' he said, grinning that irresistible grin of his. She swallowed.

'Today ... today has been the best day of my entire life. I'll always remember it ...' she whispered emotionally, tears filling her eyes.

'It's not over yet, darling,' he replied gently. 'You see, I have a certain little surprise of my own for you, but I seem to have been upstaged – I'm afraid I can't compete with flying family and friends around the globe,' he mocked.

Grace looked at him through shining eyes. 'What surprise? I don't think I could cope with another today. But what is it?' she cried, the suspense getting the better of her.

'You'll see. James!' he cried, summoning his friend. 'Would you do this crippled wimp a favour and get Grace's present from the villa?' he said, winking at him.

'What present? Oh *that* present,' he joked, heading off to the house.

'Lloyd, I've been so spoiled today and ...' started Grace, smiling lovingly at him.

'Well it can't wait until tomorrow, and I definitely can't take it back,' replied Lloyd, pointing over at James, who was standing outside the kitchen door with a golden labrador puppy in his arms.

'Oh Lloyd!' she exclaimed, breathlessly as she rose to her feet. 'Is he for me?'

'*She*!' he corrected. 'And yes she is.'

'She's beautiful, she's just like ...'

'Just like one of the pair you had at The Gables, when you were a little girl?' he asked gently.

Grace nodded, moved beyond words as she knelt on the ground, calling to the puppy. James let the animal down and she pattered, floppy eared, across the lawn into Grace's waiting arms.

'Oh Lloyd,' cried Grace, burying her head into the blonde bundle of mischief. 'She's so beautiful, I love her already.

You couldn't have given me a gift that would mean more to me,' she said, gazing up at him warmly. 'Would you mind if I called her Lana?'

Lloyd shook his head, revelling in her happiness, and the others gathered round to inspect the lively young pup.

'Everything is just too, too perfect!' sighed Grace, sidling up to Lloyd. 'Except for one thing,' she added slyly.

'What's that?' he asked, curious.

'Weelll ...' she began coyly. 'Having a puppy is just as much of a responsibility as having a child. I wouldn't dream of bringing a dependent into the world without a secure and loving family environment.' She bent to pick up the pup, who licked her chin furiously. 'I would hate for this poor misbegotten mutt to be gossiped about, so I think we should make an honest pup of her, don't you?' Grace said bravely, looking shyly up at Lloyd.

Lloyd looked at her blankly. 'Are you asking me to marry you, Grace?'

'I, er ... yes, I suppose I am,' she replied nervously.

Lloyd looked away into the distance scratching his chin ponderously. 'If it's a question of legitimising this pooch, I'll need time to think about it.' Grace's heart sank. 'But in the meantime, why don't you have a look at her pedigree?' he suggested, handing her an official document from his shirt pocket.

Hurt and embarrassed at his cool reaction, Grace blindly opened the certificate. There in black and white beside 'Owner' was written, Mr and Mrs Lloyd Davies. 'Oh, you horror!' she cried gleefully, throwing herself at her future husband as the rest of the party looked on in silence. 'Kiss me, you devil.'

'Aagh, my leg,' he cried out, teasing her again, and turned to their audience. 'I hope my wife will show me more sympathy when we're married.'

And with that he took her face in his hands and kissed her slowly, deeply and passionately, oblivious to the cries and echoing cheers of 'Bravo' and 'Encore' all around them.